Smokin' Situation

E.L. KOSLO

Copyright

TW: Wildfires and mentions of destruction of property; Injury, burns, scarred MMC; Orphaned FMC (mentions of previous death of parents/grandparents); Cheating adjacent (she's in a non-exclusive FWB situation with the MMC's little brother); accidental mistaken identity

PROOFING: THE ROMANCE DOCTOR - Brittni Van @the_romance_doc

Cover and Interior Designed by E.L. Koslo

Custom Illustrated Vector Characters by Qamber Emporium

Depositphotos: @TeddyandMia, @Elisanth, @aprilianzee4@gmail.com

Envato Elements Fonts: Rustling Trees & BaskervilleBT

Table of Contents

Dedication

SFW Dedication:
This book is dedicated to all of the hard working, selfless, coura-geous firefighters who live and work in our communities to keep us safe.

NSFW Dedication:
This book is dedicated to all the people pleasing girlies who want to order a hunky, brooding firefighter-cowboy to his knees and tell him to get to work.

Chapter One

Annie

I SPUN THE EMPTY glass in my hand, focusing on the bar top in front of me. Typically, I was the person behind the bar, but not tonight. With the Butterfly Ridge summer festival starting in the morning, I was granted a brief reprieve from bartending duties and was spending the evening at the distillery a few miles from the small cabin I shared with my sister. But judging from the look on my on-again, off-again friend-with-benefits' face, I would not like what he was about to say.

Things had been weird between Jayden and me for the last month or so. I wasn't sure exactly what happened, but he'd started acting weird after he'd recently gone to meet with a head chef candidate to run the kitchen at his new restaurant. It was still in the early planning stages of construction, slated to be built on the other side of the large warehouse building that housed the distillery. When he'd come back from his trip a little distant, I'd chalked it up to the fact that he'd returned empty-handed, but now I was wondering if there was more to it.

"Are you sure Hudson doesn't mind you taking over my booth? I know you were supposed to be running the kegs in the beer tent, but I really need to make this trip now. I'll only be gone a week, but if he needs you, I can always see if Colette minds covering for me. She's supposed to be home for a few days between trail tours."

This was one time in my life that I wished I could say no to people. At thirty-one, you'd think I would have stopped trying to be a people pleaser, but I said yes to things more often than I wanted to.

"Yeah, he got Reid and Hazel to take over service. Unless you'd rather have Reid run your booth instead."

His cousin had pitched in a lot over the last few months since Jayden's schedule had become a little more unpredictable in the aftermath of the accident his older brother, Tristan, had been in during February. Jay didn't share a lot of details, but I knew he was injured in a fire where he worked in Wyoming and had been burned badly.

While Jay and I had been more than just friends for years, we both knew the score and didn't muddy the waters with things like involving our families, so I'd never met his brothers or his parents. I obviously knew his cousin Reid because we'd been in the same grade and his friendship with Hudson. But I'd never met Tristan because he had left town before I'd dated Jay when we were still in high school.

I didn't blame Tristan for his accident, but it was another thing that had made the situation between Jayden and me more difficult. Tristan had moved in with Jay after he'd recovered from his skin grafts, and had just recently moved out a few weeks ago to start his new job. But that meant that Jay's place had been entirely off limits for hook-ups and my sister Reese hadn't been thrilled at the idea of guys staying over at the cabin we shared.

So that left very few options for us to connect. My truck may have had a roomy cab, but I was beyond the days of backseat hookups.

Jay's growing distance meant he hadn't tried to initiate anything in a while. We hadn't always had a purely casual relationship. In fact, we'd dated our senior year of high school before separating for college. He'd come back home after dropping out of culinary school nursing a wounded heart. I'd also had a similarly messy breakup around the same time, and our arrangement had been a way for both of us to let off some steam without the worry of any unnecessary emotional attachments.

"No, of course I wouldn't rather have someone else. I trust you. And you know just as much about the product as I do." He was right, I'd been around since the early days when Jay set up a small still in his parent's garage, and I'd even helped him christen the bar when he bought the warehouse that now housed his growing whiskey distillery.

At the time, he was busy trying to get his business started, and I was training to help my friend Hudson take over his dad's bar. Since then, we'd both protected each other from having to deal with dating in a small town to scratch an itch. I loved him dearly, but I'd realized early in our arrangement that I'd never be *in* love with him.

He was as chaotic as they came, and I preferred life to be a little quieter when I wasn't at work. Jay was a daredevil, spending his downtime skiing black diamonds with his best friend Colette, hiking remote mountain ridges at high elevations or jumping out of planes and recording it to post on his YouTube channel and Instagram account. I'd rather curl up somewhere with a book or watch a movie at home than go chase down the next adventure.

It was only a matter of time before one of us called it quits for good to pursue an actual relationship. And now that we were both over thirty, the thought that I might want something more than just casual was getting louder.

"I know this was a huge ask, and typically I would have just told the planning committee I wasn't able to run a booth this year, but with how many roadblocks Noreen has already thrown up with the city council, I don't want to rock the boat."

I understood where he was coming from. Noreen, the head of the city planning board, had been a bit of a monster when she found out he had hired someone outside the ridge to design his expansion. He was bringing in his friend Garrett—who was a commercial architect—to design the restaurant and run the construction project.

She'd falsely assumed her son would be used for the project, but her son designed log cabins, so he wasn't exactly qualified to design a restaurant that was built into the side of a mountain. But good luck convincing her of that.

"It's really not that big of a deal, Jay. I've helped you before, and honestly, your booth is easier to manage than the beer tent. If I need help, Mikey will be around, and I know Charley will help if I need it." That was one of the convenient things about living in a small town, if you needed something, there was never a shortage of people who were willing to pitch in.

It also helped that all the booths serving alcohol were grouped together behind the temporary fencing they used to keep the teens and underage college students from trying to sneak a taste. The last thing we needed was a bunch of drunk college students on summer break creating havoc.

"Yeah, you keep saying that, but I know how you get. You'd help me whether or not you want to, and I don't want to take advantage of the fact that you're a bit of a pushover. You *can* tell me no sometimes." His voice was teasing, but there was a kernel of truth to his statement. I *was* a pushover when I wasn't cosplaying a badass female bartender.

"It's like you think you know me or something," I muttered, only stiffening slightly when he walked around the bar and wrapped his arms around my waist from behind, nuzzling the side of my neck.

"Well, I know we haven't had much time alone for the last few months, but we could try to change that when I get back from this trip."

The flutters of anticipation I normally felt around him had been fading, the once intense passion had settled into near dormant embers. I was still attracted to him, but it was also starting to feel like maybe continuing whatever was going on between us was just setting us up for a messy break down the line.

Obviously, our relationship wasn't emotional, so it wasn't going to be a *breakup*, but he *was* my friend, and I didn't want to have to start avoiding him when our situationship fizzled out. Our friend groups overlapped, and I wasn't looking forward to when things inevitably got weird.

"We'll see," I evaded, letting out a heavy breath when he moved away. Typically, when he was getting ready to go out of town, he would invite me over to get a fix to tide him over, but I wasn't in the right headspace to deal with it right now. And he wasn't offering either. If he wanted it, I would have already been bent over his desk, laid out on top of the bar, or straddling him on the mats in the warehouse where he practiced kickboxing and riding him until we both...

"You okay? You look tired. Maybe it's time to go home and get some rest. I know you've been taking on a lot of late shifts lately."

But I'd taken those shifts voluntarily. My boss—and mutual friend—Hudson had decided that maybe work-life balance was something important, so he had cut back on late nights at the bar to spend time with his new live-in girlfriend, Charley. And his little sister, Hazel, who typically ran the food service aspects of the bar, had fallen in love with her brother's best friend and now only worked sporadic late-night shifts.

We'd trained some new servers, and I'd taken on a barback along with a new part-time bartender for extra coverage on my nights off, but I didn't really have a lot going on in my personal life. And the last few months, with Jay being less available, had made that clearer. So, I'd done what any other workaholic does, I'd thrown myself into extra shifts so I could pretend that I wasn't lonely.

"This *should* be my last trip for a while. If this chef finally commits to moving to the ridge to run the restaurant with me, then I won't have to chase her all over Colorado anymore."

There had been grumblings that Jay had a history with the chef he was trying to coax into moving to Butterfly Ridge. I only knew what I'd heard from other people, because he was uncharacteristically tightlipped about the situation, but I knew once he had his mind set on something, he rarely let it go. That was part of why he'd been so successful in getting his distillery operational and all his plans for expansion in motion in such a short time. I admired that kind of drive, but it also felt like maybe I was getting left behind as he transitioned into this new part of his life.

"You know, I think the two of you would work well together," he casually mentioned, not looking at me while he ran a cloth across

6

the smooth wooden surface of the bar. "I'm going to need someone who can develop a cocktail menu. Know anyone who might be interested?"

It wasn't the first time he'd mentioned working together, but I didn't want to mix business with pleasure. Especially with how unsettled our situation felt lately. I'd seen how awful it could turn out when a relationship ended with a coworker, and even though I'd been much younger then, I didn't have anywhere to go if things turned out like that again.

"I'm good where I'm at," I whispered, not wanting to elaborate. "But thank you."

He nodded and dropped the subject, thankfully able to take a hint. I appreciated he thought I was capable, but working with him on a full-time basis was not a risk I was willing to take.

Reese had built a life in Sage Springs, and since my sister and I were all each other had left, I was happy maintaining the status quo and continuing to run the bar with Hudson. I didn't have grand plans to open my own business, so I was comfortable right where I was. And despite being an introvert when I wasn't working, I liked the challenge of it. Sure, it could get tiresome dealing with the college students, and every once in a while, we had some stubborn asshole tourists who created chaos, but I had bouncers—and sometimes servers—I knew would take care of it.

"Want me to follow you home?" he asked, tossing his dirty cloth toward the bin underneath the counter.

"Nope, I'm a big girl. I can handle navigating dark country roads at night."

He nodded, pursing his lips while he scratched at the scruff covering his chin. "Just be careful. I know you can handle your own, but with the festival and the holiday coming up, sometimes people get behind the wheel when they shouldn't. Just promise to text me when you get home."

"You worry too much."

The fourth of July was less than a week away, and every extra cabin in the county was currently rented out to the summer tourists who came to admire the beautiful mountain views. It was good for business, but there were also dangers when you had new people driving on poorly lit mountain roads at night in a place they weren't familiar with.

Reese had been telling me the same thing with her job as a nurse at the hospital. She'd dealt with her fair share of the usual sprained ankles from inexperienced hikers and heat sickness from people who didn't hydrate themselves at an increased altitude. She'd also mentioned she already had treated some nasty burns related to fireworks—even though we were currently under a burn ban.

It was something I hadn't mentioned to Jay. He was still reeling after seeing what had happened to his brother and I didn't want to stir up bad memories since he'd told me he had reservations about his brother joining the volunteer fire department now that he was back for good.

"Sometimes I feel like I don't worry enough," he sighed, then flipped off the lights over the bar before he led me toward the back door of the warehouse. "And I just want to make sure that you're safe."

At the door, he backed me against the frame, pulling me into a tight hug and kissing the top of my head. I squeezed him back, appreciating that he was so concerned, but I'd been alone long enough that I could handle myself.

"Text me when things wrap up tomorrow," he whispered into my hair.

Nodding, I released him and leaned back, looking into his eyes. "Everything will be fine. There are usually enough volunteers around that I'm sure if I get busy, I can rope someone into helping."

He cupped my cheek, rubbing the pad of his thumb across my skin as he stared down at me. "I'll be back before the end of the week. My schedule will be less hectic after the festival, and we can spend some more time together. I promise it'll be different when I come back."

But his schedule wasn't the only thing different when he returned.

Chapter
Two

Annie

"WOW, AND I THOUGHT I'd had a rough night," Reese chuckled from across the room where she was curled up on the couch. "What happened to having the night off?"

"Insomnia strikes again," I sighed, trudging toward the coffeemaker and going through the motions of changing out my sister's decaffeinated tea pod for my extra dark brew. Despite working regular twelve-hour shifts, she rarely drank caffeine and often lectured me about my consumption. With our family's history of heart disease, and the generational curse of dying young, we kind of had the deck stacked against us. *If you believed in that kind of stuff.* I wasn't convinced, but most of the people in our family hadn't celebrated their fiftieth birthdays either.

"You need to talk to Dr. Foster about that. It's not healthy for your sleep schedule to be as disrupted as it is with how much you've been working. You're going to burn yourself out."

That was how Reese had handled the aftermath of our parent's death. By being extra diligent about every aspect of her life. She lived a regimented lifestyle of maintaining a clear work-life balance, regular exercise, and a very strict diet.

I, on the other hand, regularly ate cereal because I was too tired to cook and lived on a steady diet at the bar of chicken fingers and tater tots. Part of the perks of working in food service, you never have to worry about paying for a meal. Even if it was probably unhealthy to consume mostly bar food.

I *occasionally* had a salad. Key word being occasionally.

"Yes, Mom," I sighed, returning my attention to my coffee cup and adding a splash of flavored creamer that I knew my sister would never touch.

"Well, maybe if you listened to me just once about your health, I wouldn't have to act like your parent. You're not exactly a child anymore. I shouldn't have to tell you a balanced diet might help you feel better."

Rolling my eyes and biting back the sarcastic remark on the tip of my tongue, I took a deep breath before I responded. "Can you not pick a fight with me this morning? I'm going to have a long day, and I just need to drink my coffee in silence so I can muster the energy to pretend I'm an extrovert for the next ten hours."

"You *could* have said no to working at the festival."

She wasn't wrong, I could have. But I didn't. And now I was going to force myself through it so I could come back home and pass out before my shift at the bar tomorrow night.

"But I didn't," I sang, heading toward my room to pull on my clothes for the day. Hazel had recently designed a new logo for the distillery to prepare for the expansion of the restaurant, so it was the first time I was debuting it to the town on my new cropped T-shirt and baseball cap.

Jay had also invested in all new signage for the event, which was stashed in the bed of my truck along with the pop-up shelter and cases of whiskey that I was sure would be empty by the end of the day.

While Butterfly Ridge and Sage Springs were your typical quaint little mountain tourist towns, the locals also liked to socialize and foster community spirit. I was sure I'd have just as many locals paying me a visit today as the tourists here for the fourth.

Reese was in her bedroom when I came back out, clearly ready to crash for the day until her next shift started later in the afternoon.

I'd donned my battle armor in the form of a cropped, short-sleeved plaid shirt pulled over the distillery tee artfully tied beneath my cleavage, showing off a sliver of my stomach above a pair of high-waisted denim shorts. I'd begrudgingly thrown on my beat-up brown leather cowboy boots, leaning into the country girl look. My long brown hair was split into two braids, the distillery cap covering the top of my head, thankful it'd provide a bit of protection from the brutal sun.

I would be under a shelter for most of the day, but I'd still slathered myself in sunscreen. My diet may have left a lot to be desired, but I took sun care seriously.

The drive into Butterfly Ridge was short, but the hair on the back of my neck prickled when I crossed the ridge and headed toward town. It felt like there was something in the air lately, some sense of foreboding that change was on the horizon, and it heightened my already tense mood. I was sure I was just being overly dramatic because I was sleep deprived, but I'd also felt like this driving into Sage Springs multiple times before—usually followed by an awful night at the bar.

Pulling into the parking lot a few blocks from the city center, I followed the hand signals of the volunteer firefighters who'd been assigned to act as security for the festival. After I'd pulled into a parking space, I took a deep breath as I prepared myself for the chaos of trying to set up for an event.

A knock on my driver's side window startled me, and I was met with a set of striking dark blue eyes peeking up at me from beneath the brim of a Sage Springs Fire Department hat. There was something almost familiar about them, but he was not someone I recognized. As my eyes traveled down his face to the tight navy-blue shirt stretched across his strong pecs, I knew I would have remembered this man if I'd seen him before.

Hitting the button to roll down my automatic window, I took a deep breath and plastered on the fake smile I used as my daily mask.

"If you fold back the cover on your truck bed, we can unload everything. Once you give us your booth number, we can deliver it all." His curt response showed it was all business with this one, he didn't even say hello. Not waiting for a response, he turned and walked toward the back of my truck.

I shut off the engine, opening the door and hopping out. Mr. Super Serious Firefighter and a few of his coworkers had already opened the back hatch of the truck bed and started loading cases of whiskey onto a small trailer attached to the back of a gator truck.

"Please be careful with those, they're full of glass bottles."

Three sets of eyes shot in my direction, and I stood there awkwardly while they did the typical male sweep of my outfit before they finally settled on my face. One set of familiar hazel eyes twinkled mischievously as my sister's former best friend grinned at me, but we'd mutually decided years ago that it was easier to pretend we didn't know each other than face the wrath of my sister.

"But thank you," I hastily added before I nervously rattled off the number of the booth Jay had been assigned. Feeling useless while they did the heavy lifting, I folded back the tonneau cover over my truck bed and pulled out the small, wheeled cart I kept in there. I could use it to load up the signage and marketing materials while they got the alcohol transported for me.

A large set of hands met mine, the contact startling me as I pulled the case holding the six-foot collapsible standing sign out of the back, preparing to hoist it into the wagon. "I can get this. We're here to help, ma'am."

"Well, first of all, don't call me ma'am," I responded, trying not to react when the calluses on his palm grazed the back of my hand, sending a shiver down my spine. "I'm in my early thirties, not my sixties."

He didn't react, taking the bag out of my hands and pulling the long strap over his shoulder.

"And second, I'm a perfectly capable adult. I can handle carrying some signage."

But he didn't respond, just continuing to unload items from the back of the truck and transferring them into my cart and another one he pulled over from the pop-up tent set up in the corner of the parking lot for the volunteers.

13

"Not a talker, huh?" I mused after I settled the cover back into place and locked the clamps before I slammed the tailgate, dusting my hands off on my shorts.

When I looked back up, I was met with an impassive stare, the imposing firefighter waiting for me with his arms crossed over his broad chest. He was dressed almost head to toe in dark colors, navy blue tactical pants tucked into black combat boots and a long-sleeved tech shirt covering his upper half.

Before I could think about the other way my words could be misinterpreted, I blurted out the first thing his outfit made me think. "Aren't you hot?"

His eyes widened, and one eyebrow disappeared underneath his hat, his head tipping to the side, but he still didn't open his mouth to respond. If he wasn't so insistent on being helpful, his imposing stature would have been intimidating.

"I mean, how can you stand to wear that?" I asked, gesturing at his outfit. It was supposed to get up into the high eighties today, which was hot for late June at this elevation. We mountain folk enjoyed our mild summers because we had such brutal winters on the other end. "Not that it doesn't look good, but I'd be suffocating covered head to toe. It's already warming up and this afternoon the temps are supposed to be in the..."

"It's my uniform, ma'am."

His voice was gruff, but I could tell he was amused, the slight quirk at the corner of his lips giving him away.

"I know, but everyone else is wearing shorts and short-sleeved T-shirts. You're covered head to toe in dark colors; you're going to bake once the sun comes out." It had already started emerging from the treetops in the distance, a warm orange glow filling the sky even though it was barely six in the morning.

"I'll be fine. I'd rather be warm than end up with a nasty sunburn."

Nodding, I picked up the handle of my cart, walking to the exit of the parking lot and toward the street where the festival booths were set up. He followed suit, pulling his cart beside mine, his gaze solely focused on where he was going. Not on the awkward woman at his side who kept asking him unwanted questions.

"Are you new around here?" I asked, unsure why I was trying to get him to have a conversation when he clearly did not want to talk. The question was, did he not want to talk in general, or did he not want to talk with *me*?

"Not exactly," he responded, and I waited for him to elaborate, but he never did.

"You look a bit familiar. Have we met before?" I couldn't shake the feeling that I somehow knew him.

"Not that I know of, ma'am."

"I work at the only bar in Sage Springs. Have you ever been there? Sometimes we get guys coming off a long shift from the firehouse."

"I haven't been there in a long time. Not really a big drinker."

"So, you *are* from around here?" I rephrased my earlier question, focusing my gaze on the side of his face.

There was a layer of darker pink skin behind his ear that trailed down the side of his neck and disappeared beneath the high collar of his shirt. He noticed me looking and his eyes darkened, his jaw twitching before he returned his gaze forward.

"Not exactly. Was born here, but I moved away when I was eighteen and haven't been back for more than a day or so in about a decade."

"Sounds like there's a story there," I mused, but he didn't take the bait. It also gave me the idea that he was probably around my age, but the faint lines at the sides of his eyes indicated he might be further into his thirties than I was.

Glancing down the street as we crossed an intersection that'd been closed and barricaded off for the festival, I noticed that the cases of whiskey had been neatly stacked at the back of the marked off space where I needed to go.

The beer tent next door had already been set up, but Reid and Hazel were missing. Since his bike was in the lot we'd just come from, I didn't think they'd be off doing naughty things, but I also

15

wouldn't go looking for them to find out. Been there, walked in on that.

The other volunteer firefighters were nowhere to be seen, so it seemed the man of few words to my side was stuck with me for a little while. At least I hoped he'd take pity on me to help get the pop-up shelter in place.

"Where's your shelter?" he asked, parking the wagon off to the side of the marked off space.

"Not interested in spilling your traumatic backstory to a stranger?" I teased, but he still didn't crack. He slipped past me, still not making eye contact, and unzipped the bag with the shelter inside.

I helped him pull it out of the bag, following his brief cues to stretch it out. I watched while he silently clipped the roof onto the frame. He was about a foot taller than me, so I just stepped back to stay out of his way, since he clearly had things handled.

The independent part of me wanted to insist I could handle it, but his size had me clearly at a disadvantage.

"Grab that corner and I'll pull it out," he instructed. "I'm hoping you brought some weights for the poles. Winds are supposed to pick up this afternoon. This thing will be a hazard if it's not weighted."

That was the most words this man had said to me all morning, and he was talking about the weather and pop-up shelter weights.

"Yeah, they're at the bottom of a few of the crates. Let me get the tables set up and I'll dig them out."

He nodded, and I worked on putting up the two folding tables the festival provided for each booth.

Going into autopilot, I covered them with tablecloths, carefully smoothing the new table runners across the top before I hoisted the first crate of whiskey onto one and started unpacking.

The shelter overhead only seemed to exaggerate the cool morning air, goosebumps cropping up on my skin while I worked. Sensing eyes on me, I glanced up, noticing him watching me.

It was a little unnerving to have him standing a few feet away, arms crossed on his barrel-like chest and those dark blue eyes tracking my every move.

Biting my tongue, since he obviously didn't want to engage in small talk, I emptied the crate and held out the weight. Unsuccessfully, I tried not to react as he bent over to secure it around the first pole, showcasing the snug fit of his tactical pants.

The silence between us felt charged as I continued unpacking, my eyes flitting up to meet his occasionally before they returned to what I was working on. My cheeks felt like they were on fire, and I had to stifle a laugh when my brain thought that maybe he'd like to put them out with his big hose.

Clearly, my nerves were bringing out my inner teenage boy. I should not be objectifying a virtual stranger who was *not* interested.

Not that I should be interested, either.

Technically, I was involved, although that was a flimsy excuse at best. Jay and I were the furthest thing from exclusive. Just because I'd never strayed from our arrangement didn't mean that was true for him. Although he'd never said anything, even I could acknowledge that Jay was an attractive man and would likely garner some attention from other women. Neither of us mentioned other partners, but that wasn't what our no-strings-attached relationship was about.

We provided each other with companionship, whether that meant sex or just sharing a meal together, we both knew the score.

For all I knew, he could be with someone else on his business trip this week, and the thought of that didn't spark jealousy from me in the least. Maybe that was the sign I needed to finally stop messing around with him. While it'd been a way for me to escape from having to invest emotions in a relationship when I needed it most, now it was just delaying the inevitable.

If I truly wanted to have a relationship like my parents had shared when I was a kid, I needed to put myself back out there.

But how did you tell the universe you were finally ready to meet your other half when you'd been hiding from it for so long?

"You okay over there?" an amused voice asked, my eyes widening before I glanced up at my grumpy firefighter. Wait, no. He was most definitely not *my* grumpy anything. I'd only just met him and...

"Yeah, I'm good," I squeaked, the heat in my cheeks doing the heavy lifting in dispelling the morning breeze that'd been making me shiver. Now, under his intense, but suddenly filled with mirth, stare, I was anything but chilled.

"You got another one of those weights for me?"

Redirecting my attention, I dug out the last few weights, try-ing—and failing—not to watch him bend over to fasten them to the legs of the shelter. I was suddenly craving cake.

My fingers fidgeted with a shot glass in my hand as he turned and aimed the full force of those penetrating eyes at me, the corner of his lip quirking into something that was decidedly not grumpy. I couldn't recall a time I'd ever had such a visceral reaction to any man, much less one I didn't even know.

He glanced around the booth, seeing the space take shape, and I was at a loss for words, afraid I'd start babbling again and scare him off, not that he'd be staying here with me. He was here to help with the event, not here to help me. Even if I was suddenly having visions of him pushing up the dark sleeves of his tech shirt and shouldering me to the side as he started pouring tasting shots to pass out to the hum of festival goers looking for a little buzz.

"I think you're set here," he said, voice even because he probably never got nervous like I felt right now. "Unless you need me for something else, I'm going to head back to the welcome tent and see where they need me next."

Nodding absently, I watched as his head tipped to the side, his fingers reaching up to scratch the side of his neck. A flinch barely flitted across his features before it was gone, and he stared down at his hand with something that looked like irritation. I wanted to ask him what was wrong, but swallowed the words as he returned his expectant gaze to me.

"I'm good, I can take it from here."

"I'll see you around then..." he trailed off, lifting his hand toward his neck awkwardly, then blinking hard and returning it to his side.

"Rhey," I blurted, my eyes widening slightly as my grandmother's nickname for me slipped from my mouth instead of what people had called me for over a decade. Everyone around here knew me as Annie, not Rheyanne.

He nodded, the smirk reappearing as he turned to go, catching sight of my sister's arch nemesis, Baker, headed in our direction.

"You done, Tripp?" he asked, but Baker was looking at me, shooting me a secret wink and an eyebrow wiggle.

Shaking my head, I tried to get my act together, because despite his complicated relationship with my sister, Baker would tease the shit out of me if he'd seen how awkward I had been around his coworker. Annie, the bartender, wasn't awkward. She was sarcastic with a quick wit and a no-nonsense attitude.

A bar full of unruly drunks never got my feathers ruffled in the way a single man I didn't even know had during the last ten minutes. And I needed to get my act together if I was going to make it through the next eight hours with my mask in place.

Chapter

Three

Tristan

"**D**UDE, YOU DON'T WANNA go there." Baker's voice cut through the fog in my head, and I turned toward him with a frown. "Go where?"

"*Her*, trust me. She'd eat you alive. The Thomas sisters are not for the faint at heart," he replied with a significant nod toward the beauty in the cutoff denim shorts that'd scrambled my brain the second she jumped out of that big ass truck she drove.

"She can eat whatever she wants," I muttered, suddenly cursing my brain-to-mouth filter.

Baker laughed loudly, slapping me on the shoulder, and I winced as the sensation of fire licked up my arm and across my back. Nerve damage was a fucking dick punch. I knew I was lucky that I could still feel it. My burns could've been worse. I could've been carrying around much worse damage than surface burns. My once smooth skin was puckered, pink, angry, and still hurt like a bitch, but I was grateful to still be alive.

"Trust me, there're plenty of other available women in this town who would be interested in the brooding, mysterious new cowboy firefighter. Just start talking in a southern drawl and wear a cowboy hat when you're not on duty and you won't know what to do with all the attention you get."

"Not interested," I grunted, briefly glancing over my shoulder, my eyes meeting Rhey's dark ones before she broke my stare, her cheeks flushing a deep shade of pink. I wanted to say it was the heat of the day, but there had been a vibe we'd both been dancing around while I helped her get set up. I'd been kind of a dick, trying to keep our focus on getting her booth set up while she was just trying to be friendly.

Most people would say that someone driving a truck as huge as hers was overcompensating for something, but I couldn't see a damn thing about that woman that didn't set my brain on fire. But I was here to help today, to prove to the chief that I didn't need a damn probationary period or to be "eased into duty" or whatever else bullshit he'd spouted off at me when he'd reluctantly hired me for the volunteer squad.

But I was having a hard time focusing, even though I knew I needed to. It'd been months since I'd touched a woman, and I wanted—no, I *needed*—to touch that woman. But it was probably also a terrible idea since I should've been focusing on getting my new life settled and trying to do whatever stupid bullshit the Chief wanted to get in his good graces.

Part of me also wanted to text my brother and demand the details on his employee, since she currently had his brand stretching across her ample chest. A chest that my baser instincts had imagined burying my face in while she was adorably rambling on the way to her booth.

"Yeah, your mouth might say that, but your eyes are undressing her, dude. Get it together. As far as I know, she doesn't do relationships, and I'm not one to perpetuate rumors, but there are other reasons she might be off limits to you."

"I'm just here to help people get set up and prove that I can handle being on duty."

"Mm hmm, sure. Not here to ogle pretty brunettes that blush the moment you make eye contact at all. But for real, don't let Chief's restrictions get to you, he just wants to make sure you've got a second to breathe before he metaphorically—well, maybe literally—throws you back into the fire."

"I've had more than enough seconds to breathe over the last four months. Sitting around on my ass has only made it harder to move past it," I gritted out, my jaw tense.

"Well, then, since you're not sitting on your ass anymore, go make yourself useful." Leave it to Baker to give me some tough love. At least he had a permanent position in the department. He didn't have to worry about the politics of trying to earn your spot. Not that I was sure I really wanted a full-time spot if one miraculously opened in this tiny ass town.

"Yes, Lieutenant," I quipped sarcastically and headed back to the festival coordinator for my next assignment.

The first two months I'd been trapped in my brother's place had been torture. It hurt to breathe, every minute stretch of my damaged skin felt like being stabbed with needles. I was constantly exhausted. And I hated all I could do was lay on my stomach in the bed in his tiny guest room and watch countless hours of streaming shows I didn't give a shit about.

When the forestry service had cut me loose with a fat severance check early in the spring, I'd fallen into a depression that I was still finding it hard to shake. I'd been on a crew of jumpers for over a decade. I lived, ate and breathed the job, and to suddenly not have a purpose was excruciating. What was even harder was realizing that there was nothing keeping me in Wyoming. That I'd spent a significant chunk of my life building a career with nothing to show outside of the job. Only the stinging reminder I was a *liability*.

Most of my friends were other jumpers or worked for the forestry service, and while their lives had moved on, mine had come to an abrupt halt. A few had texted me since I'd left, but I was having a hard time letting go of the lingering anger, which meant keeping in contact rarely happened. They had done nothing wrong, and it made me feel like shit, but they were living the life I wanted while mine had gone in reverse.

Which meant after more than a decade after leaving Sage Springs, I was forced to come back to the tiny ass community I'd grown up in with nothing to show for myself other than the scars I now wore on my back and a few duffel bags worth of belongings.

I'd left a young, idealistic man ready to prove himself, but had returned a scarred shell of myself. From the outside, everything seemed fine, but with every ounce of gratitude and praise from the people who found out about my career serving others, it just drove home the fact that part of my life was over.

Financial stability wasn't a problem either. It wasn't hard to save money when you got hazard pay and didn't have a social life. The problem was that there wasn't much of a career pivot available for a smoke jumper who'd been grounded. Permanently.

One who woke up in the middle of the night covered with sweat and had panic attacks when he let the memories of that day creep in. There weren't enough deep breathing exercises in the world that'd help you forget the feeling of being trapped like I'd been. There wasn't a sleeping pill strong enough to block out the phantom feeling of a wildfire out of control and threatening to consume not only the surrounding landscape, but your own body as well.

When my dad had reached out to the county fire chief on my behalf, I'd been pissed. But it got my foot in the door. I just had to decide if I wanted to continue to be a firefighter. This career wasn't one you easily walked away from. Over the years, it became a part of me, a calling I felt compelled to fulfill. An unshakable sense of duty that permeated the fiber of my being.

I'd appreciated that he was trying to help me find a place to land, but it'd just felt like an epic fucking demotion. Being a pro- bationary officer on a volunteer squad was like hitting rewind on my career and starting at the bottom again. Actually, since my first assignment had been ground support in a full-time position for the forestry service, it was below the bottom.

Sure, it was career adjacent to what I'd spent more than the last decade doing, but I couldn't survive on a volunteer firefighter's meager earnings. At this point, I only got paid a fraction of what I'd been paid before, and while the health insurance I'd negotiated was decent, my passion for jumping wasn't in my job description anymore. And it likely never would be again. I'd lost faith in my ability to make quick decisions, and in this line of work, it was a skill that meant life or death.

But along with my career trajectory being thrown in reverse, I'd also been forced to branch out to support myself. Which brought my new coworkers endless entertainment. They'd started calling me *cowboy* since I'd taken a ranch manager position at one of the local horse ranches. So now I babysat junior ranch hands and tourists who wanted to try their hand at ranching before they went back to their cushy lives at the end of their stay.

It wasn't a terrible job so far, and it got me out of my brother's place since they gave me a small cabin to live in as a part of my salary, but it wasn't the life I'd envisioned for myself. Being back here wasn't part of what I'd imagined for my future.

Although surveying the way the community was coming together to put on this festival, maybe I just wasn't giving it a fair shot. Growing up here had been idyllic, but it'd never been part of my plan to stay here long term. I'd wanted more for myself, to make my mark on the world.

Shaking my head to clear the constant anxiety that seemed to be my new companion, I refocused on what I was getting paid to be here to do, not on the things I couldn't control anymore.

A S THE DAY WENT on, I realized the pretty brunette who'd been lingering in my thoughts had been right; it was hot as fuck. And I was itching, literally, to pull off the long-sleeved shirt I'd carefully pulled on this morning, but with the sun high overhead, I couldn't risk it.

While I'd been lucky enough to only need spot graphs where the fire did the most damage along the back of my neck and under my arms, I couldn't risk further scarring or graft site rejection by getting sunburned. It was bad enough that I'd wear the marks of one split-second decision on the skin for the rest of my life. Even if that decision had ensured someone else had got to experience the rest of theirs.

Wiping sweat from my brow, I pulled my water bottle from the side pocket of my pants, trying—and failing—to keep my eyes away from the tent on the other side of the town square. The line at her booth was wrapping around the side of the aisle, blocking a few of the booths to her side, and even though the owners of said booths didn't seem bothered by the line blocking a clear path to them, I was duty bound to clear the traffic obstruction.

At least that's what I told myself when my feet started carrying me through the dense crowd and straight toward the person I'd been trying to ignore all morning. Baker's vague warnings about her complicated social life weren't at the forefront of my mind, because I wasn't interested in doing anything other than helping her clear the line at her booth.

It didn't matter that my eyes were laser focused on the small dimples that flashed when she smiled or laughed as she poured drinks. Or that I could see small droplets of sweat on the side of her neck that my depraved mind envisioned licking off while she rocked in my lap.

Fuck.

Getting a hard on in public probably wouldn't endear the new probie to the Chief, so I shut down those thoughts and navigated my way through the crowd.

Walking past the beer tent, I paused, surprised, as I watched my cousin filling a table full of glasses from a tapped keg. I knew Reid helped his best friend Hudson at the bar sometimes, but I hadn't realized that he'd also apparently helped himself to his buddy's little sister, who looked wildly different all grown up. Hazel had been in middle school when I'd left town and seeing her now made me suddenly feel old as fuck.

I probably should've made time to see him since I'd been back in town, but I'd hidden away in Jay's apartment for the last few months. My parents had tolerated my turning down invitations to family gatherings while I was still recovering, but with the annual family barbecue for the fourth approaching, I knew I'd have to bite the bullet and start showing up. Especially since my aunt and uncle lived down the road from the ranch.

"You going in?" a deep voice startled me, and I paused, looking over my shoulder into Baker's highly amused face.

"Fuck off," I laughed while he bounced his eyebrows, tilting his head toward the distillery booth. "Her line is becoming a problem, just trying to do what the Chief asked me to do and manage crowd control."

"Is that what gets you hot? Control?" Baker cackled, not deterred by my glare. "You gonna go back there and tell her what to do?"

"You're a sick fuck," I growled, but he just laughed, bumping my shoulder as he moved past me and disappeared into the crowd. But he wasn't necessarily wrong, I did like control. Just not in the way he was probably expecting.

As I locked eyes with Rhey, her cheeks turning pink as she held my gaze, I wondered what her thoughts were on the matter. But I didn't have time to find out, because she broke my stare, her eyes frantically scanning the line of people still waiting to sample my brother's whiskey.

Myself, I wanted to sample something else of my brother's, since his employee was becoming a very welcome distraction.

Maneuvering through the tight space between booths, I made my way behind the tables I'd greedily watched her set up this morning. Her eyes flitted in my direction as I quickly packed the empty bottles in the crates underneath, replacing them with full bottles.

"What are you doing?" she asked in a low voice between pours, looking at me with concern. "You're not certified to serve. You need a—"

Moving around her, I collected the empty plastic shot glasses that hadn't made it into the large barrel trash can at the corner of the booth.

"And I'm not the one serving," I answered, flipping up the table-cloths until I found one with extra napkins and cups.

27

"Stop rooting around under that table, I don't have time to straighten up the mess you're making under there."

Flashing her a smile, I neatly stacked the napkins in my hand, fanning them across the table to her side. "Seems like I'm the one cleaning up the mess, not making it."

"Little busy here, haven't exactly had time to straighten up," she clipped, looking irritated briefly before she turned on the charm with the next set of customers. She moved like having a bottle in her hand was an extension of who she was. When she said she worked at the bar over in the Springs, I hadn't realized that she was clearly the bartender there.

Maybe I'd have to pay regular visits to the River Run Tavern, where she worked, now that I was back in town. I'd only been there a few times over the years; on the rare occasion I could come back home for the holidays. Those visits had been few and far between, the schedule in my previous life dictated by Mother Nature, much to my mother's dismay.

"Seriously, why are you back here? You're making me anxious."

That was the last thing I wanted to do, even if she inspired the same feeling. Although if I were to have to put a more specific name to it, I'd probably use the word anticipation.

"I'm here to help."

"I don't—"

Cutting her off, I reached out to take payment from the next guest, placing it in the cashbox that looked just as chaotic as the rest of the table when I'd forced my way back here.

"Thank you, hope you enjoy that one. It's got a bit of a kick but goes down smooth."

Reluctantly, and with no small amount of side-eyed glances, Rhey let me help her clear the line, her pouring countless shots and mixed drinks while I handled the cashbox and payment app, replenishing supplies in the very brief lulls between groups.

I could tell by the curious stares that some people recognized me, but thankfully, no one said anything. Thank goodness, because the last thing I wanted to do was encourage the small-town gossip mill. Even though I was in uniform, I hoped people would view my assistance as helping my brother, not trying to put the moves on the local bombshell bartender.

It was bad enough I was the oldest Harding of the second generation and hadn't brought a wife with me when I'd returned home after so many years. My transient career had kept me so busy I hadn't had time to move past the superficial parts of a relationship before. And finding someone who could cope with me being gone—and in an unpredictable, dangerous environment—was a lot for the ones who lasted more than a few dates to handle.

Working side by side, the line eventually dwindled as the sun crept behind the trees. It was still sweltering outside, kind of an anomaly at our altitude, but nothing about my life lately had felt typical.

Blowing out a breath as the last person took their cocktail and retreated into the lively crowd, I looked over at Rhey. She was leaning against the support post of the tent, eyes closed, and cheeks flushed.

"You doin' okay over there?" I asked, watching as she took a deep breath, the logo tightening across her chest. Definitely not something I should be admiring. I'd come over here to help her, not to ogle her. But there was something about her that made it impossible to look away.

"Just tired," she whispered, her eyes blinking open. She swayed slightly as I watched her, alarm bells going off in my head.

"When was the last time you drank something?"

Her eyes slipped closed again, and she leaned her forehead against the metal pole gripped between her hands. "I'm fine."

The first responder training kicked in, noticing that while I'd seen her sweating this morning, her neck and chest looked suspiciously dry, the sweat marks on her shirt were long gone and I could see the pulse thrumming in her neck.

Pulling out my phone, I texted Baker.

Tripp: Can you bring me a chair, electrolyte tablets and some water?

29

Baker: Where are you?

Tripp: Distillery booth.

Baker: Still playing hero for our sexy town bartender?

Tripp: ETA

Baker: Someone over-served?

Tripp: More like the person doing the serving didn't serve herself any water.

Baker: Need me to send over someone from the ambulance crew? Rhodes isn't busy.

Tripp: I can handle her, just bring me that water.

Baker: I'm sure you can, cowboy ;) I know how much you like the "hands on" part of the job.

Tripp: Quit fucking around and get over here.

Baker: OMW

When I returned my gaze to Rhey, my eyes widened as I watched her sway to the side. If someone could look flushed, eerily pale, and beautiful as fuck all at one time, that was how I would have described her right at this moment.

"Fuck," I grunted, lunging to her side just as her grip on the pole loosened, her body swaying into my arms.

Chapter Four

Annie

"**I**S SHE OKAY?" A familiar high-pitched, feminine voice was way too close to my head, but I couldn't muster the energy to open my eyes to look at Hazel. My head throbbed as colors danced across my closed eyelids.

"She will be," a deep voice responded, fingers tracing across my temple, a cool palm covering my forehead in a way that felt oddly comforting. "We just need to get her to drink a little more."

"Wha...?" my voice cracked as I tried to speak, my tongue feeling dry and heavy in my mouth.

"Open up, pretty girl, we need to get you rehydrated," he whispered, and I would have swooned if I hadn't already.

"Did you just call her pretty girl?" Baker asked, letting out a borderline obnoxious laugh that made my headache worse.

"Shut the fuck up, man. I'm trying to comfort her," Tripp hissed.

"Yeah, sure, whatever you say, cowboy."

The fingers from my forehead disappeared, and I fought to open my eyes, the canopy of a tent above my head blurring as my eyelids lifted slowly.

"There we go," Tripp whispered, and I blinked, trying to focus. "Just open your lips so I can get more fluids in you."

A choking sound from my right drew my attention, and I struggled to focus on Baker standing a few feet away, trying to hold back laughter. Hazel was standing beside him, wringing her hands, and I tried to catalog where I even was.

"If you're not going to help, go do your job," Tripp growled. He dragged a wet cloth across my forehead and a cooling sensation followed in its wake.

"I'll let the Chief know you're off duty," he replied, nodding at me before he turned and left what appeared to be a white tent.

"Where am I?" I whispered, wincing as I swallowed.

"We're in one of the medical tents next to the visitor's center. You passed out, and we needed to get you out of the sun."

"How did I even get here?"

A smile pulled across Hazel's face as she nodded toward the man whose lap my head was currently resting on. "*Someone* caught you before you passed out and carried you through the festival. It was quite the sight."

An uncomfortable flush filled my already hot cheeks, and I wasn't sure if I could be any brighter red.

I knew I should have been better at making time to drink water, but I hadn't realized exactly how long it'd been since I took a drink when the line from hell finally let up.

I'd never admit it to him, but the moment I noticed Tripp moving through the crowd with a determined look on his face headed in my direction, my pulse had raced. I should have texted Hazel to send Mikey over to help long before then, but I had been determined to do it myself. Jay would be pissed if he knew I'd literally worked until I passed out. He'd blame himself for not being here, but as I tilted my head and glanced up at the man still looking down on me with concern etched across his features, I pushed Jay out of my head. I didn't want to think about him right now.

"You ready to drink some more?" he asked, holding the tip of the bottle to my lips. I nodded and craned my neck up slightly, sighing as the cool liquid filled my mouth. "Good girl, just small sips."

After a few swallows, he pulled the bottle away, brushing my sweaty hair off my forehead. I didn't know where my hat had gone, but as his rough fingertips traced across my skin, I honestly didn't care.

"Do I need to take her to the hospital?" Hazel asked, and I slowly turned my head in her direction.

"Nah, I think she'll be okay. If I can get her to drink the rest of this, and maybe another one, I think she'll be okay."

Hazel nodded, taking a relieved breath. I hated that I'd worried her. In all the years I'd known her, she'd probably never seen me like this. "Reid and I can pack up the booth with Colette, she heard what happened and came to help. Hudson and Charley took over breaking down the beer tent, so I can stay here if you want me to—"

"Breathe," I chuckled, wincing when I swallowed against my dry throat. "If you can pack up, that'd be good. Colette knows how to get into the distillery to drop it all off. Jay won't be back until next week."

"Did you want me to call—"

"No, you don't need to call him," I cut out, avoiding Tripp's curious gaze. With my head in his lap—as innocent as it was—I didn't want to talk about another man around him. Much less one who was making every interaction I was having with Tripp awkward. Jay was the elephant in the room that Tripp didn't even know existed.

"I was going to ask if you wanted me to call Reese. Do you want to have her come get you?"

"What time is it?" I asked, looking around, but the darkened tent made it hard to tell if it was still daytime outside.

"It's almost seven, and since the fireworks show was canceled, people are clearing out."

Frowning, I wondered why the annual fireworks display was canceled. It was a tradition that had been around longer than I'd lived here.

"Red flag warning," Tripp filled in, holding the bottle back to my lips. "The Chief called it off around the same time you collapsed."

"Well, I guess at least people were distracted by that and didn't have to see me getting—"

Hazel giggled, shaking her head. "Oh, no. Don't worry, plenty of people still saw you getting carried through the crowd by a firefighter. Don't think that gossip is gonna go away anytime soon."

"Shit," I hissed, closing my eyes and pinching the bridge of my nose. Being the center of attention in a small town that couldn't mind its own business was not my idea of having a good time. I was the one people told the juicy gossip to, not the one who the gossip was about.

"I guess if you're going to load up the booth, I'll just wait until you're done and then I can head home."

"You're not driving anywhere." Tripp's voice had lost the gentleness he'd been using since I woke up with my head in his lap, replaced with something a little sterner. It shouldn't have had me reacting to it, but goosebumps cropped up along my arms, regardless. "You need to be taking it easy until you're rehydrated."

Hazel shot me a look, her eyes bouncing between the two of us. "I know you have to be back in town tomorrow for work—want to just stay in the apartment at the bar tonight? Then I can keep an eye on you if you need it. Reese is probably at the hospital overnight, right?"

My sister was likely already at the hospital by now. Hopefully, this incident had managed to stay off her radar, or she'd be giving me endless amounts of shit for not taking care of myself. You'd think as my younger sister, I'd be the one lecturing her on taking care of herself, but that was definitely not the case.

"Do you have a car here?"

Hazel shook her head. "No, Reid and I took his bike over, but I can drive your truck back to the bar."

"Do you even know how to drive a stick?" I asked, figuring she probably didn't. Hazel was more of a passenger princess, or I guess a biker backpack, with Reid's chosen method of transportation. "And I'm not talking about the one in Reid's pants or in the drawings you think no one knows about."

Her cheeks turned pink, clearly embarrassed that I'd outed her penchant for drawing male genitalia to a stranger. It was the worst kept secret around Sage Springs now that people had found her hidden Instagram page.

"I'll take you home when the time comes," Tripp commented.

Without even thinking about it, I blurted out. "Do *you* know how to handle a stick?"

Tripp chuckled along with Hazel, and I felt my cheeks flame again.

"I can handle a stick just fine. Your larger than usual equipment doesn't scare me."

"On that note, I'm gonna go and let everyone know you're awake. If you're making dick jokes, then I think I can tell them you're gonna be fine," Hazel said, backing up slowly.

She left the tent, and an awkward silence suddenly loomed, the sounds of the dwindling festival muted through the heavy tarp sides.

"You don't have to drive me. I'm sure I can..."

Tripp scoffed, returning the cool cloth to my forehead, droplets of water trailing down the side of my face. I watched as one landed on his leg, absorbing into the navy-blue material of his tactical pants. "You don't let people take care of you very often, do you?" He didn't sound mad, just curious.

"No. I don't like people telling me what to do. I like to be the one in control."

"You don't say," he chuckled, holding the opening of the water bottle to my lips and encouraging me to take another drink. "I never would have been able to tell the woman—who literally made herself sick because she didn't want to ask for help—liked to be in charge."

"I can do that." My hand closed over his on the bottle, and I tried to ignore the sensation I felt suddenly rushing up my arm. I wanted to blame it on the heat exhaustion, but I had a feeling it was just my body's reaction to him.

"I know you can. But you don't need to. Just drink. Me holding a water bottle for you isn't going to compromise your independence."

After taking a few more sips, I settled back down, my headache still making it hard to keep my eyes open, but I felt better than I had when the dehydration had caught up with me earlier. Typically, I was pretty good at drinking water during events, especially since we were at a higher elevation, but I'd been a little more distracted than usual this morning. And while I'd warned him about the day being hotter than usual, clearly, I hadn't heeded my own warnings.

"You don't have to stay here with me. I'm sure you have better things to do right now."

He leaned forward, waiting until my eyes made contact with his. "My job today was to help and keep people safe, so I think I'm right where I need to be. Now let's finish this bottle and work on getting you to sit up. Once I get another one of these in you, you can direct me to where I'm taking you."

"But what about your vehicle?"

"It'll be fine. I'm sure I can get one of the guys from the station to bring it to me or pick me up. I'm more concerned about you getting rehydrated right now."

Nodding, I did as he instructed, slowly taking sips of the electrolyte drink until the bottle was empty, waiting patiently until he had another one mixed before I let him help me sit up. He stayed close, moving a chair in front of me and letting his large thighs bracket my knees while I rested my head against the side of the tent, closing my eyes and taking deep breaths.

The nausea I'd felt earlier had slowly subsided, and as the liquid in the bottle diminished, my headache eased. Now I was just left with the lingering embarrassment I felt at having fainted in this man's arms. He spent the morning trying to escape my awkward small talk, but was now having to spend the evening babysitting me because I was too stubborn to take care of myself like a normal human being.

"I'm sorry I derailed your day," I whispered, trying to avoid his steady gaze.

But he dipped his head, moving into my line of sight as his large hand closed over mine. "Are you kidding? This made me feel useful for the first time in months."

"Well...thank you. Clearly, your timing was impeccable since you showed up right when I needed you."

"I should have trusted my instincts and shown up earlier instead of watching you from across the crowd. Maybe if I'd been a little more proactive, I could have helped you out sooner."

Biting the corner of my lip, I worried the dry skin between my teeth for a moment before I looked up at his gentle smile. "You were watching me?"

"You're kind of hard not to notice."

He held my gaze, his fingertips grazing my knee, and my stomach flipped, a wave of something completely opposite of the nausea I'd felt earlier causing my breath to stutter.

"Hey, I—" Baker's voice cut through the sudden tension, and I averted my gaze as Tripp sat upright, turning toward his coworker with a frown. "Sorry for interrupting."

"You're not—"

"It's not—"

My voice overlapped with Tripp's, and Baker's eyes widened as his shoulders shook, clearly entertained by the scene he thought he'd interrupted. It *had* seemed kind of like a moment, but it'd been so long since I'd had one of those with another guy, I'd almost forgotten what that felt like.

"Anyway, now that most of the crowd has cleared out, I wanted to see if you could come help break things down so we can get out of here before it gets dark. I got one of the EMTs to spare a bag of IV fluids for the patient here." He motioned to the woman I hadn't noticed standing behind him. She stood at the entrance of the tent, a bag of fluids held above her head in one hand and a small bag of supplies in her other.

"Sure thing," Tripp confirmed, squeezing my knee before he stood. He pinned me with a significant look. "I meant what I said earlier, you're not in any condition to drive. When I return, you'd better be here."

"Yes, Sir, I'll be a good girl," I joked, and his eyes flared with heat before he nodded and followed Baker out of the tent.

"Hey, I'm Daisy. I'll get this hooked up and let you rest for a bit."

Nodding, I held out my arm for her to get the line started, knowing that I needed to go along with it because I couldn't afford to be out of commission with the fatigue I knew would eventually hit me.

She reached up on her toes to hang a hook from the bar above our heads, going through the motions I'd seen my sister do countless times for our grandmother toward the end of her life. I'd also been Reese's pin cushion when she was in nursing school and wanted to perfect her IV skills.

"I'll check back in on you in a bit to take it out. Do you need anything?"

Waving her away, I sat back, closing my eyes and drifting off as I let the IV do its thing.

"**D**O YOU NEED HELP with her?" Baker's voice was much quieter than I was used to it sounding as I tried to wake myself up.

Reaching for my arm before I opened my eyes, my fingers met a Band-aid in the crook of my elbow, the fluids clearly long gone. I wondered how long I'd been asleep, but I felt much better than I had the last time I'd awoken in the same tent.

"Nah, I got it. Once I get her keys, I'll take her back to the Springs. Sounds like she was planning to stay at the apartment above the bar tonight." Tripp's voice was a low whisper, but it still had the same effect on me as it had earlier.

"Okay, I'll drive your truck over there and leave the keys with Hudson if you're not back by the time I need to head to the station. The Chief is worried about this weekend and wants to make sure the rapid response team is briefed in case something happens that we need to mobilize."

"Do I need to come back to the station tonight?"

"No," Baker sighed, his gaze flitting to me briefly as I blinked against the haze of fatigue. "This is just for the salaried squad. Volunteers are back on call as needed. Just keep your cell charged in case they need to call you in."

Tripp nodded and then turned his attention back to me, a small smile pulling at the corner of his lips while he crouched down and picked up my hand, inspecting the Band-aid with a gentle fingertip. "Looks like they got ya all patched up. You ready to go?"

When I looked over his shoulder, Baker was long gone, presumably to take Tripp's truck to the bar so he could finally escape the train wreck he'd been stuck with for half the day.

"Yeah, but are you sure it's not too much trouble? I'm sure you have somewhere else you'd rather be right now than babysitting me."

"Nah, just headed back to an empty cabin, so you've saved me from another long night of boredom."

"No roommates?" I asked, unable to stifle my curiosity about this man.

"Nope, not unless you count the spiders I've been re-homing back in the wilderness all week." Of course, he would be the type to rescue spiders instead of killing them. I had a feeling the sense of chivalry ran strong in this one.

"You don't have anything better to do than be my knight in shining armor?"

He shot me an amused look as he stood to his full height, slowly pulling me to my feet. I was not a short woman by any means, but my eyes barely crested his shoulder, my breath stuttering in my chest as his stubble scraped against my temple.

"Nope, unfortunately you're stuck with me, but we both know you're not a damsel, even if I did technically rescue you...from yourself."

"Ha, ha." Looking up at him, I rolled my eyes, earning a deep chuckle that I could feel since our chests were brushing up against each other. Bracing my hand on his pec, I tried to fight the urge to squeeze the firm muscle beneath my palm. "I guess if you insist on continuing to expose yourself to my hot mess, the least I can do is offer you dinner once we get to the bar."

His palm grazed my side, and I swayed at the contact, gasping when he pulled me firmly against his strong, muscular chest.

"You gonna cook for me?"

Laughing, I shook my head as I looked up into his eyes. At some point, he'd flipped his hat around backwards, and I was trying to ignore how hot it made him look. "Not unless you're into cereal for dinner. But I can offer you some top-notch chicken fingers and tater tots. They're quite popular amongst the college kids."

"Do I look like a college kid to you?" he asked, the movement of his thumb against the bare skin on my side making me shudder.

"Nope." His smile widened at my squeaked response. "Definitely a man. A very, *very* tall, fully grown man."

"Glad you noticed."

"Hard not to," I whispered, taking a step back, my knee giving out as I backed into the cot behind me. He caught me before I toppled backwards, pulling me back against his chest.

"Careful there. Don't need you doing anything else to hurt yourself tonight."

"Guess it's a good thing I've still got you around."

"Guess so," he murmured, taking a few steps back to let me pass him, but keeping a hand on my side to steady me. If it were anyone else, I would have shaken off his touch and insisted I was fine, but I had to admit it was nice to be the center of his attention. Even if it was to keep me from hurting myself.

Thankfully, as the sun sunk down below the ridge, the temperature had also dropped, a breeze prickling my skin as we walked through the remains of the festival and toward my truck in the parking lot that seemed a lot further away than it had this morning.

Shivering, I crossed my arms, knowing that it was just my body trying to regulate my temperature again. But as Tripp pulled me into his side, rubbing his hand up and down the side of my arm, the chill was the last thing on my mind.

Chapter Five

Tristan

W HILE SHE STILL LOOKED exhausted, the color had returned to Rhey's cheeks, and she seemed in better spirits than before the medic had given her the IV.

Baker had wanted to call her sister, who was apparently an ER nurse at the hospital, but I had a feeling the independent woman currently fidgeting with the hem of her shorts in the passenger seat of her truck would not have been on board with that. She didn't seem like the type who wanted to draw a lot of attention to herself. And I could relate to not wanting to have younger siblings in your business.

Jayden had graciously let me stay in his guest room instead of being stuck in the purgatory that would have been living in my childhood bedroom under my mother's care for months on end. He'd mostly just checked in on me to see if I needed anything, but I'd hated that feeling of being under a microscope.

As soon as I'd found out from Marty West, the owner of the ranch I now helped manage, that a small, dated cabin came with the position, I'd been ready to check it out the next day. It'd been a few weeks since I took possession, but now that the cobwebs were cleared out—and hopefully most of my arachnid friends—it was feeling like home.

And I didn't have to worry about cramping my brother's style anymore. He hadn't brought a single woman back to his place in the four months I'd lived there, and I had a hard time believing he went that long between partners. My baby brother had been a total slut in high school even as a freshman while I was a senior, so I doubted that'd changed much in the last twenty years.

"Do you need me to tell you where to go?" Rhey's quiet voice cut through the silence in the truck cab, and I glanced at her briefly as I took the turn that'd take me up the mountain pass that separated Butterfly Ridge from Sage Springs.

"While you're welcome to boss me around," I teased, returning my eyes to the road and pressing the gas, the engine of the over-sized Ram purring. "I know where I'm going."

"Just wanted to make sure since you said it'd been a long time since you lived here."

"I could come back in another twenty years, and it'd probably still be mostly the same," I commented, resisting the urge to watch her because I needed to focus on the road.

"Isn't that the beauty of small towns?" she asked, but her tone was melancholy. Almost like she didn't exactly feel like she was a part of things, just an outside observer.

"Or the curse. Didn't you notice all the people watching us when I came to help earlier?"

"Um, I was kinda passed out when you took me to the med tent, so no, wasn't exactly aware of people watching that. Although it'd be normal anywhere to be a little curious when a big strapping firefighter is carrying an unconscious woman through a crowd."

"I meant before you passed out while I was just helping you get the line down," I chuckled, although carrying her through the crowd had been a memorable moment. But I'd been more focused on her than the crowd parting to let us through. "It was the same when I was in high school, everybody in everybody else's business. I'm sure there will be some rumors circulating tomorrow."

"Well, coming inside for your gourmet meal of fried bar food will surely get the tongues wagging."

Instead of the panic I thought I'd feel at being the subject of additional scrutiny from the members of the small community we lived in, I kind of wanted to double down and give them something to really talk about. It wouldn't have been the first time considering how I had returned to town after over a decade of being on my own.

When I woke up this morning, trying to quell the panic that usually came after the nightmares that had plagued me for months—breathing through the chaos—I hadn't expected my day to end on a vaguely enjoyable note.

Was I happy that my passenger had passed out from heat exhaustion? Hell no, but I wasn't sad about the fact that I got to be the one to feel useful for the first time in months and come to her rescue. And making sure she got back to the bar safely where she'd invited me to eat with her was better than the alternative of heating a can of soup on the outdated appliances I needed to update in my new home.

"Let them talk. I have nothing to hide."

She let out a labored breath in response, leaning her head against the window in the passenger side door. I suddenly wondered if maybe *she* had something to hide. But I left her secrets alone, carefully navigating the dark roads while she drifted off in the passenger seat.

HUDSON, THE OWNER OF the bar, was waiting at the back door, leaning against the brick wall with his arms crossed, as I pulled Rhey's truck into the alley behind the building. I could see my boss' daughter—not so little anymore—Charley West, standing beside him inside the doorway, bouncing on her toes as I downshifted and engaged the parking brake.

Rhey didn't budge as I pulled the keys out of the ignition on the late model Ram, reaching over to drop them inside her open purse on the seat between us.

"Wake up, pretty girl," I whispered, squeezing her kneecap light-ly. When she didn't budge, I figured our plans for the evening were going to have to be put on hold. I'd never been so disappointed to miss out on tater tots before. But hopefully since we lived in the same small town, and I knew where she worked, we'd see each other again.

Sighing, I unbuckled my seatbelt, slipping out of the driver's seat and locking the manual lock on my side before I walked around the front of the behemoth and carefully opened the passenger side door.

"You want me to take her?" Hudson offered as he stepped for-ward, holding his hand out to take her purse from me.

"Nah, I got her." Stepping onto the running board and leaning across her sleeping form, I unbuckled the seatbelt, her soft breaths tickling my neck as I pulled back. She was completely asleep as I lifted her out of the truck. Instead of hanging limply in my arms like she had before, she tucked her face into my neck and grabbed a fistful of my shirt.

"I'll show you where you can lay her down," Charley whispered before she led the way up a back staircase to a modest apartment above the bar, holding the door open for me before she flicked on the living room light. I followed her down a small hallway and into a sparsely decorated room, laying Rhey down after she pulled the covers out of the way.

Charley and I worked to remove her boots and get her tucked in. She only stirred briefly as I tugged off her hat. I had to fight off the sudden urge to kiss her on the forehead before I pulled the covers up to her shoulders.

Watching how exhausted she was, I had a feeling it had more to do with her stubborn refusal to do everything on her own than just a simple case of heat exhaustion. It endeared her to me even more, because until I got hurt, I'd also been a stubborn asshole who didn't like to ask for help. Maybe that was just another thing we had in common.

"Thank you for driving her back here, Tripp," Charley whispered after she led me out of the apartment and down the stairs to where Hudson was waiting for us in the back hallway of the bar.

"Thanks, man," Hudson echoed as he joined us, pulling me in for a half hug and back slap that had me fighting off a wince.

"Did Baker stop by yet?" I asked, knowing I probably needed to get back to the ranch and get some sleep before I needed to be up at the ass crack of dawn tomorrow.

Hudson dropped my keys into my hand, tilting his head toward the front of the door. "Drinks are on me if you've got time."

Shaking my head, I pocketed my keys. "Maybe another time, I've got an early morning. But someone told me I'll need to stop by for some tater tots sometime."

He chuckled, thankfully letting me off the hook. "Tots on the house then next time. I'm sure my fainting bartender who works Thursdays and Saturdays would love to help you out with those."

"Real subtle, ding dong, why don't you close out the bar so we can get out of here," Charley laughed, flicking his arm and shaking her head. Hudson shrugged, nodding at me before he took off down a side hallway. "Sorry, he's kind of oblivious sometimes. But for real, I'm sure Annie is thankful you were there. Hazel told me you went all white knight and carried her halfway across the town square with everyone watching."

"Annie?"

"Did she not tell you her name?" she asked, looking confused.

"Her name isn't Rhey?"

Charley shook her head. "Well, I guess it kind of is. Her name is Rheyanne, but everyone around here calls her Annie. Wonder why she told you Rhey?"

And now I was wondering the same as well. She hadn't corrected me when I'd called her that all day, and I kind of liked that she wanted me to call her something different from everyone else. I hadn't exactly been honest with her about my name, either. I had told the guys around the fire station to call me Tripp because that was what I'd gone by for years when I wasn't back in Colorado.

"Can I give you my number to give to her when she wakes up?"

"Gimme your phone and I can put hers in there for you." Her smile widened, her eyebrows dancing as she held out her hand. Passing over my phone, I watched as she pulled open a new text message filled with a local number and then handed it back to me.

"Thanks, I guess I'll see you around."

She nodded and shot me a grin before she turned to follow Hudson to the front of the bar, leaving me to let myself out the back door. The sun had finally set, but the wind had picked up, rustling the trees in a way that almost sounded ominous.

While the winters in Wyoming could be a little more brutal, I was used to the weather changes in the mountains. But as I drove back to the ranch, I couldn't shake the feeling that everything was about to shift.

A BLARING SOUND FROM my phone at 4:30 in the morning, when my alarm was already set for 5:15, was not the ideal way to be woken up from a nightmare. My already frazzled nerves were on edge when it went off again moments later, which sent me scrambling for it on the nightstand. Pulling open the notification app the fire station used, my stomach dropped as I read the push alert that had been sent to my phone.

> *Active fire alert for Eastern Chaffee County. County roads north of US Hwy 50 east of Monarch Pass are closed to thru traffic. All on call officers need to report to checkpoint to help set up detours and alert affected residents.*

Adrenaline kicked in as I threw off the covers, pulling out a clean class B uniform and getting dressed while I tried to run through the list of protocol that I'd studied last week during my onboarding with the fire department.

I needed to notify Marty I wouldn't be around the ranch this morning, but we'd discussed the logistics around me being a volunteer firefighter before he'd hired me. He knew I might need to take off at a moment's notice, I just hadn't expected it to be this soon.

> *Tristan: Being called in, I'll send you an update once I know more.*

> *Marty: We have things covered here, let me know if there is anything we can do to help.*

Hesitating, I pulled up Baker's number, firing off a text before I shoved my utility knife in my pocket and clipped my gloves to my belt. Everything else I'd need, like my turnout gear and my breathing SCBA, were locked in a chest in my truck bed. Typically, if there was an active blaze I'd be reporting in full turnout, but since I was still a probationary officer, I knew the Chief wouldn't let me suit up.

> *Tripp: You already on site?*

Baker was typically assigned to search and rescue, so I knew he likely wouldn't be a frontline report to the actual fire. Not unless they really needed him.

> *Baker: You on your way? Chief just told us he sent out the volunteer alert. I've been up on the ridge for the last two hours directing traffic like a fucking meter maid.*

> *Tripp: Meter maids don't direct traffic, they write tickets, dipshit. We get that much traffic through the pass in the middle of the night?*

> *Baker: No, but I'm bored as fuck and want to feel useful. You better get your ass up here so you can direct traffic, probie.*

Tripp: Fuck off. Thanks for reminding me how low I am in the ranks.

Baker: No problem. Now get your ass in gear, bitch boy.

Choosing not to react, I finished getting myself ready, hopping into my truck and pulling up the location pin that had been sent to my phone before I took the access road from the back side of the ranch to the highway.

Heading north of town, the roads were quiet; the sun hovering low behind the trees, an ominous orange haze hovering across the pavement. The wind had picked up overnight, rustling the trees and making the windows in my truck vibrate in the frame. While it'd helped bring down the uncharacteristic sweltering temperatures we'd had lately, it was only going to make containing this fire more difficult.

Under normal circumstances it was a bad time of year for wildfire, but with the lack of rain, higher than normal temperatures, and now the wind gusts that were strong enough to shake my truck while I was driving, I did not have a good feeling about this. There were certain instincts you honed as a specialty firefighter, and reading the environmental conditions was something I'd learned a long time ago. Things were about to get very real about my new assignment.

Chapter

Six

Tristan

PULLING ONTO THE SHOULDER, I eyed the line of cars along the side of the road and then craned my neck to the side to see above the skyline through the windshield. A winding column of smoke was visible in the distance and my training kicked in, calculating the risk of where we were located and the distance to the fire.

It didn't appear to be very large yet, but that didn't mean shit when you were dealing with an uncontained blaze and the high winds that hadn't improved as I ascended the mountain pass.

Climbing out, I shoved my phone in my pocket and filled my cargo pockets with two bottles of water and my compass.

Since I wasn't cleared for interior work, I doubted the Chief would let me go up with the ground crew that was likely up on the ridge working containment.

We were still a few miles outside of town, but there were acres and acres of kindling in between that could go up in the blink of an eye. I was hoping the natural barriers of the river and the reservoir south of the ridge would help us keep it from jumping the road, but nature didn't always like to play by the rules.

"Officer Harding, glad to see the alert system works." The Chief nodded as I hiked up the remaining incline and ducked underneath the flap of the temporary pop-up shelter they'd set up on the gravel shoulder of the road.

"Where do you need me?" There was no point in beating around the bush or trying to convince him I needed to be on the ground crew. He'd made his stance clear during my initial interview; he thought I was a liability until I proved otherwise.

It didn't matter that I had more extensive field training than almost every single officer in the department, including him. Once that PTSD label had been slapped on my file, it took away the one thing in my life I'd worked literally decades to achieve. But the only thing I could do to prove myself was to keep showing up. To deal with whatever he threw at me and say thank you with a smile. And hope that I didn't have a panic attack while on duty that would put the final nail in the coffin of my calling to be a firefighter.

"Baker and Rhodes are running the current motorist barricades, and I have another crew setting up detour signs before the turnoff for the pass that'll keep traffic from getting up here. We'll need some guys south of the ridge to direct traffic if we end up requiring an evacuation, but right now I could use someone to do gear checks on the supply rig. Go with Officer Ford and he'll show you what I need done."

"On it," I nodded, following an officer almost a decade younger than me toward the mobile supply unit that'd stay close to where the fire containment crew was working. We spent over an hour checking valves, filling tanks and making sure that the ground crew could quickly grab any supplies they needed. It was busy work at its finest, but it was better than sitting on the ranch feeling useless.

At one point, we all donned particulate masks because the wind changed directions and started raining down ash particles on where we were located. But I just put my head down and focused on what I could do, helping fill in the supplies that'd save other officers time in an emergency. Every fiber of my being wanted to be up that mountain surrounded by smoke, figuring out how to run a containment line, but that wasn't my life anymore.

After what felt like forever, but was really a few hours, the Chief pulled us all to where the pop-up shelter had now been broken down and loaded into the back of a department pickup truck headed toward town.

"We're going to swap crews and push back to the barriers. The high winds are reducing visibility and we're going to have to enact an evacuation zone. Lake County crews are coming at the fire from the north, but the wind is causing spot fires to crop up outside the containment zone. It's better to be safe than sorry, so we need to get the civilians most at risk out of the way while we can do it easily."

He barked orders to different crews, and the crowd thinned out quickly, officers springing into action for their assignments. Baker took off for one of the emergency rigs, ready to start residential evacuations north of the pass, but I knew his job wouldn't be an easy one. There were rentals all over the mountain, some up winding sparsely accessible roads, so it wasn't like your typical urban evacuation where you just went house to house and banged on doors. This was driving into remote areas, not knowing who or what you'd be encountering.

"Harding, I want you to head back to town. I need you rested in case we need to call the volunteer crew back in to assist," Chief explained, clamping his large hand on my shoulder. Fighting the urge to wince as it set off a cascade of nerve pain down my back, I nodded, knowing I needed to stay on his good side to prove myself.

"Yes, sir."

"I know you want to be up there, but I'm sure the Wests could use you at the ranch right now to get things prepped in case we need to do a town-wide evacuation. They'll appreciate your experience if it comes to that."

Gritting my teeth, I tried to resist the urge to plead my case, knowing that it didn't matter what I thought I was ready for. He was the one calling the shots, and he thought he was doing what he needed to do to ensure the safety of his department and of the residents we were duty bound to protect.

Didn't make it suck any less. And it certainly didn't make me feel any less useless than I had since I'd woken up in the hospital four and a half months ago knowing my life as it had been was over.

"Marty would be fine with me staying out here to help where I'm needed. I know you can't send me up to the fire, but surely there are other things I can do around here or back at the station."

He flashed me with a look of pity, shaking his head. "All I need from you right now is for you to help them set up the new barricades at the detour point and then you can take off. If it makes you feel any better, I can send a radio with you so you can hear if the line shifts in your direction. You'll get another push alert to your phone if we decide to call everyone in, so just make sure you keep it charged. Hopefully, we can get this back under control in the next few hours, so we don't need to do that."

Nodding, I turned and headed back to my truck, hating that I couldn't be more useful to him. And hating myself more, because it was my savior complex that had put me in this situation to begin with.

Chapter
Seven

Annie

M Y TEMPLES THROBBED AS I opened my eyes slowly, blinking against the stream of light coming into the window that faced the parking lot. The fatigue I'd been feeling last night had lifted slightly, but I still felt like shit.

Hazel had let me crash at her apartment a few times in recent months, so I had a few tiny bottles of shampoo and body wash in the shower. Maybe getting clean would clear my head.

Raiding her mostly empty dresser, I found a clean oversized button-up shirt, but there was no way I was fitting in anything else from her wardrobe as she was tiny. I had a bit more junk in my trunk.

Stripping off my clothing from the day before, I stepped into the warm spray, washing off the dried sweat from being outside all day in the heat at the festival.

Flashes of deep blue eyes danced behind my eyelids as I washed, and I regretted letting myself get so run down. Eating chicken tenders and tater tots with Tripp would've been vastly more enjoyable than passing out from exhaustion on the way home and sleeping in someone else's bed.

It almost would've felt like a date, and I wasn't sure how I felt about that. Sure, I ate meals and did things with Jay regularly, but it'd been a long, long time since that had felt remotely romantic.

When we first started hooking up, there had been an inkling that could've led to something more, but his emotional distance and my fear of abandonment had shut that down quickly. We were well suited as friends, and he understood me in a way no one else probably did, but I'd never imagined a real future with him.

Letting my thoughts stray to Tripp, I wondered if my initial attraction would fade like that, but there was also an underlying current to our interactions throughout the day that I couldn't stop thinking about.

But maybe our flirtation had passed, too. Maybe falling asleep in the truck was the natural conclusion to the night and I wouldn't see him other than in passing. We lived in a small community, but that didn't mean we were now magically friends. And then there was the complication of Jayden to factor in. How did you break up with someone you weren't really dating? Just thinking about it made my head hurt.

Running through the things I should probably do since I was in town early for my shift, I decided now would be the ideal time to run some inventory in the liquor storage room.

Hudson usually kept a close eye on things since he was the other full-time bartender, but he'd also been actively cutting back on his hours. Not that I could blame him, this bar had been pretty much our lives for the last seven years. Now he'd moved on, with his relationship taking a priority in his schedule.

Plus, I was still here. Still spending every weekend making drinks for everyone in town who had a social life.

Rinsing my hair, I tried to reset my attitude, because I was the only person who could change that. No one else made me retreat into myself after my grandmother died. The woman who'd sacrificed her retirement to raise two preteen girls after their parents succumbed to the generational curse that had taken her husband at a young age. Not that I believed the curse was real. But if it was, I was running out of time to do something other than maintain the status quo.

Normally my purse contained an *in case of emergency* kit with a spare pair of panties, but I'd forgotten to replace them after the last time I'd stayed here—so commando it was. Thankfully, this pair of denim shorts were longer than normal and didn't have any artfully placed frayed spots that would show off my lack of clean undergarments. Not that I'd be the first person to have gone au naturale in the bar.

My hair was still wet, and I didn't have the energy to dry it, which meant two loose braids were as good as it was going to get. My little emergency kit still had deodorant wipes, so I swiped my underarms and called it adequate. Everyone in town knew who I was, so it wasn't like I needed to impress anyone other than the new firefighter who told me he rarely stepped foot inside this building, despite growing up a few miles away. Not that he'd have a reason to come to see me. He probably felt sorry for me.

"Hey, you're up. Feeling any better?" Hazel asked, startling me from her perch on the couch as I rounded the corner into the living room of the small apartment above the bar.

A dull throb still lingered at my temples, but it wasn't anything guzzling some water wouldn't resolve. At least the shower had made me feel somewhat human. I cast a longing look at Hazel's mug on the coffee table, but I knew she probably didn't have any coffee here, anyway. While I craved the caffeine to survive the day, I knew it messed with her concentration and she preferred tea.

"Kinda. Thanks for letting me crash here."

"It's not like I was using the bed anyway," she laughed, returning her attention to the tablet in her lap. I was well aware that she only used this space on her days off to draw, somewhat relieved I was no longer subjected to the sounds of raucous banging while I was doing inventory in the storage room below her bedroom.

While she appeared like innocence personified at first glance, Hazel was loud, not that it was surprising considering her boyfriend Reid's reputation. I'd never taken a spin on that pierced ride—mostly because my tenuous situationship with his cousin would have made that epically weird—but I'd overheard enough conversations at the bar to know he had some modifications to his equipment that drove the ladies wild.

"If you need to stay here again, you're more than welcome. I know Reese might have figured out something different, but the offer is there if you need it."

"Okay." The word stretched as it came out of my mouth, my furrowed brows causing Hazel's eyes to widen.

"Oh, shit. You didn't hear, did you? Of course you didn't, you've been asleep, and your phone was out here in your purse. Shit," she rambled, her look morphing into concern while I tried to figure out why she was being so weird. "They called a mandatory evacuation for everything north and west of the pass over the ridge. You live up there, right?"

Shit, indeed.

"Mandatory evacuation for what?"

"Here, let me pull up the notification," she said, quickly pulling up a web browser on her tablet and clicking on the screen a few times before she extended it in my direction.

> *Accidental fire suspected as arson spreads through Chaffee County as authorities speculate illegal fireworks ignited land near the technical college campus. The Sherriff's office is investigating leads while Chaffee and Lake County fire management attempt to contain the blaze.*

"When did this happen?" I asked, scrolling down the webpage, but there wasn't any new information since the alert had been sent out a few hours ago.

"I guess in the early hours of the morning. Roads out of town north were closed off around daybreak, and we've had a steady stream of tourists headed south along the main road. They don't want to stick around with a wildfire close by. Hudson opened early for lunch but shut down alcohol service until they get things under control. Don't need drunk tourists getting lost and ending up where they shouldn't be."

Nodding absently, I bent over and rummaged through my purse, pulling out my phone. The screen was filled with notifications, but messages from the person who I would have expected to be blowing up my phone by now were notably absent.

"When did they set up the barricades?"

"Not sure, but dad called and said they closed the road out of town north around eight when he was out checking the cabin. So maybe a few hours before that?" She shrugged, picking up her tablet to resume sketching while I started to internally freak out.

Reese had been on a twelve-hour shift that started at four yesterday, which meant she would have headed home just after four in the morning. She wouldn't have known about the fire, and if the emergency crews set up the barriers after she'd already been through, she was at home asleep, with her phone turned off, wearing earplugs and completely oblivious to the fact that she was in a mandatory wildfire evacuation zone.

Pressing the icon in my contact favorites, I dialed her number, my stomach sinking as it went to voicemail after a few rings.

"Are my keys up here?"

"They should be in your purse. Hudson said they left them in there after they brought you up last night. Your truck is out back."

"Can you tell him I'm gonna take tonight off if you don't need me to run the bar?"

I wasn't sure exactly where I was going, but I couldn't just let my sister sleep while she was in danger.

"Where are you going?" Hazel asked, looking up at me with concern. She probably should have been concerned about me, but I didn't have time to explain to her why I couldn't debate whether I was going to go on a misguided solo rescue mission to make sure my sister was safe.

I probably should have just called the non-emergency line and told them about Reese being home, but I couldn't—I wouldn't—take any chances. She was the only person I had left, and I'd never forgive myself for just sitting back and hoping that she was safe.

"Just tell Hudson I'm not gonna be here for my shift later."

Hazel's voice called out after me, but I was already halfway down the stairs, and didn't stop until I was out the back door of the bar.

Chapter
Eight

Annie

Y ANKING OPEN THE DRIVER'S side door of my truck, I hopped in, pulling hard against the strong winds to get it closed.

Navigating across the steady stream of traffic headed away from the road closures, I turned north, watching the edges of town fade away as I pressed the gas pedal, ignoring the little voice in my head that told me it was a bad idea to do this. But I wasn't the type to just sit around and do nothing.

When I got near where the state highway forked and turned toward where the article said the road was closed, I slowed. Barricades blocked the intersection, but whoever had once monitored them was long gone. I was sure they assumed most people wouldn't drive around a barricade. I wasn't most people.

And I knew the alternate road where the locals turned to avoid the traffic during tourist season, which was not blocked off. Carefully turning my truck up the old road, I navigated around the potholes left behind by the spring thaw and used it to cut across to the highway on the other side of the barricade.

My pulse thrummed as I took the sharp curves on the empty road up the ridge, knowing that I was putting myself directly in the path of something I couldn't control. And that if I got caught ignoring a mandatory evacuation, I was in deep shit. But my sister was going to be in shit so deep it'd threaten her life if she'd gone home after her shift in the middle of the night.

I should have gone home last night. I should be there right now to wake her ass up and drag her out of the house. But after weeks of insomnia fueled, broken sleep mixed with the heat exhaustion,

I hadn't even really remembered getting back to the bar last night. There was no way I would have been awake to guide Tripp to our tiny cabin off the beaten path.

We technically lived in a "neighborhood" according to the county, but the houses were far apart, and the roads were frequently inaccessible in the dead of winter because they never sent plows out here.

Coming around the bend that bordered several of the ranches north of town, I watched as a light haze of lingering smoke coming from up the mountain filled the air. I could see the road, but it just added to the level of anxiety keeping me alert. Only a few more miles and I'd be near the turn to our road, and then I could get my sister and get us the hell out of here.

The curves tightened, and I slowed my speed, only to hit the brakes hard, narrowly avoiding a splintered tree laying across the pavement. Trying not to panic, I scanned the road outside of my windows, hoping I was still far away from the fire and sheltered enough from the strong wind gusts that had knocked the tree down. My truck windows rattled as the howling wind blew smoke and ash through the air, the smell of it creeping inside the cab of the truck through the air vents.

Throwing the truck in reverse, I pulled a U-turn, heading back toward where I'd come from, trying to plot an alternate route.

"I'm fine. Everything is fine," I murmured as I scanned the tree line for answers. And if I continued repeating that to myself aloud, then maybe I'd believe it.

The smoke that'd once been far off in the distance was now moving closer with every wind gust, and I was suddenly terrified that not only was the road blocked, but the wildfire seemed to be heading straight for my home. The same cabin where my sister was currently asleep.

Twisting my hands on the steering wheel, the leather creaked as I tried to figure out the quickest alternative to get around the downed tree. There had to be some way to get around this roadblock and the last few miles to the cabin.

Steering the truck to the shoulder, I grabbed my phone, dialing her phone number again. The sound of the continuous rings was ominous. I hated that she turned off her phone when she was working the night shift.

I knew her job as an emergency room nurse meant she had to be rested for every shift, because sometimes people's lives depended on it, but right now I wished it was one of the rare times she forgot to put her phone on silent. I'd gladly face her wrath if it meant knowing she wasn't in the path of a shifting wildfire.

"Come on, Reese, pick up..."

Her voice echoed over the speakerphone, telling me to leave a message and she'd get back to me, but right now I was afraid that she'd never be able to get back to me if someone didn't warn her, she was potentially in danger.

"Fuck," I groaned, laying my head on the steering wheel briefly before I tried to formulate a plan to get back to the right side of the ridge. There were some country roads that wound through the forest that only locals knew about I could use, but since cell service out here was spotty at best, I'd potentially put myself in the path of the fire and unable to get help.

If Reese were in this situation, she'd calmly have told me to go back to town and find someone working on the emergency dispatch for the fire service. But they were busy enough trying to keep things contained with the wind that had swept through the valley in the last few hours.

Fucking careless idiots. They knew there was a burn ban and still set off fireworks, because dumbasses who were probably drunk seemed to not give a shit about the consequences of their actions as long as they got some enjoyment out of it.

Pulling up the map app on my phone, I tried to zoom in far enough to plot out a path around where I was stuck. My anxiety rose with each second my eyes scanned the screen, not seeing a clear path through.

But as the smoke swirled in the air outside my windshield, the smell of burning pine drifting through my air vents, I knew I needed to just pick a path and hope it got me out the other side.

Putting the truck in reverse, I carefully turned it around, scanning the side of the road for the break in the tree line I knew was there. I just hoped the road that'd been a shortcut to save time when we were running late for curfew in high school was still there.

I almost missed it, but I navigated the cab carefully through the gap in the trees, following what had once been a bypass to the highway from other county roads. It had clearly seen better days, the truck rocking from side to side as I slowly disappeared into the dense forest.

The smoke thinned out as I got further from the main road, but the acrid scent of the fire lingered, reminding me I needed to hurry.

The jarring sensation of the truck crawling its way through the pockmarked trail kept my senses alert, hope springing in my chest as the trees thinned out slightly as I approached the road that'd get me home.

The road on the other end appeared so close, but then I felt the front end of the truck suddenly dip and an ominous crack echoed through the cab. The sound of metal snapping made my eyes widen before my teeth gnashed together with the impact.

The sound of my pulse rushing in my ears and the metallic tang of blood in my mouth were only secondary to the sudden sense of panic that was taking over. But I couldn't let it pull me under.

"Maybe it's not as bad as it sounded," I whispered, knowing it was a lie.

Carefully unclipping my seatbelt, I shoved my phone in my pocket and reached for the handle on the door.

The cab of the truck was cocked at an awkward angle as I stepped onto the running board and looked down at where my wheel had once been inside the wheel well.

That was not the case anymore as I looked down in horror at the rubber of my tire visible in a place I knew it didn't belong.

Leaning out further to assess the damage, the truck dipped, and an eerie creak rang out as I took in the deep, crater-like sinkhole that had come out of nowhere, snapping my wheel to the side like I'd been driving a Matchbox car and not an oversized pickup truck.

"Fuck," I breathed, knowing that I'd taken a precarious situation and turned it into a fucking disaster. Not only was I still miles from the cabin, and my sister; I was now stuck in the middle of fucking nowhere with a broken axle.

A flat tire I could have handled, but now I was well and truly fucked.

And as the wind picked up, a powerful gust rocking the truck underneath me and threatening to toss me off my perch, I realized that maybe the voice of Reese in my head was right.

I should've headed back into town and let the professionals try to find my sister, because now they had two Thomas sisters to rescue.

Carefully leaning back inside the cab of the truck, I pulled the door closed after me, hoping my phone could still get a signal. Because I wasn't going anywhere in this vehicle, and heading out on foot toward where I thought my cabin was located would be epically stupid. If I didn't manage to walk straight into a fire, surely the smoke inhalation would kill me.

Dialing the numbers to 911, I swore as a set of beeps rang out over the speaker phone before the line disconnected. Squinting at the corner of my phone, I cursed again at the tiny letters in the corner saying *No Service.*

It was like the universe was mocking me for being an idiot.

"Think, think," I breathed out, trying to remember what Reese had told me to do if the cell service towers were out of order.

Since it didn't say SOS in the corner, I knew that meant there wasn't any signal to call someone, but I thought texting sometimes still worked.

Scrolling past a text from a number I didn't recognize, I pulled up Reese's contact, hoping I could get through to her too. Or that she'd at least maybe wake up to a text and know what was going on.

> Annie: Mandatory fire evacuation. Get out of the cabin as soon as you see this.

It took a few extra seconds to send, but it didn't bounce back, so I opened a new text and hovered my thumbs over the screen.

Was I supposed to send this to the fire department? The sheriff's office?

Maybe I should have paid better attention to my sister when she was trying to lecture me about safety procedures.

Typing 911 into the *To:* field, I hoped my message would go through.

> Annie: Stranded on an abandoned road in the evacuation zone in a truck with a broken wheel axle.

In seconds, my phone vibrated in my hand, a message filling the screen.

> 911: This is the Chaffee County emergency services dispatch line, do you know where you are located?

> Annie: The old bypass south of County Road 24.

> 911: Can you describe the make and model of the vehicle?

> Annie: Metallic gray Ram pickup truck.

> 911: Who am I speaking with? And can you give a brief description of the passengers in the vehicle?

> Annie: Rheyanne Thomas. I'm by myself. 31, female, long brown hair, 5'7.

> 911: I need you to open the map app on your phone and see if you can get enough signal to generate a location. Click on the little blue dot on the map and share it with a new text message to this number.

Following the rest of the directions from the dispatcher, I sent the message, hoping it'd go through.

> 911: Got your coordinates. Forwarding to emergency services. Please remain in the vehicle and keep your windows up. Is there smoke in the vicinity?

Looking out the window, I noticed a haze in the air, but I could still see the break in the trees where the road I'd been trying to get to was located.

> Annie: Not as much as there was on the main road, but there's a haze between the trees. Definitely smells like smoke, but I don't think it's close.

> 911: Turn on your emergency flashers. Keep the windows closed and set your AC to recirculate the air inside the car without pulling in air from the outside. Close as many vents as possible. If the car starts to fill with smoke, turn it off. Do you have any water or a face covering? Blankets?

Scanning the passenger seat, I spied a discarded bottle in the footwell, full of the greenish electrolyte drink Tripp had given me yesterday. He must have mixed a fresh bottle before we left the festival last night. Under the back seat, I found a blanket and another bottle of water, but nothing to cover my face with. Where were those damn Covid masks when you needed one?

Settling back into the driver's seat, I texted them back.

> Annie: Found some water and a blanket.

> 911: Good. Make sure your doors are all unlocked and then get down as low as you can in the rear seat of the vehicle. Wet the blanket with some water and keep it over your head if possible. Keep drinking to stay hydrated.

Following her directions, I climbed over the center console, settling on the floor in the back. I grabbed the strap of my purse from where it rested in the passenger seat and pulled it over my shoulder, tightening the strap until the small crossbody was tucked tightly against my chest. I guess if I died in the burned-out hull of this truck, it wouldn't matter if I was wearing underwear.

The air outside still looked hazy, and I hated I couldn't see what was happening outside the truck from the floorboards, but I'd ignored enough safety instructions for the day, so I would do whatever they told me to.

Annie: Do you know how long it's going to be?

911: Local search and rescue have been notified of your location. Just try to stay calm and do not leave your vehicle.

Easier said than done, but I tried to keep my breathing slow, sipping out of the bottle of electrolyte drink, wishing I could return to the previous day when my problem had only been dehydration. Now I wasn't sure if I was going to die stuck in the backseat of my truck while my sister was asleep in a cabin a few miles away with no one to save her.

Wanting to preserve the battery in case I needed to send another message, I locked the screen and set the phone on the seat next to me, closing my eyes and praying that someone out there was on the way to get me out of my own mess. Because the last thing I wanted was to be added to the tally of Thomas' who didn't live to see old age. Like my parents.

Chapter Nine

Tristan

T HE RADIO CLIPPED TO my belt crackled, a rough transmission from the dispatch office to the emergency rigs on the far side of the ridge catching my attention.

"Be advised. Stranded motorist on old County Road 24 bypass needing immediate evacuation. Any units available to respond?"

Frowning, I tried to recall if there even was a bypass there. County Road 24 bordered the north side of the ranch, but it'd been straightened and repaved sometime in the last five years, leaving the old sections of the road cut off and abandoned. Most of which had been reclaimed by the forest, and I wasn't even certain they were drivable.

Why in the fuck would someone be on a deserted bypass through the woods right now when it was in the middle of the mandatory evacuation zone?

There shouldn't even be cars that far north of town because there was a blockade preventing traffic from accessing that part of the ridge. I should know. I'd help set it up before the chief had sent me back to the ranch until they needed me. When I'd protested, he'd shoved a radio at me and told me I was only to report back to the mobile command center if they called all hands on deck.

Feeling useless, I'd headed back to the ranch to plot out a mitigation plan if the winds shifted and the fire turned toward us. So far, the winds had stayed north of us, but the haze that was creeping closer and closer had my senses on high alert.

I'd seen enough fires turn to know when the climate was right for absolute chaos to be unleashed. And as the smell of charred forest and lingering ash floated in the distance, it was a genuine possibility that this entire area could be engulfed in the next twenty-four hours. But I'd fight like hell before I let that happen.

"Dispatch, we're on the wrong side of the ridge to respond," Baker's deep voice echoed over the radio, followed moments later by several more rigs reporting in with similar responses.

My heart thumped heavily in my chest as I thought about what it meant for the person caught in that car.

The horse shifted underneath me, pawing at the ground while I continued to stare at the radio in my hand, waiting for someone to call in that they were en route.

"I know, you're fine, Phi. It's okay, pretty girl." Running my palm down the side of her neck, I tried to calm her, knowing she was picking up on my anxiety.

Seraphina and I were still getting to know each other, but when I'd been given the option between a younger, stronger horse and the scarred, solemn beauty that I was currently atop, it hadn't been a tough decision.

We'd been kindred spirits from the start.

"What's going on?" Marty asked, sidling his horse Ajax next to where I'd stopped after noticing I was no longer following him on the ride we'd taken around the western perimeter of the ranch. We'd been coming up with a game plan in case the fire jumped the ridge and headed in this direction.

Which was a possibility if the erratic winds kept up, but I was hoping they'd be able to keep it contained.

"There's a car stranded on the old 24 bypass."

"What in the hell would possess someone to take that route? That section has been closed for years. It's probably totally overgrown. That road was shit before it was abandoned."

"I've been asking myself the same questions, but I wasn't sure if there was something you knew that I was missing."

He shook his head, gripping the top of his hat and settling it on his lap before he pulled a bandana from his pocket and wiped away the sweat that was beaded along his hairline.

75

Martin West was probably only a decade and a half older than me, but a life involving outdoor manual labor had already carved deep lines across his forehead.

Despite being the owner of the West Ranch, he had spent his career being hands on with the operational side of things. But now that I was lined up to be his new ranch manager, he was starting to hand over the reins for me to step more into his role.

I'd thought for sure that his daughter Charley would want to continue the family legacy and run the ranch, but he'd told me she was working for her aunt and uncle in Butterfly Ridge doing event planning.

I had a feeling you could never really keep a career cowboy from the *life*, but I think he was cursing this wildfire for throwing off his transition plans. Especially with the real danger of it affecting his land *and* his livelihood.

"They gonna send someone out to get 'em?"

The radio in my hand had been silent for a few minutes, but it wasn't looking good. I knew the Chief had the evacuation and containment measures handled, but none of the crews had confirmed they could stop what they were doing to find this person.

Pulling the radio toward my mouth, I depressed the button on the side, knowing I shouldn't be interfering but also unable to stay quiet if I could help.

"Dispatch, this is radio twenty-seven. Is the call still open for the stranded motorist on 24?"

Marty shot me a concerned glance, clearly thinking the same thing as I was. One of us was going to have to find this idiot if no one from the county fire service could.

"Affirmative, twenty-seven. I have not received confirmation to reroute any of the ongoing evacuation plans."

"Radio twenty-seven, you were told to stand down," a deep baritone cut in over the line, the static barely distorting the sound of my other boss' voice. "This channel is open for active rescue personnel right now."

"I understand that, Chief, but I'm currently within the vicinity to respond if needed."

I'd have to pick my way through the woods to find them, but I knew Phi could get me there.

"Harding, you're not supposed to be operating a vehicle in the evacuation zone. I can't afford to have you getting stranded while you're out playing hero."

"Not in a vehicle, Chief. Currently on horseback inside the perimeter of the West Peak Ranch."

The line went silent, and I waited, hoping I wasn't about to get fired via radio transmission for not following the explicit orders he'd given me the last time I saw him.

"Alright, cowboy. You wanna prove yourself? Find me that motorist and get them back on the east side of the ridge. Dispatch will send you a pin of their location."

Marty patted a gloved hand against my shoulder, nodding as I gripped the radio tighter in my hand, waiting for further instructions.

It appeared our plans would have to wait; a rescue mission was about to throw my entire day into disarray.

"Twenty-seven waiting for instructions, ready when you are dispatch."

THE WOODS WERE EERILY quiet, the usual sounds of birds chirping replaced by the howling winds and an ominous haze rolling in that almost looked like fog.

Marty had shoved all the water he'd had stashed in his saddlebag, a bandana, and an extra horse blanket at me before he'd led me to the trail through the woods that'd get me closest to the GPS coordinates of the truck. Its last reported location was three miles north of the pasture we'd been in when I intercepted the radio call.

My breath echoed in my ears, the wet bandana tied across my face obnoxious, but necessary as the smoke blowing through the trees became denser the closer I got to the blue dot on my phone screen. Thank fucking God for modern technology. When I'd gone on my first search and rescue, GPS pins hadn't been a thing, and you were left to scan sizeable portions of wooded areas like this with just a fanned-out crew and a handful of prayers.

Phi was moving at a pretty good clip, and I knew while I had my face covered, she didn't, so I needed to find this person and get the hell out of here. But I didn't want to push her into a trot because the ground was uneven and the last thing I needed out here was a horse with a broken leg.

Scanning the trees, I looked for the signs of flashing lights, knowing turning on the hazards would be the first thing the dispatcher told them to do if the vehicle was still running. Which I hoped it was. Because blue dot or not, the quicker I got out of here, the better.

Phi kept moving forward, huffing as we got closer, and the smell of burning wood that had permeated my gear for years catching my nose through the bandana. Despite the winds, it was hot as fuck, since I was covered from head to toe with my hat securely on my head. I knew I had to be getting close to the fire line with the size of the ash floating in the air.

"Fuck," I exhaled, seeing the little dot blink on the screen, the corner of my phone showing that cell service was no longer available in this area. I pulled back on the reins, halting Phi for a moment as I thought about what I should do next.

Knowing I had little room for error, I tilted my hat backward and scanned the tree line, hoping for a sign I was in the right area. The traffic on the radio clipped at my side had been steady, but dispatch hadn't called me off, so I was the best hope this person had to get out of here.

"God dammit, where are you?" Phi shifted, walking off the path into a grove of trees and I held on to the end of her leads tight but gave her her head, hoping she'd sensed something I couldn't see and would lead us there.

As she broke through the dense brush, I exhaled, seeing a familiar gray truck tilted at an odd angle on the broken asphalt, my pulse picking up when I recognized the numbers and letter combination on the Colorado tags.

What the fuck was she doing out here?

My calm cracked, and I urged Phi to walk toward the truck faster. Slowing her down once we were right beside the tailgate, I slid sideways off the saddle, keeping her leads gripped tightly in my hand, so she stayed right with me.

She was typically an even keeled horse, but now that I'd dismounted, I didn't want to risk anything startling her. Even the most docile horses could panic in a moment of danger.

"Where is she?" I whispered, scanning the driver's side window, using my glove to wipe off the fine layer of ash that'd accumulated since she'd been stuck out here.

The front of the truck was empty, and my stomach sank, but there was no way she would've ignored the dispatcher instructing her to stay in the vehicle. I cleared the back window, peering inside and exhaling in relief when I saw a blanket with a Rhey sized lump curled up underneath it in the footwell.

Banging on the window, I almost laughed as she peeked out, her eyes widening when she saw me. She threw the blanket off her shoulders and moved to open the door, but I shook my head, holding my hand up.

Tying the reins on the handle of the driver's door, I reached over to pull out a bottle of water and the extra bandana from my saddlebag. When I returned to the door, I motioned for her to slide to the opposite side. Once she was in place, I yanked open the door and slid inside, slamming the door behind me to minimize the smoke I let into the cab.

"Oh, thank God," she breathed as she stared at me wearily.

Fighting the sudden urge to either shake her or kiss her, I went into emergency response mode, taking the cap off the water and dumping half of it over the bandana, using the last of the bottle to re-wet the one tied around my face.

"I'm gonna tie this around your head."

My voice was muffled, but Rhey didn't seem scared by the large, masked man wearing a cowboy hat raising a bandana toward her face. She held her hair back so I could quickly knot the material behind her head.

"Pull the blanket over your hair and wrap it around your shoulders. I'll get the horse untied and lift you onto her back first."

She nodded, shoving her phone into the back pocket of her shorts.

"I'm gonna close the door, but I'll be right back. I promise. Turn the truck off and get anything else you need."

Quickly slipping out of the door, I closed it behind myself and untethered Phi.

Patting her flank as I lined her up outside the door swing, I dragged the door open and held my hand out to where Rhey was dutifully waiting for me.

Clicking my tongue at Phi, I got her as close to the side of the truck as possible before I stepped onto the running board. Pulling Rhey in front of me, I lifted her up by the waist as she threw a leg over each side of the horse's back.

"Move forward!" I shouted so my voice would carry over the sound of the wind.

Depositing the reins in her lap, I grabbed the back of the saddle while I secured my boot in the stirrup, only letting go to swing myself onto the horse behind Rhey.

Wrapping my arms around her, I grabbed the reins and steered Phi away from the side of the truck, my eyes widening as I looked at the tree line in the distance.

Orange embers floated toward us on the next gust of wind; the glow of an active blaze visible on the far side of the road through the break in the trees. Turning the horse away from the fire, I grabbed one of Rhey's hands, securing it to the horn on the front of the saddle.

"Hold on tight!" I yelled, scanning the cluster of trees we'd emerged from before.

Phi pushed back through the brush, picking up the pace as soon as we hit the trail. She could sense the danger and probably the spike in my anxiety. I momentarily feared I was pushing her too hard with the additional weight of another rider, but she determinedly followed the path back toward the ranch without hesitating.

Rhey leaned back into my chest, her body hidden underneath the blanket wrapped around her, but I could feel her heartbeat thumping through the thick material, probably just as worried as I was about the situation she'd gotten herself into. I couldn't believe that she'd ignored a barricade to get up here and then doubled down, deciding to take an abandoned road. If I wasn't busy trying to scan the trees to make sure that we weren't headed directly into more danger, I would have gone off on her for being so reckless.

Getting yourself dehydrated because you were stubborn was one thing, putting yourself directly into a dangerous situation was just the fucking next level of idiocy.

She was lucky that I was apparently just as reckless, riding to the rescue on a fucking Appaloosa instead of waiting for an emergency rig to go fish her out of that heap of a truck. It hadn't been in terrible shape before, but if the broken axle didn't total the thing, being burned to a crisp by a wildfire would take it out.

At least she hadn't been inside at the time. Thank fucking God for that.

Pinching my eyes closed, I tried to shake the images from my brain—the sounds of phantom screams and the sharp, jarring memory of what it'd felt like as I lay helpless, pinned down and unable to move as fire licked up my gear.

When I opened them, I cursed as I watched the orange glow in the trees up ahead showing the fire had jumped the road and was headed directly for the trail we were on.

Wrapping one arm tightly around Rhey's waist, I yanked Phi's reins with the other and spun her away from the trail. If we could get across the river that bordered the northern edge of the ranch, there was a cluster of unused rental cabins hidden between the mountain and a small lake.

The smoke was too dense headed back to the ranch, and I didn't exactly have enough time to stop and see if I could get enough of a signal to navigate us out of here. There wasn't a guarantee I'd get us back before sunset anyway if we had to go around the fire, and there was no way in hell I was risking getting lost in these woods after dark. If the fire didn't catch up with us, the smoke inhalation would.

Rhey's fingers clutched the back of my glove tightly, her other hand gripping the saddle as I steered Phi through the trees and into a valley of rolling hills that stretched halfway across the property. With a quick squeeze of my thighs, the horse took off into a fast trot, eating up the distance between the forest and the river crossing, the smoke dissipating back into a light haze that made the sight of the burning mountain to the north look almost ominous.

What had just been a small plume of smoke visible on the horizon this morning had left a wake of destruction in its path. As I slowed Phi to a walk near the riverbank, I tried not to focus on the glowing horizon that had nothing to do with the approaching sunset. Acres of the mountain were on fire and unless Mother Nature intervened with some rain, acres more would be destroyed before this was all over. Sending up a quick prayer for the firefighters that were still out there working the ground crew, I focused on getting us further away.

Seraphina had likely been making this crossing long before I came to the ranch, finding a low point in the water and slowly making her way across. Once we were back out in the open, she let me guide her toward the lake, the small body of water expanding the closer we got, the cluster of cabins coming into view.

Ten more minutes and I could get her fed, watered, and bedded down for the night. And no, I wasn't talking about the infuriating woman wrapped in my arms.

Rhey's grip on my hand hadn't let up, but I wasn't arguing, it kept me present so I didn't let the wave of anxiety I could feel building inside me take over. At least for now. I'd had enough panic attacks in the last few months to know it was only a matter of time. I just hoped the adrenaline would keep it from building until I got off this horse.

The modest barn behind the cabins was a welcome sight and judging by how her gait picked up as we neared it, Phi knew exactly what it signified. Getting my heavy ass off her back and hopefully a meal. She deserved it with how calm she'd remained, and it further earned my respect and loyalty. She may have been a trail riding horse for the ranch guests before, but now she was mine, and I was going to spoil her rotten once we got back to the main ranch in the morning.

If there still *was* a ranch in the morning.

The fire was still miles out, and we were safe for now, but there were no guarantees.

Chapter
Ten

Annie

HIS EYES.

I'd recognized the eyes of the man who'd wrenched open the back door of my truck to pull me out. And while I wasn't a hundred percent certain that my rescuer via horseback was Tripp, I kind of hoped it was.

He wasn't wearing a uniform, and I didn't think that the fire department had started wearing thigh hugging jeans, riding boots and cowboy hats. There was something about those eyes, though.

But since we'd been a bit preoccupied with escaping a wildfire that had gotten too close for comfort, I hadn't exactly had time to ask him to take off the bandana covering his face and make an introduction. Although, at this point, he was probably the opposite of happy to see me, even if I'd never been so thankful to see another person in my life. I knew it was my fault that we were both in this situation, but seeing him again had sent a jolt of relief through me so bone deep that I'd happily take any amount of ire directed in my way because of my reckless actions.

Brilliant golds and pinks painted the sky above the mountain tops with a beautiful watercolor display of nature's beauty, but as I peeked out of the blanket I'd had pulled around my head and shoulders, my eyes scanned lower in the horizon, my breath catching in my chest as I saw the sheer destruction that had turned the mountain I'd lived half my life on into a desolate, charred landscape.

A desolation that I hoped and prayed my sister had escaped, because I didn't know what I'd do without her. She was the only family member I had left.

The horse slowed its pace as we edged closer to the mountain, hugging the shoreline of a lake I hadn't known existed. I guess that made sense, since it was tucked along the edge of what I knew was private property. I was pretty sure it was part of Charley's family horse ranch, but why would Tripp have been on the ranch?

My rescuer's hand pressed against my stomach, and I pulled the blanket that had been covering my head down to rest on my shoulders, turning to look back at him.

"We're gonna stop here."

His eyes held mine through the gap between the brim of his hat and the bandana covering the rest of his face, and I wished I could see more to read his expression. He had to be epically pissed off at me. If he was irritated I had gotten myself into trouble yesterday by not drinking water, I was sure it'd morphed into full-blown anger at putting myself directly in the path of an uncontained wildfire.

He pulled back slightly with the hand that had been holding the reins, slowing the horse as we neared a quaint barnlike structure tucked around the backside of the small cabins we'd passed. My heartbeat that had slowed once we were out of the forest and further away from the edge of the fire raced now that we were safe. At least I hoped we were far enough away to be safe. With how quickly the fire had spread, I was still on edge. There had been spotty fires in the mountains before, but never this close to town, and never one that had threatened everything I held dear.

"Stay put." His deep voice was still muffled by the bandana, but it held an edge that just increased my anxiety. Part of being a people pleaser was that you hated it when you disappointed people. And I had done something that warranted an emotion much stronger than disappointment.

He pulled away the large hand that had anchored me to him, still holding onto the reins with the other as he slipped out of the saddle. Despite the July heat, I felt cold without his solid presence wrapped around my back.

My fingers gripped the horn as he pulled the reins over the horse's head and led her inside the small building. It was dark, but much cooler than it'd been outside. Goosebumps cropped up along the back of my neck as I watched him settle the end of the reins on a hook outside of a shadowy stall, ducking underneath the horse's head and disappearing into the darkness.

The large animal shifted beneath me, her soft breaths the only sound accompanying the loud beat of my heart. Unsure of whether he wanted me to climb off the horse, I just waited, only jumping slightly when the hum of an engine further in the building kicked on, followed shortly by the overhead lights.

Continuing to stare at the empty stall in front of me, I waited, startled when two large hands closed on the sides of my waist, lifting me from the horse and depositing me on the dirt aisle that ran down the center of the barn.

Harsh breaths filled the air behind me, and I wasn't sure what to do as his fingers squeezed my sides, lightly digging in before he released me. He pulled away the blanket and untied the bandana that was tied around my face.

Heaving in several breaths, I turned, expecting to meet the angry gaze of the man who'd had to pluck me out of my stranded vehicle, but he was several paces away, leaning against the opposite wall with his head down.

"Are you okay?" I asked quietly, watching as he slowly slid down the wall, hunching over his knees, holding the sides of his face in his hands. He didn't answer me, struggling to pull in full breaths through the bandana still wrapped around his face.

Without hesitation, I dropped to my knees in front of him, pulling off his hat and untying the bandana, discarding them to the side. He didn't move, his shoulders shaking as he dragged in heavy breaths.

"What do you need? Are you hurt? Is there something I can do?" I asked, fighting the urge to touch him in case he was injured, and I didn't know about it.

"No," he rasped, still heaving in labored breaths as he shook his head. I sat helplessly, watching him struggle for breath, flexing my fingers. After a few moments, he didn't seem to calm any, tucking his head further into his knees and rocking in place.

Unable to watch, I grasped the back of his hands, gently pulling until he tilted his face in my direction, his panicked eyes connecting with mine. My suspicions were confirmed as Tripp met my gaze, but it was like he looked right through me, unable to focus as he was gripped by whatever was going on inside his head.

Acting on instinct, I smoothed the sweaty hair off his forehead, lowering my voice as I leaned in, trying to calm him. "Hey, just breathe. You're okay, it's okay. We're safe."

His eyes closed; the lids clenched tight as his shoulders continued to shake.

"No, look at me, open your eyes. I'm here. You're safe. Breathe, Tripp, breathe. Please."

Tears sprung to the corners of my eyes and I hated that my actions had caused this. That this strong, protective man was gasping for air, fighting off an invisible panic because of something I'd done.

"I'm so sorry," I whispered brokenly, urging him to look at me. "Please open your eyes. Focus on me. Focus on my voice and my face. You're okay. Just breathe."

Taking deep breaths, I continued to rub my thumbs across his strong cheekbones, hoping he'd just look at me and realize he wasn't alone. That he was okay. That he'd saved me.

After a few moments, his eyes slowly drifted open, but I could tell he was stuck deep in the panic attack as they frantically scanned my face, his breathing still labored. I was afraid if he didn't calm down, he'd hyperventilate and pass out.

Out of sheer panic, I leaned in, pulling him to meet me halfway, and pressed my lips to his. He didn't respond, his harsh intake of breath coasting over my lips before I leaned in again and pressed a little harder, trying to do something—*anything*—to bring him back to me.

When he didn't respond, I froze, my lips still burning from where they were nestled against his lush mouth.

Then my own panic set in. Oh my God, I just mauled a stranger. Well, he wasn't exactly a stranger. He'd spent enough time with me yesterday, so I guess we were past the stranger phase.

We'd had a stilted one-sided conversation first thing in the morning, followed with him bailing me out during the festival by jumping in to help serve people when the line at the distillery's booth got too long for me to handle. He'd seen my harried expression from across the aisle of crowded booths and came to my rescue. He'd steered me away from disaster multiple times now. And I was just returning the favor.

I recognized the signs of a panic attack. I'd helped pull Reese out of a few when we were younger. Although I'd never kissed my sister to pull her out of that panic spiral, so I guess I couldn't exactly equate the two methods.

"I'm so sor..."

I didn't even get the word sorry out again before two large, calloused palms were framing my soot covered cheeks and pulling me forward.

Tripp hesitated for a fraction of a second before he was tilting his head and plunging his tongue past my lips. Falling forward, I braced my palms on his muscular chest, my fingers itching to dig into the solid muscles as he groaned into my mouth and nipped at my bottom lip.

The frantic, wheezing man from moments before was gone, replaced by a man as crazed as the fire we'd narrowly escaped. I could have died in that truck waiting for the search and rescue, but like something out of one of my grandmother's old harlequin novels, there he was. A man, whose face was obscured by a bandana, pulling me out and practically throwing me onto the back of his horse before he rode off toward the sunset that had been nearly drowned out by smoke.

The attraction I'd sensed the night before flared brightly, burning between us as he sat upright and hauled me into his lap, his lips coasting down my throat before his teeth sunk into my collarbone.

"Fuck," he grunted into my neck as I rocked in his lap, the layers of rough denim pressing against me in a way that sent sparks racing up my spine.

It was like I was being consumed by him, the rough scrape of his facial hair marking my neck as he kissed me and pressed his hips into my movements.

"Oh God," I panted as his hands gripped my hips, his fingertips digging into my skin. "Yes."

His hands were everywhere, skating up my back, digging into my back, his large palm wrapping around one of my braids before he yanked me back down to him, taking possession of my mouth in a way I'd never experienced before. He was rough in how he handled me, but I greedily rocked into every movement, taking all the anger and passion he poured into the kiss.

Gasping for breath as I pulled away, I dug my fingers into his hair, scraping his scalp while his eyes tracked my movements, no longer gripped with panic. He looked like a man possessed, dark blue eyes hooded as his grip on my braid tightened, tilting my head back as he stared at me.

"I'm sorry," I panted, gasping as his hips thrust from beneath me.

"Be quiet," he growled, forcing my head back while his grip on my waist tightened, pulling me forcefully against him. Even through the layers separating us, I could feel how hard he was beneath me, throbbing against the denim between my legs.

"But I—" I trailed off, my nails digging into the skin on the back of his neck when he pulled my hair hard, my neck arching backward.

"Shut the fuck up." His voice was low and angry, and I worried that maybe I'd pushed this too far. Read him wrong. Acted too impulsively when I'd kissed him.

With strength I was surprised he had, he lifted me, standing and turning so my back was pressed against the wooden wall of the barn.

Bringing my fingers to the sides of his face, I rubbed my thumbs across his stubble, gripping the back of his neck as our chests heaved against each other. "Tripp, I..."

His eyes narrowed as he loomed over to me, his hips pinning me in place with my legs wrapped tightly around his waist. "I said, shut the...*fuck*...up, Rhey. Or should I call you Annie?"

Opening my mouth to apologize again, a low rumbling growl rose from his chest. He released my hip with one hand, reaching back to grab my hand, swinging it over his head and pinning it to the rough wood above mine.

"Don't talk. Just... Just don't," he panted, interlacing his fingers with mine above my head and leaning in, ghosting his lips across mine. "No more words."

"Kiss me again," I breathed, arching my back and trying to lean into his touch, but he pushed in, pinning me to the wall. He leaned forward, his facial hair scraping my jaw as his teeth latched onto my earlobe, eliciting a gasp from me—part pain, part ecstasy.

"No," he growled in my ear, scraping his teeth down the side of my neck as his hips rocked forward. "I'm so fucking mad at you."

"I'm sor..."

His teeth clamped down on my collarbone, scraping the sensitive skin as I gripped his shoulder, digging in my nails until he gasped. His lips and tongue soothed where he'd bitten me, leaving a scorching trail up the side of my neck until his lips hovered millimeters from mine again, his eyes no longer clouded. He stared down at me with an intensity I feared might be more anger than arousal. "Stop fucking apologizing."

"I..."

He swallowed the words, his lips punishing as he kissed me, teeth scraping my bottom lip before he sucked and bit down, pulling back as my neck arched against the rough wood behind my head.

"I'm allowed to be fucking angry with you. What you did..."

"Was stupid, I know," I whimpered, panting as his hips thrust forward, rocking into me in a way that sent my pulse racing.

"So, fucking reckless. You're lucky I found you," he panted, pressing his hips forward and using them to support my weight as his hand disappeared between us, frantically unbuttoning my shorts. His rough fingertips disappeared beneath the fabric, pressing lower until they reached where I was wet and aching for his touch.

"Oh God." My voice was a whimpered gasp as he circled my clit briefly before slipping lower and pressing inside, forcing our joined hands hard into the wood above my head before his lips descended on mine again.

He wasn't gentle as he touched me, punishing me with rough thrusts of his fingers as I gasped into his mouth, the tables reversed as I had trouble drawing in breaths between harsh kisses.

"Give it to me," he panted against my lips, voice low and commanding as he fucked me roughly, his hips chasing the movements of his hand. "I need to feel you fall apart."

If it weren't for the fact that I barely knew this man, I would have begged him to fuck me with something other than his fingers, imagining what it'd feel like if he were inside me.

"I..."

He braced his forehead against mine, staring down at me as he curled his fingertips, making me gasp.

"That's it, fuck my hand," he growled, pressing harder, his harsh breaths fanning against my cheeks as I moaned, my eyes slipping closed. "No, don't you close those eyes. Fucking look at me when I make you come."

Blinking against the pleasure threatening to drag me under, I locked eyes with him, helpless as he drove me closer and closer to the edge. His dark gaze sent a thrill through me, and when his thumb pressed hard into my clit, I shattered against him, falling apart in his tight hold.

"Oh fuck, Tripp," I moaned, arching my back and gasping as he continued the movements of his fingers, fucking me right through the orgasm like a man possessed.

"That's right, milk my fingers," he growled, leaning in and resting his lips against the side of my neck while he slowed his movements. "God, I love how hard you come."

My heartbeat hammered in my chest as my eyes slipped closed, my fingers clenching his tightly as I found my way back to myself.

"I'm still mad at you," he chuckled after a few moments, his lips pressed against the side of my neck, and I heaved in a deep breath, following suit with an exhausted giggle. "But I'm so fucking glad you're safe."

Chapter
Eleven

Tristan

MY COCK THROBBED IN my jeans as I drew in a relieved breath, smiling at the soft chuckles escaping Rhey as she dragged her fingertips through the sweaty hair on the back of my head.

I hadn't been lying. I was so angry with her, but relief was winning out over the terrifying frustration that she'd put herself in that deadly position in the first place. Relief that we were both safe once we'd gotten far enough away.

She put herself in danger that could have taken her from me before I got to feel her like this. Before I tasted her lips. Before I felt her pussy clench against my fingers. Before we got to spend more than one tension filled afternoon with each other, dancing around an attraction unlike anything I'd felt before her.

That fire could have stolen her from me. And maybe that was why I'd pushed things so far between us. I was running on adrenaline mixed with panic, and in that moment, relief that I'd found her converged with the anger and lust running through my veins. That one fiery kiss took over and flushed out the anxiety the flashbacks brought, replacing it with something much more potent. *Her.* Touching her...feeling her fall apart had been my new focus, and it pushed all the bad memories out.

"Oh, my God. My sister," she gasped against my cheek, her voice suddenly morphing to alarm.

Pulling away, I released her hand, gripping her waist while I waited for her to unlock her legs from my waist and find her footing.

"What's wrong?" I asked, brushing the hair that'd escaped her braids from her forehead and crouching to look in her eyes. "What's going on?"

She gasped, reaching for the pocket I'd watched her shove her phone into before, but when she pulled it out, there was just a scrap of lace in her fist. She looked at it in confusion before she looked up at me, clearly embarrassed that she'd just pulled a pair of panties from her pocket. But that would be a discussion for another time.

"Oh God, where is it?"

I reached for her other pocket, but it was empty. Stepping back, I scanned the dirt around us, not seeing anything on the ground. She must have knocked it loose at some point.

"Holy shit, how could I...? Oh God. No," she cried, her lip quivering.

"It's just a phone. We'll get you a new one once we get back to town. I'm sure—"

"No," she wailed, cutting me off, a tear streaking down her cheek, leaving a track through the sweat and grime I hadn't realized was probably covering the both of us. "The reason I was on that road. My cabin was in the evacuation zone. And my sister was at home. She was asleep, and oh my God. We have to go back. I can't..."

Pulling her into my chest, I cupped the back of her head, stroking her hair as she shook in my arms. "I'm sure she's fine. There were crews working on the evac who were checking residences in the direct path. They'll have found her."

She shook her head, sniffling as her fingers gripped my shirt. "No, you don't understand. She's a nurse. And she works the night shift. Most of the time she comes home, turns off her phone and puts in ear plugs before she crashes."

Fuck. Yeah, that'd complicate getting her out of that cabin on her own, but Baker wasn't the type to let any residence go unchecked. And from how he'd talked about the Thomas sisters, I had a feeling there was some unresolved business with Rhey's sister. "If they saw signs of someone being home, they would've pulled her out. And you don't even know if the fire got that far."

"You saw it jump the road," she whispered, voice broken, her tears wetting my shirt. "We live—*lived*—less than a mile from there. Oh my God. What if Reese is gone? And I was so distracted by..."

"Hey, look at me." Crouching down and grasping the sides of her face, I waited for her to make eye contact with me. "You wouldn't let my panic take over, and I won't let yours. Breathe."

"But now we're in the middle of nowhere, miles from where I need to be and..." her voice cut off, eyes welling with tears. I tried to figure out a way to reassure her. I wasn't sure where she'd lost her phone, but it'd happened sometime between now and when I'd pulled her out of that truck. Leaning forward, I kissed her softly, rubbing my thumbs along her cheeks until she calmed slightly.

"Let me find that radio. Hopefully, it will still work. I was monitoring the dispatch traffic earlier. That's how I found you."

She nodded, reaching up to squeeze the back of my hands before she let me pull away. Turning back toward where Seraphina was still waiting patiently on the opposite side of the barn, I reached into my saddlebag, pulling out the radio I'd shoved in there when I pulled out the bandana earlier.

The low battery light blinked at me, but I hoped I'd have enough left to get a message to the dispatch office. I was sure the civilian emergency lines were a shit show now that the fire was threatening the populated area.

"Got it," I said, awkwardly holding up the radio before I urged her to sit down. The last thing I needed was for her to pass out now that her adrenaline was wearing off. "Where is your cabin?"

"Cypress Lane, it is—was," she said with a grimace. "On the other side of the highway."

Sitting down next to her, I reached for her hand, interlacing our fingers as I pressed the button on the side of the radio with my other hand. "Dispatch, this is twenty-seven checking on the evac in progress along Cypress Lane."

"Go ahead for dispatch, twenty-seven," a feminine voice responded. I was still learning all the first responders, but it sounded like the former Deputy Chief's daughter, Kate.

"Stranded motorist on county road twenty-four bypass has been recovered. Female, possibly late twenties, with mild smoke inhalation is inquiring about a residence on Cypress Lane in the evacuation plan." Rhey frowned, shaking her head, but the dispatcher responded before I could ask her why.

"Stranded motorist from the earlier call has been recovered? What's your location?"

"Copy, we're at Spring Lake on the north side of the West Peak Ranch. We'll head back to the main property at first light," I radioed back. It was too dark for us to safely navigate back to the main ranch now, and we weren't accessible by any roads up here.

"Copy, I'll mark her call as resolved at 19:47," she paused briefly. "Per Fire Chief's orders, I'm not able to disclose details about ongoing evacuations to off duty personnel. Stand by for further information."

The radio lay silent in my hand as the dispatcher didn't respond. I wasn't sure if I should ask again, but my cell phone started vibrating in my pocket before I could. Pulling it out, I read the local phone number and answered the call, putting it on the speakerphone.

"Hey, sorry, it's Kate," she rushed out, sounding exasperated. "I stepped out for a sec to keep the other lines clear. What the fuck, Probie? Are you trying to get us all fired? I had to talk down the Chief from sending a squad car to find you on the ranch earlier when you cut in on radio traffic offering to take a fucking horse into the woods for a search and rescue."

"Kate, we both know I wasn't going to leave a stranded motorist when your guys couldn't get access. And he must have trusted me enough to give the go ahead."

"Even though I *know* you were told to stand down. There's a reason you're a probationary officer. You can't just pull shit like this if you want to stay on his good side."

I knew she was right, but in this case, I didn't give a shit about protocol or hierarchy. I never would have forgiven myself if I'd just let Rhey stay in danger, even if it was self-imposed and I hadn't known it was her at the time. Call it white knight syndrome or whatever bullshit the department psychologist had spouted at me before I'd been released by the forestry service, but I wouldn't let someone stay in a dangerous, life-threatening situation if I could do something.

"Leading edge is still to the northwest of the pass, but you've gotta get a crew doing a burn out along the river. You don't want it to jump if the wind shifts again. There's too much undergrowth along the banks right now for the water to stop it."

"I'll pass your advice along, but you know the Chief is running the show, not me."

Rhey squeezed my hand again, mouthing her sister's name when I looked over at her.

"Did the evac rig get the residences on Cypress checked?" I asked, hoping like hell Kate had gotten the information before she left the control room.

"You fucking owe me for this," Kate growled, but it didn't have any bite to it. I could hear keyboard keys in the background before she responded. "Yeah, Baker and Rhodes got the entire area checked and marked. One female was evacuated from a residence that didn't comply with the mandatory notice."

Rhey's grip tightened, and I nodded for her to ask.

"What house number?"

The sound of typing resumed on the speakerphone and Kate paused before she replied, "472."

"Oh, thank God," Rhey sighed, leaning her forehead against my shoulder in relief.

"Are they en route back to Butterfly?" I asked, knowing that the high school on the edge of Butterfly Ridge was typically where they set up the emergency shelter for situations like this.

"They're on scene for a single vehicle incident south of the ridge, but I'm sure they'll head back to the hospital as soon as they're done. EMS is a mess trying to respond to all the calls we've been getting. Fucking tourists are panicking and ignoring the evacuation routes."

"Then I'll let you go, I'm sure you have more important things to do than chat with me."

"Stay safe, Tripp. I'll let you know if anything heads your way. You've got enough supplies for overnight?"

"Yup, we'll stay in the cabins up here until first light. Not sure how much electricity we've got, but there are supplies. Thanks, Kate. I appreciate it."

Disconnecting the call, I leaned back against the side of the barn, squeezing Rhey's fingers and lifting the back of her hand to my lips for a brief kiss.

"Thank you," she whispered, rubbing her thumb across my knuckles. Leave it to trauma bonding to make you feel close to someone after a life-threatening event. I'd felt the spark between us the moment she first made eye contact with me yesterday morning, so I knew it wasn't just the situation causing my chest to fill with relief that I'd been able to get to her in time.

Seraphina softly nickered from her spot across from us, pawing at the dirt beneath her hooves.

"I know, I'm sorry. You've been very patient." Standing up, I moved across the barn, unstrapping the saddlebag and throwing it over the edge of the stall door next to where I'd hooked up Phi. Shifting to the side, I unstrapped the back cinch of the saddle next, lifting the stirrup over her back and working the knot loose on her front cinch.

She nosed my shoulder, pushing against me. "Yeah, I know. You want it off. I'm working on it."

Tracing my hand across her hindquarters, I hooked the cinch straps on the saddle and lifted it from her back, laughing as she chuffed at me while I carried it to the far wall where the saddle racks were. Her reins and bridle were next, and I wished I had a halter handy to tie her up, but I had a feeling she didn't have any plans to stray.

"Is there anything I can do to help?" Rhey asked, standing on the far side of the horse and wringing her hands together.

"Can you head out back and see if you can find the water spigot and a hose? I don't need to do a full bath, but she's gonna need some water." She nodded, headed toward the door to the barn. I watched as she peeked outside, glancing out the door to either side. "Should be around the back."

I pulled the sweaty saddle blanket off Phi's back, laying it over a post underneath the saddle and then returned with a brush. She breathed softly, occasionally pushing against my side with her nose as I brushed her down, making sure she was okay after our adventure through the woods. Rhey returned a few moments later, a worn green hose trailing behind her.

"I had to hunt down the shut-off valve to turn the water back on, but I found a hose."

She met me halfway as I walked toward her, squealing when I wrapped my arm around her back, hauling her forward to lay a searing kiss on her lips.

"What was that for?" She seemed a little dazed when I pulled the nozzle out of her hands and stepped back.

"You opened the door to kissing, if you want me to stop, just say the word."

She shook her head, her cheeks turning pink. "No, uh. You can keep kissing me."

"Good to know," I commented, stepping inside the first stall and hunting for the water bucket. Phi followed me in when she heard the spray hit the bottom, shoving her head in and drinking deeply as I filled it up the rest of the way.

I wasn't sure how fresh the hay was, so I opted for what was in the sealed feed box, scooping out a small portion and hoping it wasn't too stale.

Rhey was quiet as I worked to get my horse settled, closing her into a stall so she didn't wander overnight. She knew the ranch better than I did, but there were too many dangerous things at play to let her roam tonight.

"You ready to go check out our digs for the night?" I asked, closing the door to the barn so other animals stayed out of it overnight.

"Wow, old man, dating yourself with that lingo," she teased, bumping her shoulder with mine.

"You're not that much younger than me," I replied. "At least you don't seem like it."

"Is that your way of fishing to see how old I am?" Her tone was teasing, but she wasn't wrong. I'd told Kate she was in her late twenties, but I didn't really know how old she was.

"Did it work?" I asked, grinning at her.

"You're a lot more charming than you initially seemed. But you can put away the dimples. I'm thirty-one."

So, she wasn't much younger than me at all. I fleetingly wondered if she would have been in the same graduating class as Jay, since my younger brother was also thirty-one. But I didn't even know if she'd been around when we were in high school. Girls hadn't been my focus back then, so I probably wouldn't have noticed her. Not like I was aware of her now.

Deciding to be upfront since we didn't have much of a gap between our ages, I responded without prompting. "I'm thirty-five."

"Practically a fossil," she teased, and I fought the urge to throw her over my shoulder as we headed down the trail toward the closest cabin.

"Only thing hard about me is..."

Her laughter cut me off, making my chest warm. "Wow, maybe I preferred you quiet and brooding. Your mouth is almost worse than the guys back at the bar."

"I was going to say my head, but since you brought it up, literally. You know other things *can* indeed get quite hard around you." And they were continuing to stay hard around her. Women who could hold their own were a major turn on. Despite my lingering anger, I couldn't deny I was attracted to her even more strongly than yesterday.

"Well, keep it in your pants for now. I'm sure I'm disgusting. My skin is covered in soot."

"Not sure that's possible, but I've got a portable shower bag in my kit if we can find some clean-ish water. Worst case, we can take a dip in the lake."

She stopped walking, turning toward me with a look of disgust. "I'm not getting in that lake after dark, I don't know what's in there."

Stepping forward to hook my arm around her back, I pulled her into my chest. "Don't worry, I'll protect you from any monsters."

"Except the one in your pants," she teased, standing on her tiptoes to get closer and rocking her hips into where I couldn't control my reaction to her.

"You said it, not me." I met her halfway, my response a rough whisper against her lips before I kissed her again, unable to stop myself.

Chapter
Twelve

Annie

WHILE THE AIR WAS much cleaner at the lake cabins than it'd been where Tripp had rescued me, there was still a haze that made everything look eerie as the sun dipped behind the mountains.

And while they were still in good condition, the cabins we were approaching looked tiny.

"Let's go check things out before it gets too much darker," Tripp suggested, nodding toward a slightly larger cabin that was tucked along the water's edge, accessible by a long wooden platform.

"I don't even know where we are." I had a general idea that we were near the mountain pass that bordered Sage Springs, but once we crossed the river, I'd lost any sense of reference.

"North side of the West Peak Ranch. It's on the other side of the river. This is a natural spring-fed lake. They used to use these cabins as overflow during peak season," Tripp explained, bending down to pull a small lock box from behind a bench on the little wrap around front porch. "Now they just bring ranch guests up here for fishing day trips. They're a little rough around the edges, but it should be safe and dry."

"Why here?" Was he staying at the ranch? Or had I missed something yesterday? I was more than a little curious how he knew the Wests. Maybe he was family I'd never met. I knew Charley had cousins, but since she was an only child, I knew he wasn't her brother.

Before I could think too much about it, he started talking. "This got a body of water between us and the fire. We can stay here tonight since it'd be dark before we could get back to the main lodge, but we'll need to head out early. I'd like to get the ranch hands together and run a back-burn line along the river bordering the west edge of the ranch, so it doesn't jump."

"I can help." I didn't have the faintest idea about what a back-burn line was, or how to make one, but I knew if I gave myself too much time to think, I'd only freak out about the fact I didn't have anywhere else to go. "Don't look at me like that. I can do more than just pour drinks. I want to help. This is my community, too. And Charley is a friend. I don't want to see her home turn into what mine probably is."

Tripp nodded while he worked on finding the key to the front door of the cabin, flashing me a smile once he got it unlocked. He held the door open and motioned for me to go in ahead of him. My eyes scanned the dim space, sighing in relief when I saw it was furnished and seemed to be in good condition.

A palm cracked down on my ass, making me jump before I turned to glare at the man standing just inside the door with a mischievous smirk on his face.

"Hey, what the hell?"

He shrugged, stepping forward to tug on the end of one of my braids, wrapping it around his fist before he leaned in and kissed the skin beneath my ear.

"It looks good in those shorts. Especially now that I know what you don't have on under them."

Maybe he was more playful than I'd given him credit for yesterday. I guess he just needed a high stress rescue to get more of his personality to shine. And while I wasn't used to it, I couldn't deny that him spanking me had sent a little thrill up my spine.

"Are you expecting me to apologize for not having any clean underwear to put on this morning? You're the one who tucked me into a bed that wasn't mine."

He chuckled, running his palms along my sides and pulling me into him, his lips hovering next to my ear. "And I plan to do the same tonight, too. But you won't be going to bed alone."

"Awfully presumptuous for you to assume I'll be getting into bed with you after only a day." God, had it only been a little over twenty-four hours since I met this man? "You don't even know me."

He stepped back, framing my face with his hands as he looked down at me. "Maybe not, but we're stuck out here together, so we should change that."

Nodding, I tried to scan his expression to see if he was being sincere about getting to know me or if he was just trying to get into my pants again. I already had one complicated situationship to deal with, I didn't want to jump from one meaningless physical relationship to another. Even if he *was* making me a little weak in the knees. I'd almost forgotten what it felt like to have this strong of a reaction to another person. Things weren't like this between Jay and me. I wasn't sure they ever had been.

Despite fairly regular sex—the last four months of abstinence excluded—I wasn't sure if I'd ever had the kind of physical response I was having to this man before.

"Maybe we should get cleaned up first."

"We should." His thumbs traced my cheekbones before he leaned in to graze his lips against mine. I had to ball my fists at my sides to keep myself from reaching up and grabbing fistfuls of his hair to yank his mouth back to mine. "Even though I kind of prefer you dirty."

"Well, you kinda stink," I whispered, biting the inside of my lip to keep from laughing.

"Keep on teasing me, Rhey. It just makes me want to spank you again," he replied before he turned around and walked toward a set of closed doors at the back of the small house.

He pulled out a flashlight I hadn't known was in his pocket and clicked it on, shining it inside the first doorway before he moved to the other. I followed behind, seeing a tiny bathroom with a single vanity, toilet and a small combination bathtub/shower.

"Is there soap?" I asked, the thought of taking a warm shower taking precedence over the gnawing hunger that was trying to get my attention since I hadn't eaten much today.

"Soap is the least of our worries. I don't think they've brought any guests up here to stay the night this season, so I'm more concerned about the state of the water." Tripp turned the shower dial, and the pipes made some suspicious noises, but only a trickle of water flowed out of the faucet. He frowned, reaching around me to try the sink, but nothing happened.

"Stay in here. I'm gonna go see if I can find the shut off for the inside water. They must not have turned the supply to the cabins back on after they were winterized last year."

He'd only been gone a few minutes, but I was glad that he was here with me. I would have hated to be stranded in one of these creepy little cabins by myself. Although if I was by myself, I'd still be trapped in that pickup truck waiting for someone to save me from my reckless decisions.

The pipes made a suspicious rattling noise, followed by a rush of water spewing out of the tub fixture and the faucet. The dim light made it hard to tell, but it did not look like water I wanted to be bathing in.

Tripp joined me a few moments later, resting one hand on the side of my waist as he peered over my shoulder, aiming his flashlight at the stream of water.

"Okay, so maybe the lake looks like a better prospect for getting clean," I mused, staring at the stream of brownish cloudy water that flowed out of the tap.

"Yeah, these cabins haven't been used regularly in about five years with tourism down in the area, so I'm not surprised the plumbing needs flushed. If I had a compressor here, I could flush the lines, but..."

"I thought you hadn't been back home in years," I asked, looking up at him over my shoulder.

"But I paid attention when the Wests showed me the property a few weeks ago."

"I thought you were a firefighter."

"I am. But that's just when I'm needed. There's a reason they call me a volunteer firefighter. The ranch is my day job."

No wonder he was close by when I'd contacted 911. And it explained the horseback rescue.

"Is that what you did when you were living somewhere else? Were you a rancher? I gotta admit, the hot cowboy look is doing it for me."

If you asked me yesterday, I would have laughed at the idea of ultra serious firefighter Tripp being a secret cowboy, but today he looked the part. The tight jeans, the red button-up shirt, the cowboy hat, the scruffy facial hair accenting the mustache I'd noticed yesterday, and don't even get me started on the bandana he'd been wearing when he found me. If my panties weren't in my pocket, they would've been wet.

"Good to know," he chuckled, tickling my side. "No, I used to work as a specialist firefighter for the National Forest Service near a national park a few states north."

"Fancy."

Although it had me wondering why he went to another state, there were jobs for firefighters like that in Colorado, too. Baker had wanted to be a smoke jumper when he first started out, but after he finished his training, he came back home. Reese had returned from nursing school not long after, mostly because she wanted to be here to help me take care of our grandma, but there had been some small-town speculation about whether those two would finally end up together.

Instead, my sister had doubled down on a grudge—no one seemed to have any details on—and glared at him while he gave her a respectable distance. Which was especially awkward for two people who saw each other regularly because of their jobs.

"Not really. Once I completed my training to become a smoke jumper, I pretty much lived out of a duffel bag for about ten years. Hard to set down roots when they're sending you all over the country."

"Is that why you left?"

The warmth of his hand on my side suddenly disappeared, and he stepped back, heading toward the windows at the front of the cabin that overlooked the lake with his hands balled into tight fists. I watched him take a deep breath and then flex his fingers, looking suddenly anxious about my question. It appeared there was more to him coming home after seventeen years than he was ready to talk about.

"If we can't use the shower, I might know a place where we can get clean. Then after, we should probably get settled for the night."

Clearly, he was ready to move on from the topic of his past, not that I'd been all that forthcoming with mine either.

"The sun is just starting to set now. It can't be that late." The sun had mostly moved behind the mountains, but it wasn't quite dark yet.

"But I'll be putting you back in the saddle early tomorrow. I don't want to stick around here longer than we have to. My extra batteries probably won't last more than another day, and if that fire line moves this way, we need to be prepared. I might be sidelined for this one, but I won't leave the ranch vulnerable if I can do something."

He moved toward the closed door down the short hallway, nodding for me to go look in the bathroom for supplies. "Can you look under the sink to see if you can find any bars of soap? I'll see if I can find any towels or clean clothes left behind."

"You gonna tell me the real reason you're not out with the fire department right now?" It was clear with how he talked he wanted to be helping, but he wasn't out with the regular crew for a reason. I just wasn't sure if he made that decision, or his superiors.

"Maybe," he said, moving into the bedroom before he finished replying. "But we need to hurry if we want to get to the hot springs before the sun sets."

"As long as you're not making me get into that icy lake in the dark." It may have been July, but it was still a lake in the middle of the mountains of Colorado.

"I told you I'd keep you safe," he called out, and I could hear dresser drawers being opened while I looked in the cabinet under the bathroom sink. There was a plastic tub full of individual bars of soap and a few tiny bottles of shampoo. It wasn't fancy, but it'd work.

"And I'm holding you to your word," I hollered back. As I straightened up with my toiletry stash, he appeared in the doorway to the bathroom, holding a small stack of miscellaneous clothing and some white towels.

"I'm kinda hoping you hold me to something else," he teased with a suggestive wiggle of his eyebrows. I smiled at his playful tone until I realized that this man would most likely be seeing a lot more of me soon. And to think I'd been feeling shy with him knowing I'd been going commando this whole time.

Chapter
Thirteen

Tristan

R HEY WAS QUIET AS she followed me down the trail that bordered the far side of the lake. There was still enough light for us to find our way to the hot springs, but I knew it'd be dark by the time we finished, so I'd been pleased to find another flashlight on my clothing hunt. The haze floating over the lake looked eerie, and it hadn't gotten much worse than when we arrived, but the air outside definitely smelled like a campfire.

"Should I be worried that you're leading me into the woods at night?" she asked from behind me, and I turned, watching her nervously scan our surroundings.

"It's not very far, and we'll be fine." I wasn't about to tell her that sometimes wild animals fled fires and sought refuge near bodies of water. I hadn't noticed anything unusual as we rode in, so I was hoping anything dangerous had fled north of the mountains on the other side of the fire, not south. "There weren't any black bears when Marty brought me up here, so we'll be fine."

As the trees became denser, the trail we'd started on became more of a vague suggestion, since it hadn't been maintained in a few years. Rhey moved in closer, gripping the back of my shirt as I picked my way toward the little pools of water we were looking for, not letting go once we emerged into a small clearing near the hot springs.

"Are there normally bears on the ranch property?" Rhey's voice had taken on a tinny quality, and I shook my head, reaching out to grasp her hand after I deposited my stack of clothing and towels on a rock nearby.

"No, I've only seen a few moose, but they're probably long gone by now. Animals are usually smarter than humans and move away from the dangerous fire, not toward it."

"I'm never going to live this down, am I?" she asked, sitting down on the edge of a rock and pulling off her boots. I stared as she flexed her toes, noticing the light pink polish once she got her socks off. She let out a little noise of relief while she massaged the sole of her foot, and it stirred something in me. Then I questioned how much smoke I'd inhaled earlier in the day, because I'd never considered someone's feet adorable before.

"Do you think you deserve to move past it? You realize how dangerous that was, right?" I'd told her earlier that I was angry at her for putting herself in that situation, but I knew what I'd felt was mostly fear. There was still a healthy dose of anger mixed in, mostly because she not only put her sister's rescue efforts at risk, but she also put herself in a situation that would've ended a whole lot differently than it did tonight. One where I wouldn't have been giving her shit—because she wouldn't be around for anyone to give her shit.

"Reese would've done the same thing for me," she said in a small voice, and while I didn't doubt what she was saying was true—as I would probably do the same for my siblings—it was still really fucking reckless. And put more than just herself in potential danger.

"And if I'd rescued Reese from that truck, I'd be giving her shit about making stupid, impulsive decisions too. Then I'd probably remind her that getting herself killed only guaranteed that she'd never see her sister again."

She nodded, staring down at her lap. "Thank you for finding out she was safe."

I sat down beside her, wrapping my arm around her shoulder and pulling her into my side. "I'm glad Baker could get her to safety."

"Honestly," she chuckled, reaching over to pick up my hand. She played with my fingers, laying her head back against my shoulder.

"Baker is the one whose safety you should probably worry about. He's like my sister's arch nemesis. She avoids him like the plague, and when she sees him, the arctic is probably warmer than the cold shoulders she gives him."

"Sounds like there's a story there," I said, using the words on her she'd used on me yesterday.

"Trust me, I've tried to get what happened out of her. All I know is that something happened after their graduation that turned them from lifelong childhood best friends to strangers. Even when he treated our grandmother with kindness when she was dying, Reese wouldn't even look at him."

We both sat quietly for a few moments, staring at the water of the hot springs while she played with my fingers. I thought about how someone I'd only known for twenty-four hours had turned my life upside down. A few days ago, I was struggling to find self-worth because I'd lost my way after my accident, and now I'd found someone who was easy to talk to in a way that I hadn't experienced before.

My dedication to my line of work hadn't lent well to deep relationships, or really any relationship at all. Sure, there were other guys who'd met people, settled down and gotten married, but most of the women I'd dated weren't looking for something serious or they couldn't handle that my job took up so much of my time.

The ones who'd been okay with me being a firefighter hadn't been thrilled when they found out I jumped out of planes into fires regularly and sometimes had to leave at a moment's notice, only to return days or weeks later after having been out of contact for the entire trip.

"It's getting dark, maybe we should do what we came here to do," Rhey whispered, releasing my hand.

"And what is it we came here to do?" I asked, tucking stray hair behind the shell of her ear.

"Get clean," she whispered, turning to face me. She ran her fingertips along a scar tucked along my hairline, teasingly scraping her short fingernails down the stubble that had covered my jaw in the last few days.

"What if I enjoy being dirty?" I asked, capturing her hand and kissing the center of her palm.

"Why do I have the feeling you aren't talking about our personal hygiene?"

"Must everything be suggestive with you, Rheyanne? I thought you were supposed to be the wise small-town bartender."

She chuckled, scraping her nails down the side of my neck once I'd released her hand, eliciting a hiss from me when they caught on a raised patch of skin.

"I'm sorry," she whispered, tracing her fingertips across the scar. "Do you mind if I ask what happened?"

"Let's get in first, then I can tell you why I came back home."

My anxiety crept in as I pulled off my shirt, careful to stay turned toward Rhey so she wouldn't see the patchwork of raised scars along my sides and the puckered angry skin that had finally healed down the center of my back. Once upon a time, the scars that'd littered my back from various on the job injuries had been almost a badge of honor, but now they were a stark reminder of everything I'd lost.

"Would you mind turning around?" she asked, fiddling with the zipper on her shorts. I tried to keep my gaze on her face, but my eyes were drawn to the now unbuttoned shirt that revealed the smooth skin of her stomach and a sliver of her bra right across the center. It was taking a considerable amount of self-restraint not to drop to my knees at her feet and lick a line straight from her navel to her long, slender neck.

"If that's what you want. But you realize the water is crystal clear. I'll be seeing everything in a moment, anyway."

"Just…" she made a shooing motion, and I took a few steps away, angling my body away from her without showing off my entire back.

"Let me know when you're ready."

The woods were quiet besides the rustling of clothing being removed while I waited for her to disrobe the rest of the way and climb into the warm water. From my experience, I knew it was almost too quiet, meaning the previous occupants of this area had already fled the danger they knew could be headed in this direction.

Marty had told me on my tour of the ranch that the springs here were like climbing into a warm bathtub, and my achy muscles were anticipating the respite. It also didn't hurt that my companion was a beautiful, nearly naked siren of a woman.

"Okay, you can climb in," she whispered, and I turned to look over my shoulder, the dim light from the flashlights illuminating her face. Even after the tumult of the last day and a half, she was stunning.

"Would you mind...?" I teased, gesturing from my eyes to hers and miming covering them. She shook her head, holding a hand over her face. "No peeking. I need to preserve my modesty."

She laughed and deliberately spread her fingers apart so she could watch me get undressed. Yanking off my boots and socks, I set them on top of a nearby rock and then pulled my jeans off to fold neatly on top of them.

"Do you want me to leave my boxers on?" I asked, deciding to give her the option. It'd be uncomfortable to walk in wet underwear back to the cabin later, but if she wanted me to keep them on, I'd keep them on.

"You don't need to worry about shrinkage," she giggled, lifting her wet fingers from the water and flicking it in my direction. "It's nice and warm in here."

"Trying to respect your boundaries, sweetheart."

She was quiet for a few moments, and I turned fully, surprised when I found her leaning against the edge of the pool, resting her head on her hands along the edge. "And if I want you to disrespect them?"

E.L. KOSLO

Licking my lips, I hooked my fingers in the elastic waistband, slowly lowering the tight material, watching with satisfaction when her eyes widened as my now erect cock pointed straight at her.

I placed them on my pile of clothing, walking in her direction. She pushed off the edge of the pool, spreading her arms and propelling herself back toward the far edge.

"You're going to poke an eye out with that thing."

Smirking, I stepped into the warm water, following her once my feet touched the bottom. "You planning to get your face that close to it?"

She giggled, but it turned to a squeal when I reached forward and grasped her waist, hauling her against my chest. Her full breasts flattened against my pecs, her chest heaving as she looked up at me.

"I thought we were going to talk," she whispered, flattening her palm against my chest.

"Are we not talking?" I asked, my hands roaming her bare skin. She gasped when I put a little pressure against her lower back, showing her exactly how much she was affecting me.

"Is that what this is?" she asked, smoothing her palm over my shoulder and scratching her fingernails against my scalp.

"Our mouths are moving, and sounds are coming out. Pretty sure that's considered talking."

She grinned, bouncing her eyebrows. "There are other things that involve mouths moving and sounds coming out that are definitely not talking."

"Touché."

When she put pressure on the back of my head, pulling me toward her, my lips gently ghosted over hers and a deep rumbling hum built in my chest.

I could get addicted to kissing this woman.

And it seemed she was just as ravenous when she grasped the back of my head with both hands, yanking my hair slightly while she wrapped her long legs around my waist. It'd be so easy to lose myself in her. To shift slightly and sheath myself in her tight heat,

118

but I could be patient. There was no doubt in my mind the wait would be worth it.

Walking us to a nearby underwater rock ledge along the side of the spring, I turned and sat down, framing her face with my palms while I deepened the kiss, my tongue tangling with hers in the steam rising off the water.

"Mmm," she hummed, rocking in my lap, her pussy sliding over me in a way that threatened to end things much sooner than either of us wanted. It'd been months since I'd been with a woman, and she was too alluring. My own personal siren sent to drag me to the depths of temptation.

Skating my lips along the side of her neck, I gently bit her ear, groaning when she thrust her hips down, arching backward with a gasp. Urging her forward, I kissed along the side of her neck, whispering in her ear. "You ready to talk now?"

"Now?" she whimpered, running her fingers through my damp hair.

Leaning back, I grasped the sides of her waist, halting the distracting rocking before I did something reckless, like fucking her in this hot spring bare. "While I would love to continue exploring where this is going, I don't have protection with me. And I don't think we should go there yet."

She nodded, swallowing hard as she took a shuddery breath. Her legs unlocked from my waist, and I turned her, urging her to lean back against my chest. Interlacing our fingers, I took a deep breath, trying to decide where I should start.

"A few months ago, I was involved in a search and rescue mission along the edge of the national park," I began, enjoying how comfortable she seemed nestled against my chest. Maybe her solid presence would help me stay calm. "The trails in this section had been closed because of conditions after the snowmelt, so we had some hikers who decided to camp in a restricted area that was scheduled for a controlled grassfire burn by the forestry service."

"They should have never been there," I murmured, feeling my pulse spike as I thought back to the call we'd received from the burn team and the winds that'd battered my crew once we'd jumped. Rhey squeezed my hand, grounding me. "The burn team hadn't seen signs of their camp when they ignited the first line. By the time they realized that the area wasn't clear, the winds changed and then all hell broke loose."

"The burn boss—they're the person in charge of the controlled burn plan—had miscalculated and despite it being late winter, the fire jumped the tree line they'd built a break near. The hikers were trapped along the edge of a ravine."

"We never should have taken the mission. Our entire outfit knew that the wind shear was dangerous, but we were running out of options. The rest of my crew jumped, but I came in too hot when the wind shifted. I ended up right on top of the fire and was prepared to adjust my course to overshoot the target, but I saw someone huddled down in the path."

Closing my eyes, I took a deep breath, trying to stay calm despite the barrage of images that were flickering through my mind of that damn purple dot through the smoke. The look of panic on that woman's face when she saw how close the fire was to where she was stuck, paralyzed with fear. Me landing a few yards away in full gear, headed directly for her as fast as I could move down the hill with my gear on.

"Hey, come back to me," a distant voice broke through my sub-conscious, and I blinked, making eye contact with Rhey as she gripped both sides of my face. "Breathe. You're safe."

Nodding, I drew in a ragged breath, trying to stem the sense of panic when my body recalled the piercing, sharp pain of the fire licking up my back. Rhey's gentle touch and imploring eyes soothed the memories, so they didn't take over.

"You don't have to finish. It's okay," she whispered, stroking my cheeks with her thumbs.

"I managed to get her into my quick deploy fire shelter bag, but a wind gust took down a tree, pinning me in place when I tried to get further away from the fire," I whispered, trying to breathe through the worst of the panic, her presence grounding me. "My gear protected me from the worst of it, but the line came through too fast for them to get to me in time."

Rhey's chin quivered, tears springing to the corners of her eyes. Shaking my head, I looked away, knowing I'd fall apart if she did.

"It could have been much worse. I honestly thought I was a goner." She sniffled, and I reached up, brushing a tear off her cheek. "The pain likely caused me to pass out, and I came to in the hospital a day later."

Rhey leaned in, wrapping her arms around my neck and tucking her face into my neck. My fingers traced her back in aimless patterns. Her presence helped keep the panic from creeping in, her fingertips tracing the puckered scar tissue on the back of my neck.

"Overall, everyone was lucky. No one died. They got the fire under control before it did too much damage. But I—" my voice cracked, and I tried to choke down the emotions I'd been hiding from everyone for months. "But I knew it was my last jump. The thought of gearing up sent me into a full state of panic. I couldn't sleep. I couldn't eat. The burns were extensive, but I only needed grafts in a few places where the seams on my gear had failed. Once I was discharged from the hospital, they offered to let me back on desk only duty until I was fully healed, but I had a panic attack in the parking lot."

"I turned in my resignation from my specialist assignment the next day. I was a liability. They knew it, and so did I. An investigation was launched, so I had to relive it over and over as they took statements from everyone involved. When they told me I had to be cleared by the staff psychologist if I wanted to stay with the department, I complied, but talking about it just made the panic attacks worse. She diagnosed me with PTSD, and cleared me for light duty, but my heart wasn't in it anymore."

She leaned back, cupping my cheeks and kissing me softly. "I'm so sorry."

"I don't want your pit—" I said, shaking my head, but she held tight, interrupting me.

"Gratitude is the only thing I'm feeling right now," she whispered, tracing the scar along my forehead where my helmet cut me after it'd taken the impact of the tree. It was still pink, not as angry as it'd been after the accident, but I'd never take my equipment for granted again. My gear saved my life. "If things had been different, you might not be here at all, much less with me right now."

Gratitude had been elusive for a long time, anger and sadness ruling my emotions. The first three months had been a haze of depression and panic, my addled brain trying to cope with my entire life being sent into upheaval because of one decision I knew I'd make again if put in the same situation.

"Once I fully resigned, and they released me, I came back home. Moved in with some family, talked with the local fire department while I tried to find a job." I took a deep breath, feeling the tension fading from my body as I focused on my surroundings. The warm water. The weight of the woman in my lap. The powerful body I still had, besides it being worse for wear.

"Are you planning to stay?" she asked, scooting back on my thighs and putting a little distance between our bodies.

"If you would have asked me last week, I wouldn't have been able to give you a definitive answer."

"And now?"

"Now," I breathed, pulling her back in before I reached up to cup the sides of her neck with my palms. "I might be finding some reasons to stay."

The sweet smile she gave me in return warmed my chest in a way I knew was dangerous, but for once, I was ready to let the fear of the unknown go to chase after what I wanted.

And I wanted her.

Chapter Fourteen

Annie

TRIPP'S EXPRESSION WAS SO earnest as his thumbs gently stroked the skin of my waist, causing my heart to lurch as I thought about how a lie of omission could rip this closeness I felt to him away in the blink of an eye. Blowing out a heavy breath, I broke eye contact, shifting to stand.

He didn't let me go far, grasping my hand and pulling me back. Ducking his face slightly, he tilted my face toward him with a crooked finger beneath my chin. "What's going on?"

"There's something I probably need to tell you."

"Hey," he murmured, situating me sideways on his lap with my head resting against his shoulder. "This isn't a tit for tat situation. You asked why I came back home, and I wanted to tell you. Don't feel like you need to spill all your secrets in response."

Only this wasn't something I wanted to keep a secret from him. He needed to know, and it'd been unfair of me to let things get as far as they had without telling him. Technically, I wasn't doing something wrong, but I couldn't get more invested in things between us unless I came clean with him.

"I'm not even sure how to phrase this without sounding like a terrible person."

His fingers toyed with the end of my braids before unfastening the elastic ties and combing them through my tangled, wet hair. "Then how about let's get cleaned up, and you can say what you want to tell me when you're ready?"

Once he finger-combed my hair out, he stood, making his way across the spring, the dim light illuminating the damage the fire

124

had done to his back. I held back a gasp as my eyes scanned the angry, puckered skin, tears springing to my eyes. Seeing the marks solidified my need to tell him the truth. Because there weren't any guarantees in life, and while we were safe now, I'd regret it later if I let being worried about his reaction keep me from exploring this connection with him.

I'd spent half my life being terrified of the people around me dying, and it'd be easy to keep an emotional connection from developing, but I knew I'd regret it. Keeping Jay at arm's length had been easy, because he was doing the same thing. Tripp, on the other hand, had opened up to me in a way that felt honest and vulnerable. If I ruined that by keeping secrets, I would sabotage the first possibility of a relationship that had felt real in a very long time.

"Enjoy the show?" he asked, holding his arms out of the water as he returned, the bottles of shampoo and bars of soap looking comically tiny in his large hands.

"I think someone is looking for compliments," I teased, reaching for a bottle, but he held it out of my reach, shaking his head. He didn't need to know I was too stuck in my head to ogle him leaning over the rocks that bordered the hot spring, the taut muscles of his back and strong thighs fully on display.

"Ouch," he chuckled, settling back onto the ledge we'd been seated on. He grasped my shoulders, turning me away from him. "Can't even get one suggestive comment out of you. Tough crowd tonight."

"Pretty sure I told you earlier that you'd poke an eye out with the trouser snake you brought into the water."

He laughed, leaning close to place a kiss on the back of my shoulder. "Yet no faces got close enough to test out that theory. Such a shame. He was eager for an introduction."

"Someone stopped things before they got that far. I would've been happy to make a new friend."

His lips traced the back of my neck, settling beneath my ear. "And I will wait patiently until you're ready for me to make an introduction. But if you're thinking this hard about telling me something, you're not ready."

Tripp stepped back, and I felt the instant loss of heat from where he'd been. The sound of shampoo squirting from the bottle startled me, but then I let out a sigh of satisfaction when his fingers dug in, massaging it into my scalp. He worked my hair into a lather, his strong fingers relaxing me while they worked.

"Lean back," he whispered, moving in close and pressing his chest to my back. He dipped lower in the water, the suds dispersing into the clear water around us, the floral scent of the shampoo clouding my senses.

His fingers gently worked the shampoo out of my hair, and suddenly I couldn't keep it in any longer. This had to be one of the most romantic moments of my life, and I didn't want to spoil it, but not saying something wasn't fair to him.

Turning in his arms, I ducked underneath the water, using my hands to smooth the hair back from my face. He waited patiently, studying me as we stared at each other, the steam of the hot spring rising into the air between us.

"I was—kind of am—involved with someone," I whispered, forcing myself to maintain eye contact so I could see his expression.

"Like a boyfriend?" he asked, finding my hand underneath the water and squeezing it, but not moving any closer.

Shaking my head, I tried to figure out how to phrase exactly what Jay had been to me. "No, it was never romantic. We had a super brief relationship in high school before we went off to different schools, so we were familiar with each other. We've been friends for a long time, and I love him, but I've never been *in* love with him. Nor do I see that changing."

"And he knows that?"

Nodding, I tried to step back, but he held firm, not letting me escape just because this conversation was uncomfortable. "I think he's attracted to me physically, but we see each other as a means to an end. You know what living in a small town is like. I think I've

126

used him more as a shield than anything. He's never seen me like that."

Tripp let out a chuckle, arching an eyebrow, but I was certain that Jayden had never, and would never be in love with me either. His heart belonged to someone else, and I doubted it would change, even if she hadn't been in the picture for years.

"He's like my best friend..." I trailed off, whispering the next part. "But we have sex."

"Is that something you plan to keep doing?" he asked, scanning my face in the dim light reflecting off the surface of the water.

Shaking my head, I hesitantly took a step forward. "No. We haven't been together like that in several months, and I have no desire to go back to how things were. Not now that..."

He reached forward, pulling me toward him until our chests brushed together. "Now that *what*? What's changed for you?"

"Now that there might be someone else."

"Hmm," he hummed, running his nose down the side of my face, his lips grazing my earlobe and setting off goosebumps along my arms despite the heat of the water. "And who is this someone else? Anyone I know?"

"I think you might," I whispered, wrapping my arms around his neck. His hands gripped my hips, one of his palms pulling my thigh up to wrap around his waist. Relief coursed through me as he smiled, rubbing his nose playfully against mine. It was then I went in for the easy joke because it scared me how attached I was getting in such a short period. I'd just met him, and I was falling fast. "Do you think Baker is single?"

A loud laugh tore from his chest, and he squeezed me tightly, his mouth lowering to cover mine with a possessive kiss. When he broke for air, he pinched my butt, narrowing his eyes. "Baker couldn't handle you. And he's never going to get the chance, either. You're mine."

"Someone sounds a little possessive," I sassed, but pulled him back in for a kiss, my pulse racing at the way he took over, taunting me with smooth strokes of his tongue against mine until my head swam.

When he leaned back, our chests heaving against each other, his low voice solidified my feelings, and there was no stopping the way I was falling for this man. "As far as I'm concerned, there is no other man. Because someone who won't commit to you has no idea what kind of mistake he's making. But his loss is most certainly my gain, because I can't imagine walking away from you now."

"I don't want you to," I whispered, combing my fingers through his wet hair. The way he looked at me was addictive. There was just something insanely attractive about a man who didn't mask his emotions.

"And just so we're clear." His voice was low as he leveled his gaze with mine. "I won't share you."

"I'm not asking you to. If you want to pursue this, I'll talk to him." As soon as Jay was back in town, the first thing I would do was tell him I'd met someone, and we couldn't keep up the physical part of our relationship. I wasn't sure what it meant for our friendship, but we'd been drifting apart for a while now. Soon, the restaurant expansion would keep him busy enough he wouldn't have time for me, anyway.

"Now can we finish getting cleaned up so I can take you to bed in that cabin? I believe we have some overdue introductions to make."

Laughing, I nodded, clinging to his shoulders as he swam backward to where we'd abandoned the soap.

Washing each other was like an extended game of foreplay, wandering hands lingering in places that had me aching for him by the time we'd both cleaned the sweat and lingering soot off our bodies. He climbed out of the spring first, drying his strong, muscular body while I watched him, feeling a bit like a voyeur as his hard cock bobbed with his movements.

Now that things were out in the open, it felt like a weight had been lifted, my attraction to him no longer something forbidden. He knew my situation and didn't judge me; he'd just made his thoughts on me having other partners clear. I had a feeling a man like Tripp would be more than enough to keep me satisfied.

The only part that worried me now was the emotional attachment I could feel forming. While his job wasn't nearly as dangerous now as it had been before he came home, would he ever decide being back in Sage Springs was too tame for him and leave to go back to that life? What if he decided he really didn't want to stay here long term?

My entire life was here.

Reese was here.

She loved her job at the hospital, and I doubted she'd want to leave. And while I could technically bar tend anywhere, I felt like I'd helped Hudson build something special at the bar that'd been in his family for generations. It wouldn't be the same anywhere else. But things wouldn't be the same here either. I was probably homeless. The next few months would be about starting over and figuring out where Reese and I went from here. Would a new relationship survive all the changes that were coming my way?

"No frowning." Tripp's deep voice broke the distracted trance I'd been in, and I focused on where he now waited at the edge of the spring, an open shirt and jeans covering him. I hadn't even realized he'd finished getting dressed. "I know it's disappointing I put away your new friend, but I promise you can take him back out once we're at the cabin."

Shaking my head, I swam to the edge, took his extended hand and let him pull me out. He wrapped a towel around my shoulders, his hands pressing the soft cotton into my skin as he leaned in and kissed my neck.

"But seriously, Rhey. Out of your head. Stay present with me tonight. We can figure all that other bullshit out later."

Turning in Tripp's arms, I laid my head on his chest, wrapping my arms around him beneath the damp shirt now concealing his firm muscles. His heartbeat was an anchor, the steady cadence keeping me focused on the here and now. "I'm sorry."

"No apologizing either," he whispered into my hair. "You laid your cards on the table, and now I'm laying mine down. I want you, and I don't give a shit about anything else right now but exploring this connection I feel with you. If there's anything I've learned in the last few months, it's that tomorrow isn't a guarantee and you should embrace where life takes you."

Swallowing past my anxiety, I let him finish drying me, my pulse racing with how he looked at me. Especially when he gazed adoringly at me from his knees while he dried my legs.

"I couldn't find any clean panties for you," he whispered, tracing his fingers through my slit as he stood back up. "But I don't think that's going to be a problem because I don't want you wearing them, anyway."

"Such a dirty boy," I whispered, feeling the heat coursing through my veins as his fingertips explored, pressing into me while his thumb softly rotated my clit.

"Hungry boy." His voice was a deep growl as he leaned down to nibble at my neck, his teeth scraping the sensitive skin and making me gasp. "I want this pussy on my face once we get back."

"Then I guess you better dress me so we can get back there."

His eyes gleamed in the diffused light from the flashlights. A hungry expression never left his face as he pulled a soft cotton sundress over my head, his fingers lingering on my waist, moving up to cup my breasts through the material as he stared down at me.

Feeling the same hunger, I turned, holding his extended hand while I stepped into my boots. We gathered the things we'd brought with us, laughing while we hurried through the woods, following the beams of the flashlights until we were back on the front porch of the little cabin we'd claimed as our own.

Soiled clothing and tiny bars of soap were discarded seconds after the door closed behind us, followed by a trail of our damp clothing down the hallway leading to the bedroom. Backing away as he stalked toward me, I pulled my borrowed sundress over my head, tossing it at him after I sat down on the edge of the bed.

He paused in the doorway, stroking his hard cock while he stared at me, the ravenous look in his eyes making me almost feral with need as the moonbeams coming in from the window lingered on his face.

"Spread your legs," he commanded, nodding toward them. "Show me that fucking pussy."

"Get on your knees," I countered, propping one foot up on the edge of the bed and lazily tracing my fingers through the wetness he'd caused. He didn't even hesitate, dropping to his knees on the rug before me, licking his lips as he watched me with rapt attention. A heady sense of power coursed through me as I watched him slowly make his way toward me. His submission was intoxicating.

"Tell me what to do." He met my gaze as his hands balled into fists at his sides, waiting for me to do what he asked.

"Kiss me." I met him halfway, ghosting my lips over his and tugging on his lower lip with my teeth, enjoying the groan he let out when I bit down.

Harsh breaths filled the air between us, the tension heating up with every teasing kiss, each one becoming more desperate than the last. It'd been so long since I'd let myself feel something like this. Although it'd never been exactly like this before. I'd never felt so pent up with need, and I liked he was letting me lead. It would have been so easy for him to grasp me by the waist, throw me up the bed and just sink into me. And any other night, I might have enjoyed it, but right now, I wanted to call the shots.

"I want your tongue," I gasped into his mouth, pulling him back with a handful of hair and urging him lower before I leaned back, fisting my hands in the comforter behind me. His mustache tickled the insides of my thighs as he teasingly traced his lips across my overheated skin.

"That doesn't feel like your tongue." My teasing tone shifted into something a little more wanton as glanced up at me from between the v of my legs, tracing the tip of his tongue along the crease where my thigh met my hip.

"You want this?" he murmured, flattening it and dragging it up my thigh and back down, lingering with his nose, nudging my clit before he dove in, taking a single lick up the center of my pussy. "You want me to taste how much I turn you on?"

"Fuck, yes," I gasped as he gripped the backs of both my thighs, yanking me into his face and growling while he thrust his tongue inside me. "Lick that pussy, I need you to make me come."

His feral groan of satisfaction was all the encouragement I needed to hear, suddenly craving the power I felt at his eager obedience. I'd never been vocal like this before, but there was something freeing about telling him exactly what I wanted and knowing he'd do it. He made me feel in control of him—of my pleasure—in a whole new way.

"Fingers," I panted, gripping his hair and gyrating my hips into the movements of his mouth. "Fuck me with your fingers while you lick my clit."

He whispered filthy encouragements into my skin while he did exactly as I asked, thrusting two thick fingers inside and curling them until I saw stars behind my eyelids. My orgasm gained speed quickly, barreling down on me with the raw power of a freight train. His tongue drew maddening circles on my clit as he pushed me closer and closer to release, his desperate moans and growls mixing with mine along with the filthy sound of his fingers inside my wet pussy.

"Oh God, I'm gonna come," I moaned, arching my back and pulsing my hips into his ministrations, chasing the high I knew he'd provide.

"Fuck yes, sweetheart, all over my tongue," he groaned, staring up at me through hooded eyes while his fingers hooked and pressed a place inside of me that might as well have been a detonation button. "Cover my face."

"Fuck, fuck, fuck," I chanted as I came, gasping for breath, my body shaking while the movements of his fingers slowed, his tongue lingering with languid strokes as he cleaned up the mess I'd made.

Falling back against the comforter, I closed my eyes, my pulse hammering and my thighs shaking while he rained a line of kisses up my belly and lingered on my nipples, biting and sucking while I squirmed beneath him, completely overwhelmed by the way he owned my body.

His lips lingered on the dip of my collarbone, his tongue tracing the crease before he moved to my neck, licking a path up to whisper in my ear. "How do you want me?"

My eyelids felt heavy as they opened, meeting his desperate gaze. "Inside me."

He grinned at my whisper, leaning forward to kiss me sweetly, his tongue stroking into my mouth languidly while he settled between my legs.

"I still don't have anything with me," he replied, lightly thrusting his hips against mine so I could feel how hard he was.

He may not have had anything, but I did. "Do you know where my purse is?"

"I think it's by the front door." A look of confusion flickered across his face, followed by a knowing smile. "Permission to raid your purse?"

Chapter
Fifteen

Tristan

L EAVING A WARM, SATISFIED, entirely too sexy for her own good, giggling Rhey draped across the bed without a stitch of clothing on was not an easy feat. But if it meant I would be inside her sooner rather than later, it was a sacrifice I was fully prepared to make.

Following the trail of discarded towels, clothing and boots toward the front door, I spied the purse that Rhey had been wearing when I found her inside the truck. Thank God, she'd brought it with her, because while there were plenty of other things we could do to keep ourselves occupied, I needed the closeness of connecting with her fully. I'd revealed parts of myself to her I refused to show anyone else, and I craved her like a drug.

I also respected the fuck out of her for being upfront with me about her being involved with someone else. It would've been easy for her to push it aside and let things get physical between us without saying anything. I could admit that the thought of her with someone else made me a little jealous, but it had been long before we met, and from the sound of it, things were fizzling out between them. Thank fuck for that, because resisting her was an exercise in futility. Not one to hold back, I told her exactly how much I wanted her, and soon to be *ex*-friends-with-benefits be damned, she was mine.

My fingers shook from the adrenaline, but I managed to get the zipper open, peering into the purse that from the outside seemed small. As I emptied the contents onto the coffee table, it appeared to have some magical Mary Poppins like quality as items kept appearing. Sifting through, I found another zipper pouch. Opening it, I found what appeared to be a full-blown mini sewing/first aid kit. Grabbing the discarded flashlight from the floor, I shined it inside, sighing in relief as I saw not one, but two condoms.

Grabbing both, I hurried back to the bedroom, stopping in my tracks as I took in the scene on the bed.

"Fuck, now that is a sight a man could get used to," I groaned, watching Rhey propped up against the pillows near the headboard, her fingers lazily circling her clit while she waited for me to return. I swallowed as I watched her, my mouth suddenly parched, but I couldn't let it distract me. "You, sweetheart, are sexy as fuck."

"Come here," she whispered, crooking a finger and beckoning me forward. She had no idea how much I wanted her to boss me around.

Deciding to do some teasing of my own, I reached down, leisurely stroking my throbbing cock and spreading the moisture that'd seeped out around the crown with my thumb. It wouldn't take much to get me desperately close to the edge since it'd been almost half a year since I'd been inside a woman, so I paced myself, leaving my grip loose, but enjoying the way her eyes tracked every movement.

"I'm not sure if I should be impressed or scared that I found them next to a sutures kit in that alarmingly magical purse."

She smiled, reaching toward me as I stopped beside the bed. "My sister is a nurse. So that little kit was her doing."

"Would it be in poor taste to thank your sister the next time I see her?" I joked, climbing onto the bed to brace my hand on the headboard while I watched Rhey's fingers make soft but sure strokes against her clit. There was something intoxicating about watching a woman owning her own satisfaction and telling—and showing—you exactly how to bring her pleasure.

"As long as you're prepared to hear a lecture on safe sex practices and efficacy rates of condoms when used as your primary method of protection."

"Sounds sexy, and super educational," I laughed, but if it meant she wanted to introduce me to the most important person in her life, I'd take all the lectures. I wanted to keep Rhey safe too, so we'd already have that in common. Leaning closer, I ghosted my lips along the side of her cheek, enjoying how she tilted her head to give me better access to her neck. "Is it okay if we use one of these condoms now as a primary method of protection?"

"Yes," she gasped as I sucked on her pulse point, her hand covering where I still stroked myself. "But I get to put it on. Lay down."

"Yes, ma'am," I groaned, thrusting lightly into the firm squeeze of our hands.

"Hand it over," she demanded, holding her palm out in my direction. "But don't stop touching yourself. I want to watch." She pushed against my shoulder, urging me backward on the bed.

"Into a little voyeurism, are you?" I asked, pressing them into her palm and laying back on the mattress, doing a little voyeuristic watching of my own as she moved to straddle my legs. Her neck and chest were covered with marks from my stubble, and it gave me a primal sense of satisfaction to see the little angry pink streaks. I liked the idea of marking her as mine.

"Watching you stroke yourself makes me wet," she whispered, eyes riveted as I continued to touch myself, twisting my fist as I reached the head and then slowly stroking back down, fighting the urge to thrust my hips. Having her eyes on me was a bigger turn-on than I expected, but I wanted to draw it out and really give her a show.

"Then, by all means, sweetheart, take a seat and enjoy the ride."

Feeling empowered by the way she looked at me, I concentrated all my energy into delaying my orgasm, working myself until I was throbbing against my palm, desperate for a release.

She watched with hooded eyes, the condom wrappers fisted in one hand while the other cupped her breast and kneaded the milky flesh, her nipple pink and erect as she rolled it between her fingers.

"God, you are so fucking beautiful," I groaned, my thighs flexing as I tried to hold off. "But I'm hanging on by a thread here. What else do you want from me?"

She leaned forward, bracing a hand against my chest as she loomed over me, her pussy inches from where I was stroking my cock. So close, but not nearly enough, as I wasn't inside her yet. I was aching for it. For the relief I knew I'd feel when she finally sank down, taking me inch by inch until I'd disappeared inside her entirely. "I want you to let me ride you."

"Fuck yes," I groaned, thrusting my hips, my knuckles grazing where she was wet for me between her thighs. "Saddle up, baby. I want you to ride me, too."

"Hands above your head," she whispered, pulling my fist from my cock and stretching my arm above my head, holding it still while I followed suit with the other. "Don't move."

"Can't promise that," I panted when she reached down, tugging firmly on my dick. Each stroke had my desperation rising higher and higher. Enough for my hips to have a mind of their own, instinctively flexing into her tight fist.

"Well, you need to try," she whispered, leaning forward and grasping my lower lip between her teeth. She held eye contact while she stroked me with one hand, growling against my lips as I whimpered.

"Yes, ma'am," I moaned, arching my neck as she tilted her hips forward, dragging the lips of her pussy up the length of me. She was so warm and wet, and I so badly wanted to grab her by the shoulders and throw her against the mattress to fuck her hard. But I liked how she'd taken control. Women who knew exactly what they wanted were sexy as fuck, and being the focus of her attention was proving to be addictive.

"Oh fuck," I whimpered as she rotated her hips again, my tip poised right at her entrance while she teased me. "Please. Fuck me."

"Such a good boy," she whispered, scooting back until she settled her hips just above my knees, pinning me in place. I kept my arms still, my knuckles flexing as I grasped the covers above my head, obeying her earlier instructions—just like she wanted. "Now let's see if we taste as good together as I think we do."

My hips shot up off the bed when her lips covered the head, a sweet moan echoing in the air while she sucked and licked where she'd rubbed her pussy up against me. I could only imagine how good we tasted together, my mouth watering at the memory of how good she'd tasted with my head buried between her supple thighs.

"Mmm," she hummed, sitting up and licking her lips while she smiled down at me. I was so fucking hard, but I pulled out everything in my arsenal to hold off as she ripped open the little packet and smoothed the condom down my length.

"Fuck me," I whispered, flexing my hips as she gave me a slow stroke. "I need to watch you ride me."

Rhey released me, crawling over my body, her full breasts dragging up my chest as she hovered over me, eyes locked with mine as she reached between us and poised the tip at her entrance.

"I want you to stay exactly like you are," she whispered, her warm breath fanning over my mouth. "Let me use you to make myself come."

"God, yes," I groaned into her mouth as she shifted her hips back, slowly sinking down inch by agonizing inch. "Fucking use me, sweetheart."

Her eyes closed and she let out the sexiest moan as she rotated her hips, rocking against where we were joined.

My eyelids fluttered as I watched her face, eyes clenched tightly closed, hips rotating and pressing down, making me see stars every time she clenched that tight pussy around me when my cock bottomed out.

"Fuck, you feel so good," she moaned, bracing both palms against my chest, her fingernails digging into my pecs as she sat upright. Groaning at the change of angle, I flexed my hips into her movements, enjoying each gasp and groan as she rode me, chasing her own pleasure.

"That's it, baby," I encouraged, watching a flush work its way up her chest. She threw her head back, her loose hair cascading down her shoulders, swaying as she flexed her hips. I didn't think I'd ever seen such an erotic display of beauty. "Make yourself come all over my cock. I'll wait for you."

Her eyes opened, a determined look on her face as she leaned forward slightly, fingernails scraping my chest as she lifted her hips, impaling herself on my length over and over until her movements faltered, a loud moan echoing into the air around us.

"Look at you, beautiful," I panted, watching her ride the edge, so close to coming but not quite there yet. "Touch yourself. I wanna watch you fall apart. Flick that pretty little clit for me."

Her eyes narrowed, and I almost expected her to stop, but she didn't, reaching for my hand and drawing it to where we were joined. She pressed me against her, rocking her hips into my fingertips.

"Make me come," she ordered, sitting up and cupping her tits, rubbing her nipples between her fingertips while she rocked her hips against me, chasing the high she knew I was desperate to provide her.

Bringing the pads of my fingers to my lips, I licked them, returning them to her clit and rubbing lightly, watching her for signs of how she liked to be touched.

When her head fell back, eyes clenched and mouth dropped open, I knew I'd hit the spot, concentrating all my energy into keeping my touch steady while I thrust up from the mattress into each rotation of her hips.

"Oh, fuck," she whimpered, her movements faltering as she tipped over the edge, clenching around me. "I'm coming."

Deciding to disobey her orders, I gripped both sides of her waist tightly and pulled her into my thrusts as my hips jackknifed off the bed, chasing my orgasm like a man possessed.

She moaned as I fucked her, falling forward to brace her hands on my abs as my hips faltered, my release roaring through my body. My fingers tightened on her hips, probably leaving marks as

I rocked her against me, prolonging the intense pleasure as I came inside the condom.

"Holy shit," she panted, falling forward to brace her hands on either side of my head. I trailed my fingers up her spine, smiling as she shivered at the touch, clearly as overstimulated as I was. Her lips covered mine in a drowsy kiss and I reached down to cup her ass, rotating my hips and enjoying the way she whimpered into my mouth.

She broke the kiss with a gasp, collapsing forward with her palms pressing into my chest as I wrapped my arms around her.

"Tire yourself out there, cowgirl?" I teased, working my fingers through the loose waves of hair draped down her sweaty back.

"Lasted longer than eight seconds," she giggled, kissing the skin over my heart.

"Not your first rodeo," I chuckled, bracing my hands against her lower back. While I'd been riding horses since I was a kid, I was definitely not that kind of horseman, but I'd gladly be her bucking bronco anytime she wanted. "That was some expert riding."

"Someone seems to think he's hung like a horse."

Before I could respond, her stomach growled, and mine let out a resounding answer. I knew if we were going to get any use out of that second condom; I needed to feed her.

"You wanna come see if we can find anything to eat?" I asked, not wanting to move, but knowing we needed to.

"At least you got a snack," she teased after she moved to rest her chin on my chest. I suppressed a laugh at her little eyebrow wiggle, catching her not so hidden meaning. But despite my sudden urge to test the theory, one could not survive on pussy alone.

Chapter Sixteen

Annie

EXHAUSTION HAD COMPLETELY TAKEN over my body, and I'd only been asleep for what felt like minutes when a loud, jarring noise echoed down the hallway, startling me awake.

Tripp's arms tightened around me, the cutest little growl coming out of his mouth when I shifted. "No. Stay here."

Before I could protest, the noise echoed down the hallway again, followed by what sounded like an alert siren.

"Fuck." Tripp let go of me suddenly, rolling off the far side of the bed and escaping through the open door totally naked.

The sound went off again, and I heard voices trailing down the hallway, followed by loud curses and rustling.

Tripp appeared in the doorway a few moments later, throwing a button-up shirt at me and my dusty jean shorts from yesterday.

"Get dressed. We've gotta go," he hollered, yanking his boxer briefs up and settling them on his hips before he thrust his muscular legs inside his jeans.

"What's going on?" I asked, pushing my arms through the sleeves and rolling them up so they didn't cover my hands.

"Fire jumped the ridge. We need to get back to the ranch. The ground crew pulled back to town and is trying to get a fire break in along the east side of the river."

Nodding, I hastily pulled on my shorts, reaching for the socks he held out. He left the room, returning with my boots in his hands, clipping the radio to his belt.

"Gather up anything you want to take with you while I go saddle Seraphina."

He disappeared, the slam of the screen door echoing down the hallway while I yanked on my boots and rushed back into the living room. I scooped up the contents of my purse, shoving everything back inside and pulling it over my head, cinching the strap tight.

Red paisley caught my eye as I headed toward the door and I reached down, pulling the bandanas from the stack of discarded clothing.

Moving into the kitchen, I hastily opened the cabinets, scanning the meager contents until I found what I was looking for in one of the base cabinets. I put the bandanas in the empty sink, soaking them with bottled water and shoving them into an empty bowl on the counter.

Grabbing a few extra bottles, I balanced them on the top of the bowl and scanned the cabin, hoping it'd stay safe, as well as the rest of the things in the path of the fire.

Tripp was leading Seraphina out of the barn fully saddled when I reached him, running his hand soothingly down the side of her face while he whispered something I couldn't hear to her.

He looked up, meeting my eyes, his expression tense. "The winds died down, but the smoke looks worse. We need to get out of here."

The light haze that had hovered over the lake was clouding the area and I couldn't make out the mountains on the other side anymore. It made my lungs ache as I tried to breathe shallowly, knowing that we'd be needing those bandanas to make it back.

"I found water," I rushed out, thrusting the bowl in his direction.

"Good girl."

Tripp took the bottles, stowing them in the saddlebag before he grabbed one bandana, moving behind me and tying it snugly across the bridge of my nose. He took the bowl, crouching down so I could tie his on, running back to the barn once I was done to get his hat before he rejoined me. Holding the stirrup out, he kept it steady while I put my foot inside and swung my leg over the horse's back. I scooted forward, bracing myself while he wrapped himself around my back, anchoring me to him with one gloved hand on my stomach before he grasped the reins and led the horse back to the open valley we'd come in yesterday.

My eyes widened when I saw the damage the fire had done overnight, the charred remnants of trees poking through the dense smoke, an eerie glow along the horizon line much closer than the fire we'd left behind yesterday.

"Hold on!" he shouted, voice muffled as he squeezed his thighs, his horse breaking into a steady trot as she headed south.

My pulse raced as we neared the river, but he didn't cross back over, hugging the edge of the rocky shoreline, but keeping the horse in the grass as she headed back toward the ranch. The smoke was dense, but Seraphina clearly knew where she was going, not slowing as the trees raced by.

"We're close!" he yelled, pulling the reins to the side, slowing her pace as he guided her into the woods on a trail headed to the east. The air was cleaner under the canopy of the trees, but there was something about the stillness of the woods that kept me on edge. What had once been a forest full of noisy wildlife was silent.

Eventually, the sound of chainsaws and heavy machinery reached us before the horse emerged from the trees. I scanned the tree line, suddenly afraid one would come crashing down on us.

"Hold on!" Tripp shouted, steering her over a fallen log and through a break in the trees.

After spending the last twenty-four hours alone, I sighed in relief as I scanned the hodgepodge grouping of vehicles clustered in the middle of the field, dozens of emergency personnel hard at work along the river's edge with shovels and various heavy equipment.

Seraphina's pace slowed as we passed them, and Tripp kept her headed toward a barn I could see in the distance. The familiar sight of my co-worker and friend, Charley, brought tears to my eyes, and I tried not to cry as she took off into a run toward us. Her face was covered with a mask, but I'd recognize that technicolor hair anywhere.

Tripp slowed the horse at the side of the barn, lifting me off and into the open arms of my friend.

"What the fuck, girl? You scared the shit out of us when you disappeared yesterday," she growled into my hair, but I could tell she was just as relieved to see me as I was. Her fingers deftly untied the knot on my bandana, pulling it off my face before she cupped my cheeks. "You okay?"

Shaking my head, I let the tears fall, hating that I'd made my friends worry.

Tripp's solid presence appeared behind me, his hand grasping the side of my waist as he kissed the side of my head.

"I'm gonna get Phi watered and see where Marty wants her, sweetheart," he told me, squeezing briefly before he let go and walked past us, leading the tired Appaloosa behind him.

"Damn, sounds like someone had quite the adventure, *sweetheart*. Dad told me the new ranch manager took off to rescue a stranded motorist, but I didn't know it was you until this morning."

"You have no idea," I laughed, taking a deep breath and coughing as the lingering smoke made my throat burn.

"Let's get you a mask, and you can help me get the horses ready."

"I don't want to leave Tripp," I said instinctively, wanting to help.

"Fire Chief won't let you get within twenty yards of that crew," she said, steering me toward the barn by my shoulders. "Hudson and my dad have already tried. We've been loading up the horses and taking them in pairs to the fairgrounds just in case the fire gets any closer. Even if it doesn't reach this far, the air quality is gonna be terrible for a while."

"Do you know how far up the ridge it got?" I asked, knowing the answer before she responded just by the wrinkle that formed between her eyebrows.

"I'm sorry, babe," she whispered, pulling me back in for a hug. My shoulders shook as the shock of everything set in. "Everything north of the highway is gone."

She held me while the tears took over, mourning the only home I'd known since I was twelve years old. The place that'd been a refuge after our parents died in a small engine plane crash on the first solo vacation they'd taken since we were toddlers. Reese and

I'd been orphaned overnight and sent to live with our grandmother in the middle of nowhere Colorado.

It'd been a stark contrast to the life we'd had before, leaving behind the bustling city of Denver. Suddenly, the looming mountain ranges in the distance had become our home, much to our dismay. But as we settled in, welcomed by the community our dad had grown up in, I'd slowly come to love Sage Springs.

Charley ran her gloved hand down the back of my head, letting me cry it out until a pair of hands closed on my shoulders. I didn't even need to turn to know who it was, spinning and tucking my head beneath Tripp's chin while he wrapped his arms around me.

"You gonna be okay to stay here with Charley and Marty while I go down to help?" he asked, tipping my chin toward him and using his thumbs to wipe the tears from my cheeks.

Nodding, I tried to get myself under control. "Please don't do anything reckless."

Even though I couldn't see his mouth, I could tell he was smiling from the way his cheeks pulled up, the smile lines at the sides of his eyes creasing. "You mean like riding into a fire on horseback to rescue some crazy woman?"

I nodded, wrapping my arms tightly around his back, squeezing. "I need you safe."

"Baby, I'm trying to stay on the Chief's good side, so you don't need to worry about me riding off to rescue any more damsels in distress. That was a onetime gig. And I don't regret doing it for a fucking minute."

He held me until I released him, pulling back to look up at him. "Please be careful."

Tripp pulled down his mask, reaching to tug mine out of the way before he cupped the back of my head and pulled me in for a firm kiss. He replaced my mask, pulling his back up and nodding before he turned and headed toward a beat-up pickup truck parked beside the barn. I watched as he opened a lockbox in the bed, pulling out his gear.

Charley wrapped her arm around my shoulder as we watched him get ready, my eyes tracking every movement as he stepped into his boots and turnout gear, pulled the heavy pants up, and fastened the suspenders over his strong shoulders.

"It's like cowboy firefighter porn," Charley joked loudly, breaking the tension as we watched him pull on the rest of his gear minus the heavy coat, his cowboy hat replaced with a hardhat.

Tripp took one lingering look at me, nodding as he fastened his mask into place. He reached back into the truck bed, pulling out a shovel and an axe, propping them over his shoulder as he headed into the field to join the rest of the ground crew.

After he was out of sight, Charley tugged me back into the barn and put me to work, showing me how to get the horse's gear ready for transport once the trucks returned. It was strange to watch her in an entirely new setting than I was used to seeing her, but she was completely in control, running the barn much like she ran the bar on a busy night.

It helped to have a distraction from the worry that'd plagued me since we'd been awoken by the fire station alert this morning. But at least I knew the two most important people in my life were safe. Reese was probably kicking ass in the ER at the hospital, and Tripp was doing what he loved.

"THAT'S THE LAST OF them," Marty shouted while he latched the back of the horse trailer, slapping the side hard and giving a thumbs up to the ranch hand driving the truck.

The gravel crunched underneath the tires while he drove away, leaving a trail of dust in its wake.

"What do we do now?" I asked, pulling off my gloves and handing them to Charley.

"Now we go back to the lodge and get cleaned up. You're welcome to a room tonight, Annie," Marty offered, wrapping his arms around our shoulders and steering us toward a pickup truck outside the barn with the logo for the West Peak Ranch emblazoned on the side with the outline of a mountain peak in the background. "The guests have mostly checked out because of the fire. As long as you don't mind making your own bed, you can have one of the suites."

He led us to the truck, handing each of us a bottle of water before he started the ignition. I took heavy sips of water as the trees blurred in the windows as we drove past; the smoke followed us the mile or so to the main lodge, lingering like a fog outside. It was eerily quiet when we walked inside, the typically bustling lobby empty, which was rare during the summer.

Reese and I had taken riding lessons at the ranch once upon a time, our grandmother making it known it was an essential skill for living in this area, but since she'd passed away, we hadn't kept horses in the small barn behind our cabin.

It was all gone now, along with fond memories of going on trail rides with our grandmother when she could still ride. Those trails had probably been taken out by the fire, too.

"You need anything?" Charley asked, leading me up a staircase to the second floor, but I wasn't really listening, my eyes drawn to something on the other side of the room.

A large panoramic window faced north at the back of the lodge, and I felt my tears returning as I walked through the second floor living area to look at how much the landscape had changed in such a short period. It was chilling to see it now.

Smoke rose from the trees in the distance, almost obscuring the destruction the fire had left behind, but the lower half of the mountain, once covered in vibrant green forests during the summer, was brown and gray, no signs of the once beautiful landscape that'd existed only days ago.

Scanning the horizon for where I knew my home used to be, there was nothing, just more destruction underneath the heavy cover of smoke.

"We're here," Charley whispered, wrapping her arm around my waist and leaning the side of her head against my shoulder. "You're not gonna go through this alone. Whatever you need, both you and Reese."

We were both quiet, just awestruck by how much our home had changed so quickly. All because of someone else's recklessness.

"Have you spoken to Reese?" she asked, and I shook my head.

"My phone was lost. Tripp called dispatch and found out that she was safe, but honestly, the last day has been a bit surreal."

"If you know her number, you can use my phone," she offered, holding it out to me.

I took it, letting out a heavy breath as I settled on the couch facing away from the windows. It hurt too much to look at that and talk to my sister at the same time.

My hands shook as I typed in familiar numbers, thankfully it'd been drilled into my head by my hyper protective sister that you should always have important numbers memorized, because the favorites on your phone wouldn't do any good if your phone was gone.

"Charley? Is everything okay?" Reese answered, and my lip quivered, tears escaping from my eyes as relief coursed through me. While they'd never been best friends, Reese and Charley were in the same grade back in school.

"It's Ann..." My voice cracked, but Reese's reaction wasn't much different, a sob echoing from the speakerphone.

"Oh, thank God," she breathed, sniffling loudly. "Where are you?"

"The lodge at West Peak Ranch. They're gonna let me stay the night here. My phone is gone."

"You're not hurt, are you?" she asked, going into nurse mode. "I can come to you if you need treatment. I don't have a car, but I can get someone to take me from the hospital—"

Her rambling was almost comforting, because it meant she was still here. Still safe.

"I'm okay. Tired, but okay. How are you? I heard Baker came for a visit."

She growled, and I smiled, swiping the tears off my cheeks. "That bastard massacred the front door with an axe and dragged me out of bed in my pajamas."

"So, you're still besties is what you're telling me," I laughed, imagining exactly how pissed off she must have been when firefighter Baker came to the rescue.

"Yeah, that's a hard pass," she scoffed, but something about the tone of her voice sounded off.

"Marty said you're welcome to come up here tonight. The lodge has mostly cleared out."

She sighed, and I had a feeling it was going to be impossible to drag her away from the hospital. "Actually, I'm gonna stick around town tonight in case they need to call me in. He offered me the extra bedroom in his apartment. I'm in the on-call room now, but they won't let me clock in. Stupid bullshit hospital policies about me not having enough time between shifts to be allowed on the floor."

"He who?" I asked, my intuition clueing in that it might be a certain firefighter offering his place to my sister.

"Baker," she grumbled, and I held back a laugh. "He lives above his parent's storefront in town, so it's only a short walk to the hospital. Since my car is gone, it's the only logical solution that doesn't involve me having to arrange a ride."

"Sure, sounds *logical*," I replied, making eye contact with Charley who was also trying to hold back a laugh as my sister attempted to downplay staying at the apartment of a man who she hadn't been able to stand being in the same room with for years. Everyone knew those two had been circling each other for a long time, and with the loaded looks I'd seen Baker aim in her direction, I knew he was still carrying a torch despite her frosty demeanor.

151

The sound of the chimes my sister's phone made when she was getting a page from the hospital echoed across the speaker, and she rushed me off the phone, making me promise to stay safe.

"Let's get you some clean clothes and I'll find an empty room for you, but from the sound of it, I think the last guests have cleared out."

Charley left me in an empty suite that overlooked the forest to the north with a fresh set of sheets to cover the oversized king bed and a stack of clean towels.

While Tripp and I had gotten cleaned up in the hot spring last night, we'd been very, very unclean this morning between the acrobatic, sweaty sex we'd had in the middle of the night using the last condom from my emergency kit and from our ride back to the ranch this morning.

After making the bed, I stood at the window, staring off toward the river where he was, hoping the fire break they were building would stop the spread, because I didn't want to see anyone else I cared for lose everything.

Chapter
Seventeen

Tristan

S WEAT ROLLED DOWN MY temples, my muscles burning as I repeatedly swung the axe into the stump of the tree they'd just
felled along the edge of the river. I hated we were having to destroy
so much of the tree line, but we needed to remove the fuel source
so it couldn't spread past this point.

At least the wind wasn't working against us, although it just
made the sweltering heat that much more unbearable. We were
all drenched with sweat as the sun rose, my long-sleeved soaked,
but it was staying on because it'd keep me safe from the inferno
burning in the not-so-distant tree line.

The Chief hadn't protested me joining the ground crew, assign-
ing me a few less experienced firefighters and letting me guide
them through setting up the firebreak. Most of them were trained
for situations like this, but there was a big difference between
simulation training and having to execute it outside of a controlled
environment. As far as I knew, there hadn't been a fire like this in
years anywhere near Sage Springs.

"Harding! Take a break!" The sound of the Chief's voice from
behind me was almost a relief, and I stood upright, arching my
back to relieve the pressure that had been building. This part of the
job was grueling work, but there was something satisfying about
harnessing the destruction of nature and stopping it in its tracks.

Fire wasn't inherently bad for these ecosystems, often necessary
for maintaining a healthy forest by purging the decay and unhealthy waste in the underbrush, but it could quickly become a
destructive force that took out anything in its path.

While I'd been cleared medically for over a month, today was the first time I'd done anything truly strenuous. My skin felt tight, the sites of my grafts aching at the abuse. I knew my muscles would be sore, but it felt good to do something useful again.

Jogging back toward the supply truck, I guzzled the bottle of water that'd been shoved into my outside pocket. It was hard to stay hydrated out here, but we all knew the consequences if we didn't. And we definitely didn't need anyone passing out from dehydration like my girlfriend had a few days ago.

Fuck. I'd just thought of Rhey as my girlfriend. It'd been a long fucking time since I had one of those, but I didn't hate the idea. In fact, it sounded pretty damn good. Maybe coming back home would be good for me in the long run. For once, I looked forward to finding my way back into the community with a beautiful, supportive woman by my side.

We still had a lot to learn about each other, but I was willing to put in the hard work.

"Meal break," Chief grunted, shoving a paper bag with the logo of a local barbecue restaurant into my hands once I was at his side.

"Thanks, appreciate it, Chief," I sighed, peeking at the contents. The smell of savory roasted meat had my stomach growling, and I hoped the foil wrapped sandwich inside was one of their pulled pork sandwiches.

That was another thing about doing work like this in a small town, everyone wanted to help in some way. Communities like this really came together and pitched in wherever they could when tragedy struck. A warm, hearty meal was hands down much better than the prepackaged meals that the forestry service tried to convince us were nutritious when we were out in the field. Mostly in situations like this one, I'd survive on protein shakes and power bars for days on end.

Chief Wilson patted the tailgate of the truck he was perched on, inviting me to join him.

"I know I've been tough on you since you started, Tristan, but I appreciate the way you've stepped up and done what you were

155

asked without complaining. It takes a lot of character to take a demotion like this and still be respectful of the chain of command."

"Of course, I know I need to prove myself to earn a spot. I never wanted you to just hand me a job," I replied, holding back a groan as I unwrapped my sandwich. My eyes rolled back in my head when I took a bite, and the Chief laughed while I chewed.

"I know you've got years of experience on some of my guys, but I also know what kind of mental toll an injury like yours can take on a person." I wasn't sure what to say, so I nodded, feeling like he wasn't done talking. "You've proven to me this week that you're not ego-driven and I respect that."

"Thank you, sir. That means a lot."

He reached up, lightly squeezing my shoulder. "And while I was about to chew your ass out for that little stunt on horseback you pulled, I knew you wouldn't have volunteered if you questioned your ability to respond to a situation like that."

Biting my tongue, I refrained from telling him about the panic attack I'd had in the barn after I knew Rhey was safe. There were plenty of people I'd worked with before that had the occasional meltdown after a life-threatening situation. It didn't mean you were weak; it meant you were human.

As long as you didn't let yourself get caught up in that negative headspace, it happened from time to time. It was a natural response to the things we saw and did.

"Today, you've proven to me that your leadership skills are solid. You didn't complain when I threw some inexperienced officers at you, and I've watched you working with them."

I didn't know where he was going with this, so I just patiently listened while he got to the point of pulling me aside.

"I want you to think about what you'd like your career to look like from now on. I'd like you to consider a position as a field training officer, if that's something you'd be interested in."

I'd been a training officer before, mentoring new jumpers in the specialist program. It had been hard and rewarding work, but I wasn't sure if that was what my future held. It was a job that involved months of training, planning and mentoring before one of your trainees could go out on their own. Building a relationship with a recruit was vital and time-consuming.

Looking around the field we were in, at the rolling hills south, to the barn in the distance where I knew Rhey was working hard inside right now, and I wasn't sure what path to take. Did I build a future that led back to me being a full-time firefighter? Or did I stay on at the ranch and forge a fresh path?

"Don't decide anything right now," he said, patting my shoulder again before he pressed a bottle of electrolyte drink into my hand. "But the position is there if you want it. And we can even make it a contract position for when we get new officers if you'd like to stay on at the ranch."

"I'm honored, really, Chief, but—"

He held up a hand, interrupting me. "I won't take a no today. Sit with it for a while. The offer will still be there when you're ready to decide."

His words lingered long after I returned to my crew, well after we ran the burn line and put it out, hoping it'd be enough to stop the fire that'd slowed down significantly. They were in the back of my mind as I helped pack the gear back into the department trucks and gathered my equipment and headed back to my truck.

The purpose in my career that had been illusive for months suddenly felt like it might spark back to life, but I still needed to think about what I really wanted in my future. And I knew one person who would help me gather my thoughts and talk through it without judgement.

With her in mind, I loaded my gear back into the truck bed and headed toward the lodge, breathing easier in more than one way as the smoke thinned out on my way to her.

Since Jay had offered to let me stay at his place while I was recovering, I'd never actually stayed at the lodge, my new place a short walk down a path behind the building, tucked into the forest. But that wasn't where I wanted to go right now.

I needed to see her.

Feel her again.

Remind myself that my developing feelings weren't crazy.

That it wasn't insane to be half in love with a woman I'd known for a few days.

"She's upstairs in 206." Marty didn't even look up from his seat at the reception desk, the grin on his face the only indicator that my situation was providing him with a certain amount of entertainment.

"Not sure if I should pretend I don't know who you're referring to, but I feel like you're on to me, old man."

"Not so old that I forgot what it was like to fall hard for a beautiful woman, Tristan. But my daughter will have words with you if you step out of line," he warned, glancing up with an arched eyebrow. "And I would not fuck with that girl if I were you. I made her and she still scares the shit outta me sometimes."

"Noted," I replied, fighting back a grin when he shook his head and returned his attention to the papers spread out across the desk. I knew he was probably trying to figure out how this fire was going to affect the ranch, and I hoped I'd still have a job here once this was all over. Because he was going to be missing at least a few weeks of tourist income because of the cancelations falling during our peak season. I didn't know Charley, since she was almost a decade younger than me, but from the brief impression I'd gotten when I'd left Rhey with her at the barn earlier, you could tell she cared about her friends.

"Nelly took up a tray of food earlier, but Annie was passed out cold when she checked on her. All the guests who hadn't left yet checked out this morning, and bookings are light this week," he said with a heavy sigh. "If you're hungry, the chef left some prepared meals in the staff refrigerator. Anything else you need, I'm sure you can find it on your own. I'll probably head out in a bit, but the place is yours tonight."

Pulling off my dirty boots, I left them on a tray by the front doors, taking the steps two at a time until I reached the second floor. The sun had dipped below the horizon, the back windows lit up in a kaleidoscope of oranges, pinks and purples, the peaks of the distant mountains barely visible above the haze of the lingering fire.

Soft snores greeted my ears as I slowly swung the door to suite 206 inward, the room cast in shadows. The curtains were still open, so her slight form curled up under the blankets wasn't hard to make out, her chaotic hair fanning across the pillow she was half tucked around.

Watching her sleep, I wanted to do nothing more than climb into that big bed and curl myself around her, blocking out the rest of the world, but I smelled like sweat, sawdust and smoke, so I reluctantly made my way into the attached bathroom.

The scent of whatever shampoo she'd used in here while I was gone and something that was uniquely her lingered in the air. I closed my eyes, breathing it in before I tiredly stripped out of the rest of my clothing, my filthy, soot covered shirt and jeans discarded into the oversized bathtub.

Turning on the spray in the walk-in shower, I winced, pulling my hand back at the scalding temperature, knowing that'd have to be the first thing we addressed as a couple. I couldn't bathe in hellfire like she clearly could, so we'd have to come to a compromise, because after having a taste of a wet, soapy, pliable Rhey in the hot spring, I was not willing to give up shared bath time.

Visions of her in my much smaller shower in the cabin, our bodies pressed tightly together, sliding effortlessly as the soap bubbles multiplied between us, my lips on her neck and my hand in between her thighs had my cock thinking it was playtime again, rising to thoughts of her. But I didn't want to settle for an unsatis-fying shower tug.

And when a warm body settled against my back, Rhey's cheek pressed against my shoulders, her lips grazing the battered skin of my back, I knew I wouldn't have to.

Chapter
Eighteen

Annie

T HE ROOM WAS DARK as I stirred, slowly opening my heavy eyelids. Falling asleep wasn't my plan, but once I hit the plush bedding after my shower, the exhaustion had taken over. Food was a secondary need, although a gnawing hunger was making itself known, my tummy grumbling as I sat myself up against the pillows. Trying to regain my bearings, I scanned the room. Something was different.

The lingering scent of wood smoke seemed stronger than when I'd taken off my dirty clothes, but I could've just been imagining things.

Sliding my naked body from beneath the warm covers, I walked toward the dresser on the other side of the room, scanning a tray filled with food. Grabbing a bundle of grapes and some crackers, I inspected the pile of clothing next to the tray as I ate, thankful for the soft sweater and terry cloth shorts. A smile drew at my lips when I realized there weren't any underwear in the pile, but at this point, I wasn't sure why I bothered worrying about it. Tripp hadn't seemed to mind my lack of appropriate undergarments.

Squinting as I looked across the room, I tilted my head at the closed bathroom door. I was sure I left it open earlier when I practically sleepwalked to the bed after finally washing my hair with actual water pressure.

When the sound of the shower starting carried through the room, my heart skipped a beat.

He was home.

Well, not *home*, per se. Still, he'd returned to the lodge and to me.

As of yesterday, I no longer had one of those, but I was starting to think that maybe home could be a person, and not just where you laid your head at night. That thought had broken open something inside of me that'd scabbed over after we lost our parents and our grandmother died a few years ago. I began to see past all the trials that life had thrown at me, hope blossoming in my chest that maybe the future wasn't something to dread. Reese was safe. And we'd both escaped from a dangerous situation where things could have easily ended differently, so there was a lot to be thankful for.

While I was not one to jinx things, maybe we'd both escaped the family curse.

Knocking on the wood of the dresser top, I stared at the door to the bathroom, debating whether I should join him.

But it wasn't a hard decision, and I was across the room within seconds. Careful to enter quietly, I slowly pushed the door inward, but Tripp was facing away from the door, the room shrouded in darkness.

He was standing with his forearm braced on the tiles, his other palm gripping the solid length of his cock. Heat rose to my cheeks at the thought I'd interrupted him, but then I noticed his arm wasn't moving.

My bare feet were silent on the wooden floor, my body drawn to his like a magnet. He didn't move when I slipped into the shower behind him, laying my cheek against his back and wrapping my arms around his chest.

His skin still smelled of fire, like smoke and destruction, but if the firebreak he'd worked on half the day worked to halt what we'd already lost, maybe it could be the smell of rebirth.

We'd learned enough about ecology in high school science, and I knew not only the fictional phoenix rose from the ashes. The growth after a fire could be a rebirth for the forest. A new chance for life to flourish.

Maybe that's what this fire represented for both of us, a way to start anew.

His warm hand covered mine, and I kissed the center of his back, just savoring this innocent moment of connection between two people who had felt lost in their lives. Maybe his appearance in Sage Springs was a divine intervention of some sort. For both of us.

"Are you okay?" I whispered into his skin, and he shuddered, inhaling a shaky breath.

"I am now." His voice was rough—raspy and tired. "I missed you."

"Do you think the break will help? Are we safe here?"

He turned, cupping the sides of my jaw with his large, warm, calloused hands, rubbing the pads of his thumbs across my cheekbones. "I promise I'll keep you safe, Rhey, wherever we end up. But I don't want to talk about the fire. I just want to lose myself in you."

Closing the distance, his upper lip nestled between mine, caressing my mouth softly. Lingering at an almost drowsy pace, he kept the kiss slow and sensual, dipping in further with each pass of his lips.

My head swam, his presence entirely intoxicating, but I didn't push further, enjoying his closeness. It'd been a long time since I just enjoyed kissing someone without rushing through it. Not wanting to bring anyone else into this time together, I pushed the thoughts of men who'd come before him out of my mind and concentrated on how he made me feel.

Tripp spun me away from where I stood inside the shower door, pinning my back against the cold tiles, and I gasped at the sensation. I tipped my head backward as his palm dragged down my overheated skin, cupping my neck firmly while lips and teeth nipped at my lobe, his pants heavy in my ear.

"You have no idea what you do to me. How much I crave you."

While he'd given me the freedom to lead in the cabin, he was clearly taking it back, holding me possessively and using his hips to trap me in place, completely helpless to the way he was owning my body.

His hips rocked forward as he reclaimed my lips, kissing me roughly.

"I need to be inside you," he growled, his throbbing cock trapped between us, a heavy reminder of his attraction to me against my stomach.

"Here," I gasped, bringing my thigh up to wrap around his waist. "Now."

"Fuck, baby. I—" he broke off, his groan reverberating off the tile. "You know I want you, but I don't..."

"Bare. I want nothing between us this time." Slowly drawing back to look at my face, he searched my eyes, a crease between his eyebrows. "I get the shot. It's safe."

His jaw clenched, something almost feral flickering in those deep blue eyes before he dragged his palm down the center of my chest, lingering between my breasts before he trailed it lower, his fingertips easily sliding to where I was warm and aching for his touch.

He teased me, circling where I was desperate for him, but still holding back. "Are you sure? We don't have to have sex. There are plenty of ways for me to make you come that don't involve my cock."

"I know," I whispered, pressing my hand above where his heart thumped steadily. Slowly, I slid it upward, my fingers lingering on the rough skin of his scar before I grasped the hair at the back of his head, gripping it firmly between my fingers. "But right now, I need you to fuck me. Show me how much you need me."

"Rhey." My name was a feral growl in his throat, but that was all the permission he needed, his large palms grasping the backs of my thighs and lifting, my back sliding up the tiles effortlessly.

He pressed forward as he reached for one of my hands. Interlocking our fingers, he pinned it to the tile above my head. Strong hips supported my weight as he reached between us, lining himself up and teasingly pressing the head to my clit before he dragged it lower. "Is this where you need me, pretty girl?"

"God, yes," I panted, fighting to keep my eyes open and focused on him.

"Do you need me to make you come?" He was watching me with a glint in his eyes, enjoying teasing me when I just needed to be connected to him.

Well, two could play that game. Lowering my voice to a throaty whisper, I looked up at him from beneath my wet eyelashes. "Be a good boy and make me scream your name."

"Fuck." The word was low and drawn out as his hips shifted, his bare cock sliding inside me. "Oh, fuck. You're so fucking warm. God damn. I'm not sure how long I'm gonna last this way."

"Then I guess you'd better concentrate."

And concentrate he did, tilting his hips and thrusting into me hard enough my back slid up the tiles. Anchoring myself to him, I held on tight as he fucked me, growling into my ear, his fingers squeezing mine tightly.

There were still so many things in my life that were unsettled, but I didn't want to regret anything with him. Being with him like this, trusting him without any barriers between us, may have seemed reckless—and although the timing was terrible and circumstances lingered at the back of my mind—I was so glad I met him. In the aftermath, I'd found refuge.

"What do you need?" he asked, nipping at my ear, hips slowly rolling, his cock hitting a place that had me breathless.

"Just keep doing that…" My voice was a breathy pant as he slowed his pace, grinding into me.

"You mean keep fucking you?" he whispered in a rough tone, and I lit up, the feeling of being surrounded my him, held captive to his thrusts with his deep voice in my ear, was intoxicating. "Keep driving into you with my hard cock and watching you lose your mind with pleasure when you shatter around me?"

"Fuck, Tripp…" His hips tilted and I lost my words.

He let out a rough chuckle at my breathy exhalation against his strong, muscular shoulder.

"Yes, Rhey," he growled into my neck. "I am absolutely the man fucking you right now. And I'm going to be the man coming inside you bare as soon as I feel that pretty pussy flutter around my dick."

"Oh God," I gasped, squeezing his hand tight as I met each hard thrust, my legs locked tightly around his waist. I was lost in him, absolutely at his mercy and so close to the edge when his teeth bit down on my earlobe, a feral groan from him sending me flying, my body pulsing around him.

"That's right, baby. Come on me. Your moans make me so fucking hard. You're just desperate for me to fill you with my cum, aren't you?"

Gasping in his ear when he picked up the pace, I dug my nails into his scalp and the back of his hand. He drove into me like a man possessed, his grip borderline painful until he stilled, groaning into my ear as he throbbed, emptying himself inside me.

Rough pants filled the steamy shower as we clung to each other. I wanted to capture this moment and hold it tight. Tears escaped the corners of my eyes as his lips ghosted my shoulder, our frantic coupling turning somewhat tender. He released my fingers, smoothing his palm slowly down my arm, cupping my breast in his rough hand as he rained kisses along my neck and toward my mouth.

Languid kisses made my head spin, and I knew right then I could get lost in this man. It was easier to keep love at arm's length before to save what little love was left inside me, but now...

Now, I could see the possibility of life and love...with him.

"Let's go to bed, sweetheart." Tripp's voice sounded tired, and while I was anxious about the fire, knowing it was still close, I wanted nothing more than to wrap myself up in him and sleep for like a week straight.

"Someone just made me dirty," I teased, reaching for the body wash when he lowered me back to my feet.

Lingering touches while we washed ourselves—and each other—had me feeling relaxed and drowsy. I'd never felt so comfortable with someone, especially a man I'd just met. There was still something that felt familiar about him, but maybe that was just how you felt when you found the person you clicked with after waiting for so long.

After he turned off the shower, I leaned against the wall, watching him dry himself while I halfheartedly did the same. He noticed where my gaze was focused, shaking his head with a smile before he tucked his towel around his waist.

"Hand it over," he demanded, holding his hand out and tugging the towel from my grip.

He moved close, lowering to a knee at my feet. Pulling one onto his thigh, he returned the towel to my skin, slowly wiping away the moisture, watching me the entire time.

"I think you like being on your knees for me," I teased, running my fingers through his damp hair. "Such a good boy."

He tilted his head to the side, arching an eyebrow. "You might be teasing me right now, Rhey, but I do like it."

His grin widened at my reaction, and he leaned forward, kissing my stomach as I stroked his hair. The rough stubble that had filled out in the last few days tickled as his lips lingered. My towel was forgotten when his rough palms cupped my calves and slowly traced upward, kneading my ass as his mouth moved lower.

"I want to worship you," he whispered, kissing the soft patch of hair.

"Kiss you..." His hands wrapped around the backs of my thighs, fingertips brushing softly where he'd only just left.

"Pleasure you..." My head dropped back to the tiles as he teased between my thighs with the tip of his tongue, groaning at the taste of us together.

"Make you desperate..." He licked harder, sucking my clit into his mouth as my fingers tightened in his hair.

"Fuck you until you scream..." His dark chuckle when my knees almost gave out, my stomach muscles clenching as he thrust a finger inside me from behind.

"Watch you fall apart and come..."

"Oh fuck," I panted as he found a place inside me that had me barreling back toward a finish line he'd already pushed me over once tonight. Pressing into it with his fingertips while his lips left hot open-mouthed kisses on my clit, he pleasured me until stars danced behind my eyelids.

"That's it, baby," he groaned into my pussy, only leaning back to watch me fall apart. "Feel it. Ride that wave, knowing I'm desperate for it every time I touch you."

After a few breathless moments, he chuckled, rising to his feet with my towel in his hands. Finishing the job he'd abandoned to show me exactly how much he enjoyed being on his knees for me, he carefully dried my skin.

"Now it's time for the bed," he whispered, opening the glass door of the large walk-in shower before he scooped me up and carried me back into the bedroom.

His cock was hard as he slipped underneath the covers behind me, gripping my throat with one large palm.

"You're not too sore, are you?" he asked, rocking his hips forward.

"No," I moaned into the soft cotton of the pillowcase, arching as he pulled my leg backward over his, slipping inside me.

"I can't get enough of you," he panted in my ear, his hips driving into me. The fingers on my throat tightened when his movements became more frantic while he chased his release. "I never want to... You're all I can think about."

Gasping through another climax, I wondered if he possessed some kind of sexy firefighter sorcery, because no one had ever made me feel this way.

"Come," I gasped, my body vibrating as he just kept thrusting at a punishing pace. "I need to feel you come in me. Please."

"All you had to do was ask nicely," he taunted, groaning into my shoulder and squeezing my neck until he came, his hips pressed tightly against mine.

Panting against the pillowcase, my eyelids drifted shut briefly but flew back open at the almost jarring sound of an aircraft engine passing the building. "What is that?"

Tripp's lips traced the nape of my neck, his voice low and rumbling against my skin. "Overhead air support. They're dropping fire retardant west of the break line. Fire department must have cleared out of the area. They usually wait until the ground crew is clear to run a drop."

"Does that mean it's here?" My heartbeat picked up at the thought of us having to leave.

"No, it's a good sign, sweetheart. It means they're ahead of the spread," he whispered, wrapping himself around my back and tucking my head beneath his chin. "I told you I would keep you safe. And I'm a man of my word, Rhey."

With his warm body at my back, sleep wasn't as elusive as it once had been.

Chapter
Nineteen

Tristan

A STREAM OF SUNLIGHT arced from the crack between the curtain panels, painting colors across Rhey's shoulder. Picking up a few strands of silky hair, I traced the streaks of light across her skin, enjoying the way she burrowed further into my chest with a quiet moan.

"You planning to sleep the day away?" I whispered against her forehead, smiling when she mumbled something incoherent into my skin.

"We need to get up, sweetheart. I'm gonna have to do my job at some point today. Those horses won't exercise themselves, so I need to head to the fairgrounds."

The quiet exasperated whine that met my ears clued me in that my girl might not be a morning person. Although, after glancing at the clock on the nightstand, saying it was still morning might be a stretch. It was nearly ten am, and on any other day I would have been knee deep in horse shit or sweating my ass off somewhere else on the ranch, having been at it for hours.

I guess it made sense that she'd sleep in later, given that the livelihood of a bartender depended on late night drinking habits.

"Rhey, I'm gonna smack that sweet ass of yours if you don't get moving."

Her chest shook against mine, her chin tipping up so she could see my face. Her voice was raspy and warm, and as my eyes connected with hers, I felt deep inside my gut that this woman was going to be my everything.

"You think threatening to spank me is gonna get us out of this bed?" she teased.

Shaking my head at the naughty glint in her eyes, I squeezed her tighter, trying to fight off the urge to test it out. My fingers trailed down her back, lingering on the dip of her waist before they moved lower, gripping her ass until she squeaked.

"Then maybe we need to *UNO reverse* it. I *won't* spank your feisty ass when I get you alone tonight if you continue to refuse to get out of this bed."

"M'not sure I like you right now," she grumbled, but it turned to a moan as I rolled her backward, pinning her to the mattress. Her body was soft and warm, and I wanted nothing more than to lose myself in her, but we both had responsibilities, and she had to be sore with all the sex we'd had in the last two days.

"And right now, I'm okay with that."

After pecking her on the nose, I pushed myself to a seated position, surprised for once that my shoulders didn't ache like they normally did in the mornings. There was still lingering nerve pain, but maybe the local lore of the hot springs in this area having healing powers was true. If that was the case, Rhey and I were going to be making naked hot spring bathing sessions a regular part of our routine.

Shaking my head as I stood, I tried to push back the pessimistic part of me that wondered if maybe things were too good to be true. I'd been in that honeymoon phase of a new relationship before, completely smitten with a woman until some hidden part of her personality surfaced. But Rhey hadn't given me any indications that she hadn't been truthful to me, already opening up about her life in a way I knew made her feel vulnerable.

"I'm gonna head back to the cabin to change. You wanna come with me?"

She looked adorably rumpled as she sat upright, her hair an absolute disaster. The covers slipped to her waist, and I held back a groan at how sexy she looked, determined to get things done today.

"I don't have anything I can wear in a barn," she replied between yawns. "Or underwear."

"There's some riding gear in the tack room I can set you up with." It kind of blew my mind that some guests just left behind boots and jeans at the ranch because they didn't use them in their daily lives. But since Rhey only had the clothing she'd been wearing yesterday, I was thankful for the easy access. "But you won't hear me complaining about the lack of panties."

I'd have to take her into town for essentials eventually, but I was kind of enjoying staying insulated in our little bubble for now. If we showed up in town together, the gossip train would inevitably start monitoring our every move. While I didn't want to hide her, I also didn't want to share her just yet. Especially with my mother and aunt being some of the worst gossips in town.

T HE LINGERING SMOKE FROM the day before had mostly cleared, making it easier to breathe outside. Today was going to be a scorcher, the sun high overhead while we walked hand in hand down the trail that led to my cabin. Rhey had found something a little more ranch hand friendly during our barn excursion with the help of a belt on an oversized pair of Wrangler jeans.

"When do you need to go back to work?" I asked, secretly hoping she wasn't needed so I could keep her to myself for a while longer. Not that I was opposed to taking up residence at the bar to keep her company. I knew she wouldn't need me there for protection, because she could handle her own, but I wasn't ready to let her out of my sight just yet.

"I'm not sure. Charley told me she could help cover my shifts, but I don't want to take advantage."

"Sweetheart, you've had a shitty few days, take the time to reset if they're offering it."

"Yeah," she sighed, leaning her head against my shoulder as we walked. "I know, but honestly, the distraction might be good. Too much alone time and I know I'll start dwelling on all the things I'm gonna have to do over the next few months."

"Even more of a reason to prioritize some time away from everything."

"I probably need to talk to Reese today. We need to call the insurance company. I wonder if they'll have opened the roads back up, and..."

Squeezing her hand, I stopped, leaning my head to the side so I could make eye contact. "It's gonna be a few days, maybe even a few weeks, before they let you up there. Even if they've got the fire mostly contained, crews are going to need to assess the safety of the roads before they let anyone but emergency personnel past those barricades."

"But I know how to..."

"Rhey, no more off-road adventures. I don't care what shortcuts you think you know. That area isn't safe right now. I promise once I hear something, I'll drive you up there myself, but right now, filing insurance reports can wait."

"I don't even know where I'm going to live," she whispered, and I tugged her into my chest, holding her tight.

"I know. I know this is hard, and there are so many unknowns right now, but there are enough people in this town who love you that you're not gonna have to worry about that stuff." She sniffled, nodding against my shirt. "I'd love for you to stay with me, sans panties, if you want, for as long as you need." *Or indefinitely.*

Pulling back, she swiped at the tears on her cheeks, scanning my face. "Living together already, you sure you're not gonna get sick of me?"

"Sweetheart, who says I'm not already?" I joked. "You're kind of a handful."

Her eyes narrowed, but a small laugh escaped her lips, so I knew I'd done my job of distracting her.

"Fine. I'll just go live with Baker and Reese," she taunted, but we both knew that was the last thing she wanted to do. Especially if her sister and her arch nemesis ended up banging like I thought they might with all the built-up tension.

"Might wanna invest in some earplugs, then. Cause whether they're fighting or fucking, that apartment of his is not big."

She sighed loudly, "Looks like I'm on my own."

Not if I fucking had anything to say about it.

Her somber mood seemed to lift once I'd led her inside my new home. It wasn't huge, and definitely needed some work, but it was mine as long as I was at the ranch. And when I came back out of the bedroom after changing into fresh clothes, the sight of her on my couch, with a paperback open on her lap, just seemed natural. Like that beat up old leather sofa was just waiting for her.

"Can I use your phone before we leave?" she asked, seeming hesitant. "I need to talk to Reese, but I can see if I can use the one at the lodge if you don't—"

"You don't need to ask," I responded, cutting her off. Picking up the device from the coffee table, I extended it toward her. "Whenever you need it, feel free. We can stop while we're in town to get you a new phone."

There was a flicker of uncertainty in her eyes when she took it, and I wondered if there was something deeper to her hesitation.

She slipped out the front door and settled into the lone rocking chair with my phone pressed to her ear. I was taken aback by how much I wanted more of her. I had told her she could stay here for as long as she wanted, which appeared to be a temporary offer, but I couldn't imagine her presence here as casual. Although, I hoped I wouldn't be left disappointed if she didn't feel the same way.

I'd never lived with a woman before, and I knew our schedules would rarely align, however, I couldn't deny how normal and natural it felt coming "home" to her and curling myself around her last night.

My large frame settled into the spot she once occupied, wanting to feel closer to her in her brief absence. I was lost in the thoughts of a rambling future when she settled on my lap, wrapping her arms around my neck. I didn't even hear the door click behind her when she came back in.

"So, with the evacuation order still in place and not wanting to put possibly intoxicated people on the roads, Hudson started closing the bar at 8."

"Probably smart on his part." The last thing you needed was buzzed tourists getting lost with everything going on.

"And I talked to Reese..."

"Is your sister going to take you from me already?" I asked, nuzzling her neck and earning myself a breathy whimper.

"Not exactly. She wanted to know if we would come with her and Baker to a bar a few towns over for line dancing."

"Tonight?" While I was not a fan of the idea of sharing her time, I also thought maybe it'd be a break for both of us to get out and focus on something other than our uncertain futures. And any excuse to put my hands all over her in a sundress was something I'd be on board with. Which meant a trip into town was in order sooner rather than later.

"Yeah, I guess a group of guys from the firehouse that aren't on duty are going, and Baker is making her since the hospital took her off the call list. She was pissed they're making her take off until her shift on the fourth for the holiday."

I'd seen something mentioned this morning in the group text Baker had added me to when I started at the station, but I hadn't really been paying attention when I'd checked my phone earlier.

"We don't have to go if dancing isn't your thing, but Reese didn't want to go alone and..."

"Then I guess we'd better get moving, since you're going to need something to wear." Kissing the side of her neck, I enjoyed the way she seemed to melt into my touch. "Because you're going to put on a sexy dress for me if we're going dancing."

"I am?" she asked, her voice breathy.

"Mhmm," I hummed against her soft skin. "You won't wear panties again... And when we get home, I'm going to be so desperate for you after watching that tempting body of yours move all night that I'm gonna bend you over the railing on that porch."

"Then what are you going to do?" Her chest heaved as she squirmed in my lap, and I wasn't sure if I could hold out until tonight.

"I'm going to draw up the back of that dress and slip inside you bare..."

"Uh huh..."

"And I'll fuck you deep and slow until you're so wet it drips down your thighs."

"Mmm..."

"And when you come, the stars in the sky won't be the only ones you see."

She let out a heavy breath, fisting my collar tightly as she tilted her head to look in my eyes. "You promise?"

"Fuck yes, sweetheart. Now gimme a kiss so we can get going. Then you can torture me by making me watch you try on dresses while I try to fight the urge to fuck you in a public dressing room."

She laughed, shaking her head before doing what I asked, her lips eager as she kissed me breathless.

"But just so you know, it'd be worth it to get arrested for public indecency."

And that was the problem, I knew it would be. Keeping myself in check all night was going to be next to impossible, but I was going to try, because my girl needed a night out to distract her from everything that had been going on.

Chapter
Twenty

Annie

"**Y**OU KNOW, I FEEL like your chauffeur with you sitting back there," Tripp chuckled, eyeing me in the rearview mirror as his truck idled on the street in front of *Ice My Cakes,* the bakery Baker's family ironically owned.

I knew his parents hadn't started the small business until well after he was born, but he had been made fun of relentlessly when we were all younger for being the town baker's son.

"It's not my fault you offered to drive," I teased, shifting into the center seat to refasten my seatbelt.

"I didn't know that meant you wouldn't be in the seat next to me. How am I ever going to survive if I can't caress the smooth skin of your thigh on our drive?"

"I'm sure you'll manage," I chuckled, shaking my head at his playful banter. Boy, had things changed in our interactions in the last forty-eight hours. He'd gone from barely speaking to me to an insatiable flirt in what felt like no time at all.

Tripp and I spent a few hours this afternoon at the fairgrounds, walking the horses who'd stayed there overnight and then feeding them before we left. Seraphina seemed relieved to see him, and he showered her with attention, brushing out her beautiful brownish gray speckled coat in the time it'd taken me to brush out three other horses.

The big softie had even hidden apple slices in his pocket when we left the cabin that she had gone feral over. We'd almost needed another shower after we were done since the barn was hot in the early July weather, but we'd settled for wiping off in the bathroom before we went into town to find me something to wear.

He'd been a good sport, dutifully sitting in a chair outside the dressing room of the lone dress shop in downtown Sage Springs. The small mountain town had been half deserted, the typical bustling tourist presence missing, but at least there was still a town standing. It was going to take months for a lot of these businesses to recover from the loss of tourist income, and with having limited hours, I knew the bar would be no exception. I only hoped that Hudson could keep on the new bartender, because with him gone more often, I was dangerously close to burning myself out.

I wondered how things were over in Butterfly Ridge, but since there wasn't an easy way to get there until the roads reopened, it wasn't like I could check.

Jayden's impending return had been weighing on me, but I was almost relieved he wasn't due home for a few more days because I wasn't sure how to talk to him about the changes that'd happened in his absence. It wasn't like he had a way to contact me at this point because the phone store had been closed when we got into town and wouldn't reopen until after the holiday in a few days.

Even if I had his number memorized, there was no way I was using Tripp's phone to contact him, because that would be crossing way too many lines. My new beau may have been understanding that I was casually involved with someone else when we met, but I doubted he'd be so understanding of me texting him on his phone.

"You better keep those legs crossed, sweetheart, because otherwise Baker is going to get an eyeful of those luscious thighs and I'm going to have to murder my new friend."

Giggling, I wiggled my eyebrows, crossing my legs at my ankles as my hands slid over the fresh fabric covering my thighs. The dress was long and dark blue with a large floral print. Tripp had urged me, once again, to ditch my panties because of the sexy slit that went halfway up one thigh. I'd quietly protested, but he spun me around the dress shop until we were both laughing to show that our secret would be safe.

The salesclerk—someone I'd recognized as a regular at the bar—had looked on, amused by our antics. While she'd smiled at our interaction, I was sure the gossip would run wild. The new in town, sexy and brooding firefighter who'd taken up residence at a local horse ranch shopping for a sexy dress with the elusive bartender was bound to be in text message threads across town before the week was over.

Though I still had my purse and generous tips from the festival, Tripp had insisted on paying. He wouldn't guarantee the condition of my new dress would be intact by the end of the night.

Such a gentleman.

"You realize he won't be looking at me, right?"

He eyed me again, shaking his head. "He's gonna have to look past you to see Reese, so I'm not taking any chances."

And I suddenly regretted telling my sister I'd try to be her buffer from Baker tonight.

The truck door opened to my left, my sister's scowling face meeting mine before she huffed and reached for the handle above the doorway to hoist herself into the large pickup truck.

Climbing into the ranch truck earlier, I'd been a little melancholy, knowing my truck was totaled where we'd left it, and probably a burned out husk of what it had once been. It'd been my first big purchase as an adult, and even though it was used when I got it, and over a decade old, I'd still loved it.

"Hurry and go before he gets down here," Reese growled, yanking her seatbelt over her chest. She looked much different than she had the last time I'd seen her a few days ago.

"Nice to see you too, sis," I teased, grasping her hand. She was wearing a skin-tight white dress with a neckline much lower than I was used to seeing on her. It wasn't a dress I recognized, but that made sense since all her belongings would have been in the house we just lost.

"I'm sorry, Annie," she huffed, squeezing my hand back, but leaning her head against my shoulder. "I'm just...overwhelmed."

Tell me about it.

Tripp quietly watched our interaction, shooting me a wink when I met his eyes in the mirror.

A loud thump on the hood of the truck startled all of us and I laughed, watching Baker smack his hands on the metal and then flip us off with both hands when we were looking in his direction.

"I hate him," Reese hissed, glaring at her savior out the windshield.

"Dude," Tripp scolded when Baker opened the rear passenger door on my other side. "What the fuck? This isn't even my truck, and I'd prefer to not have to explain to my boss how the town dumbass scratched the hood because he can't behave himself."

Baker laughed, tipping his head at me and flashing me a wink before he removed his cowboy hat and slid into the seat beside me. "Ann, beautiful as always."

"Don't hit on my girlfr—" Tripp's voice broke off and Baker made a loud whoop noise.

"Woo, cowboy has got himself a girlfriend," he teased, reaching past me to smack Tripp on the shoulder. He winced, and I wanted to scold Baker for not being considerate of the fact Tripp still had lingering pain from his burns, but I also knew he wouldn't want me to bring unnecessary attention to him. I wasn't sure if Tripp even knew he flinched when someone touched the shoulder where his skin grafts were. "Whatever will all the single ladies do when they find out you're off the market so soon?"

"I'm sure Slutty McSlutterson over there would be happy to console them," Reese grumbled under her breath, and I turned in her direction.

Even though she was quiet, Baker knew she was talking about him. "What was that Reese's pieces?"

"Don't call me that," she hissed, clearly still hating the childish nickname that'd once followed her around.

"We're going to have fun tonight, thundercloud," he responded, leaning forward to look past me at my scowling sister. "Because you need a night out to shake that stick out of your ass. Unclench already."

Maybe I shouldn't have volunteered to be their buffer for the evening. The tension between the two of them was a lot.

My sister leaned forward, aiming a glare so cold I felt a draft at Baker. "I'm about to shove something up your ass." Her hissed growl had me biting my lip to keep from laughing out loud.

"Let's not scar the kids with what you like to do to me in the bedroom," he quipped, and my eyes widened as I shot my sister a concerned look.

She leaned back into her seat with pink cheeks, and I wondered if Tripp might have been correct earlier about the tension between Reese and Baker being sexual in nature. The real question was whether it was unresolved or if something had happened already.

"On that lovely note, where am I picking up Rhodes?" Tripp asked, shifting the truck into gear. I shouldn't have found the fact he knew how to drive a stick attractive, but I shamelessly ogled the way his forearm flexed when he shifted the oversized pickup into first.

"He dropped Emi off at his moms for a sleepover after his shift, so he should be back at his apartment. Just head to the station, it's only a few blocks away," Baker replied, typing a text message out on his phone. Probably telling Rhodes to head to the fire station for us to pick him up.

Elias Rhodes had been a few years ahead of me in school, but he was the quintessential golden boy. Honor society, a three-sport athlete, volunteered at the senior center and had been wildly in love with his high school sweetheart.

I'd only seen him in the bar a handful of times over the last few years since he'd returned to Sage Springs, but the death of his wife, Jasmine, had changed him. His five-year-old Emilia was the spitting image of her mother, and while I'd had a few classes with her in high school, we never ran in the same circles.

I couldn't even imagine what his life was like. Thirty-three and back in his hometown, raising a kid by himself. Both his parents and Jasmine's were still living in town, and I knew they helped him out a lot, but raising a kid alone had to be hard.

Rhodes was waiting in the parking lot, quietly climbing in the passenger seat and waving at us in the backseat while Tripp headed toward the road that led south out of town. The roads were quiet on the trip, and I sat twisting my hands in my lap while trapped between my sister and the man I wasn't so sure she hated anymore.

Both were absorbed in their phones, but I had a sneaking suspicion they might be texting each other when my sister's furious texting was countered moments later by a chuckle from the man on my right and a lazy response.

The two of them couldn't be more different, but there was also undeniable chemistry between them, and there had been since they were children.

While I didn't know adult Baker, I had known preteen and teen Baker. He and my sister had once been inseparable, and I wondered if they'd ever find their way back there.

I guess only time would tell.

"WHAT CAN I GET you to drink, sweetheart?" Tripp whispered in my ear, his large, warm hand resting in the middle of my back. His thumb rubbed the skin just above the neckline of my dress, and I fought the urge to shiver at his touch.

Tipping my head back, I leaned it against his shoulder. "What are you having?"

He leaned close, his lips ghosting the shell of my ear. "Just water for me tonight. I'm driving and I want to remember every second of ruining this pretty dress later."

Well, wow... talk about sending a girl from zero to sixty-nine in 2.2 seconds.

"What if I like this dress?" I asked, unable to control my smile as I turned to look at his smirking face.

"Then I'll buy you another one, but I have plans for this one later."

Lifting my hand, I rested my palm on his neck, my thumb absently rubbing his scar. He tilted his head into my touch, and I suddenly wanted to abandon my sister in a country bar with her arch nemesis and retreat to Tripp's tiny cabin in the woods to make him fulfill the promises he'd been making all day.

"What happened to my good boy, who wanted to cherish me?"

He chuckled, tucking his face into my neck. "This good boy wants to be bad tonight and ruin you for anyone else, Rhey."

"Too late." He'd already done that.

"Come on, fuckers. It's time to dance," Baker announced, clapping loudly from his seat on the barstool next to me. "I didn't come here to watch your foreplay. I came to have some fun tonight."

"Dance with my sister, then," I told him, enjoying how Tripp had wrapped himself around me possessively.

"What the fuck, Annie?" Reese practically shrieked, clearly not liking my suggestion that she dance with the man she wanted to avoid tonight.

Glancing over at her, I fought the urge to laugh at her murderous expression. "I'm going to remember this the next time you need my help with something."

"I'm sure you will," I replied, but maybe there was some merit to Baker dragging her out tonight. She'd forgotten how to have fun.

"If you don't want to dance with Baker, I'll take you out for a spin," Rhodes offered my sister, tilting his head toward the dance floor.

"That sounds like an excellent plan," she chuckled, sliding off her stool to take Rhodes's extended hand. They disappeared onto the crowded dance floor, Reese laughing as she shot an arched eyebrow at the dejected man to my left.

"On that note," Baker growled, pushing his stool back from the high-top table we'd found when we came in, and we watched him turn toward the bar. "It's time to get fucked up."

Since he was taller than half the patrons surrounding us, it wasn't hard to see him make a beeline toward the bar. He took two shots of a brownish liquid the bartender poured for him and then scanned the occupied stools, his face lighting up briefly before he settled into the space between two women in short skirts. He propped his elbows on the bar top behind him while he introduced himself, his eyes briefly flicking to the dance floor where his friend was spinning a giggling Reese in circles in a skilled two-step.

"While I'm enjoying the show just as much as you," Tripp whispered, ghosting his lips across my bare shoulder. "I'm gonna need that drink order or you're coming to dance with me."

"You dance?" I laughed, turning to look at him.

He smiled, raising an eyebrow. "I might be a bit serious, but I know how to have fun occasionally."

"Oh, I know exactly how much of a good time you like to have, but I wasn't sure if those sexy hip movements of yours extended to the dance floor."

"Why don't you take me for a spin and find out," he whispered, and I was once again reminded why I was falling so hard for this man. Just when I thought I had him figured out, he surprised me in the best possible ways.

Grasping my palm in his, he helped me stand, lifted my hand to his mouth, and placed a delicate kiss on the back. Before I could anticipate his next move, he'd spun me into the empty space surrounding our table and back into his chest. His large palms grasped my waist and spun me so my back was to his chest. With his arms around my waist, he swayed his hips against mine to the fast-paced country beat coming from the band playing on the opposite side of the dance floor.

"Believe me now?" His deep voice was a teasing whisper, and as I met my sister's eyes across the space between us, I couldn't keep the grin off my face. She shook her head, rolling her eyes before she let Rhodes lead her back into the sea of bodies.

I was in trouble with this man with a capital T.

Baker passed us, leading both of his friends from the bar toward the dance floor, laughing loudly before he stopped near where my sister was smiling at Rhodes and spinning both ladies out before he pulled them back in to grind against his solid thighs.

And that was when I knew my sister had enough trouble of her own, her jaw dropping at the blatant display Baker was clearly putting on for her benefit. He tipped his head at her when he noticed her looking and gyrated his hips to the beat, much to the delight of his dance partners. But I wasn't convinced my sister was as unaffected by him as she wanted to appear, her eyes revealing that his actions cut deeper than she wanted to let on.

"Maybe Baker needs to ride in the front seat on our way home, because I am not driving home with the two of them fucking in the backseat of Marty's truck."

"Ew, just no…" Laughing at his crass assessment of where the night was going, I led him toward the edge of the dance floor, ready to enjoy those fluid hip movements of his until we could leave.

Chapter
Twenty-One

Annie

T HE TRUCK WAS QUIET on the way home, but my mind was buzzing. Reese had talked me into having one mixed drink with her about an hour into our night, but three hours later, the effects had long worn off. And since I'd actually slept last night, with the sexy man driving the truck wrapped around me, I wasn't tired.

"Look behind us," Tripp whispered, squeezing my knee.

Shifting, I glanced into the back seat, stifling a laugh when I noticed the scene behind me. Baker was seated with his back braced against the window and had an arm draped across the back of the seat, Reese was tucked under his shoulder with her head buried in his chest. Her fingers gripped the open placket of his buttoned shirt possessively, and he seemed to enjoy her unconscious attention.

Baker noticed me looking and grinned, winking as he picked up a loose curl and twisted her hair around his fingertip. Soon after his display with the two ladies from the bar, he'd excused himself to go to the bathroom and come back out to the dance floor alone, cutting in on where my sister was still dancing with Rhodes.

His friend had taken it in stride, escaping outside to take a call while Baker pulled my sister into his arms, swaying closely to a few slow songs until she'd practically sprinted to the bar when the music picked back up. This continued throughout the evening. Baker somehow convincing Reese to take another turn on the dance floor, followed by her rushing back to the bar for an escape after.

189

Despite wanting to watch their interactions like a tennis match, Tripp had kept me on the dance floor until we were both sweating and laughing, my somber mood from the morning was nowhere in sight.

Tripp squeezed my knee again, and I returned my gaze forward, giving my sister some privacy.

Watching the horizon as we drove north, I scanned the tree line for the glow that had once accompanied the sight of the mountain range to the north. But it never came, the stars nearly visible through the lingering haze that'd blocked the sky out for days.

As much as I hated the fire for its destructive nature, I could already feel parts of myself ready to sprout and bloom under all the changes that'd happened in my life in such a short period. While almost everything in my future was uncertain, I knew two things wouldn't change. My growing attachment to Tripp, and the job that'd grounded me for years. Along with my sister and my friends, I could figure everything else out as it came at me.

Rhodes was quiet as he climbed out of the truck at the fire station, heading down the block to a newer apartment complex with a backward wave.

Reese was still out cold when we stopped in front of the bakery, her grip on Baker unwavering.

"You need some help with her?" I asked and tried not to swoon when Baker ran his fingertips along her hairline, whispering into her hair.

She let out a little growl, but didn't wake, which caused the burly firefighter to grin. "If you open the doors for me, I can get her tucked in."

The air outside had cooled, feeling good on my overheated skin as I rounded the front of the truck and pulled open the back door. Baker shifted my sister fully into his lap, wrapping an arm behind her back and his other underneath her knees before he slipped out to the sidewalk.

"My keys are in my pocket," he whispered, nodding to his right.

"I've got it, sweetheart." Tripp's voice was quiet from behind me, and I hadn't realized he'd turned off the truck to help us.

"Try not to get too turned on while you've got your hand in my pocket, cowboy," Baker teased, cocking his hip to the side and easily lifting my sister higher so Tripp could get access to his pocket.

He pulled them out gingerly, turning and leading us toward the door to the bakery. The three of us were quiet as we walked through the shadowy shop that smelled faintly of flour and something sweet.

"Up the stairs there," Baker whispered, following behind Tripp.

Baker's apartment looked like a quintessential bachelor pad, but it was neater than I expected. Which was good for him, because my sister hated that chaos in the house—and I could be a bit of a gremlin. At least I kept it confined to my bedroom. Not that it mattered at this point, because neither one of us had a bedroom anymore.

"Door's to the right," Baker nodded at a closed door, and I walked forward to open it for him, surprised that my assessment had clearly been wrong. I may not have a bedroom, but this one looked like Reese already.

There were neatly folded scrubs on the dresser, and the duvet was a rich blue color, eerily like the one she'd just lost. A shower caddy had all her usual products neatly tucked inside and two pairs of familiar white shoes she specially ordered to wear at the hospital were placed just under the window that overlooked the alley beside the shop.

"Do you guys want to stay for a drink?" Baker asked while he carefully pried my sister's fingers from his shirt. I should have offered to help, but he seemed to have it under control as he laid her down on the sheets, gently pulling off her high-heeled sandals and neatly leaving them next to her other shoes.

"Nah," Tripp whispered, tipping his head toward the bedroom door. "We're gonna head back to the ranch. Early morning tomorrow."

"Thanks for coming out with us tonight," he whispered, following us out of the bedroom before he left one last lingering glance at my sister and pulled the door closed. "I think she needed it, despite all her arguments against it. She's barely slept since she's been here."

For someone who thrived on routine, I could see this situation being hard on my baby sister, but at least she had a someone to help her through it. "Thank you for letting her stay here."

"Not sure if it was *let* as much as it was forced. The head of emergency medicine told her she wasn't allowed to stay at the hospital if she wanted to be put back on the schedule. I just happened to be within earshot right before she lost her shit and offered my place."

"Well, thank you. I can tell she appreciates your hospitality."

"Yeah," he chuckled dryly, looking at her closed bedroom door. "She's just full of gratitude toward me."

Baker followed us back down to the front of the shop, locking the door after he let us out. Tripp held open the door to the truck while I climbed inside and then jogged back around to start the truck.

"You know I was serious earlier when I offered you a place to stay, right?"

Reaching across the center console, I laced my fingers with his where his hand rested on his thigh, squeezing briefly before I let go. "I know."

"Your sister seems settled for the time being, so I don't want you to feel pressured to find something right away."

"That's the only reason?" I asked, only partially teasing.

"And I selfishly want to wake up to you every morning," he confessed, and I sighed in relief. I wanted the same thing.

"Then I guess you're stuck with me."

He shifted the truck into gear to head back to the east side of town where the ranch was located, the tension in the air increasing with every mile closer we got to that front porch of his.

Chapter
Twenty-Two

Tristan

R HEY WAS CURLED UP in the passenger seat by the time I pulled the truck into the oversized garage, where all the ranch trucks were stored during the winter. Marty had moved all of them in during the fire because of the ash spread. And since I didn't feel like hiking the keys back to the lodge right now, I returned his truck to where I'd borrowed it from and pocketed them to return tomorrow.

"Sweetheart, we're home," I whispered, leaning over the console to unbuckle her seatbelt. She stirred, curling up tighter against the doorframe where she'd leaned her head after we left Baker's.

Guess both Thomas sisters were going to need carried to bed tonight. But at least I got to join mine in the bed, unlike my coworker who was clearly smitten with Rhey's younger sister but hadn't cracked through her hard shell yet.

Reese had watched me interacting with her sister earlier in the night, but we hadn't really talked much. She was distracted by spending the first half of the night avoiding Baker, and the second half pretending she wasn't just as attracted to him as he was to her.

But I wasn't concerned about my friend's relationship—or lack thereof—right now, I was worried about mine. Surely it wasn't normal to be this in sync with someone days after meeting them. Spending a night out sober wasn't uncommon for me. Back when I was in Wyoming, it was usually done spinning a glass of water while I was seated at the bar all night waiting for my former friends, whereas tonight, I'd danced and laughed with this feisty woman until we were both breathless.

A few months ago, I'd dreaded coming back home, feeling like I was starting over, but now, pulling Rhey out of a pickup truck—yet again—felt like returning to Sage Springs was *coming home.*

There wasn't any other way to describe it. Meeting her at the festival and then the events of the crazy forty-eight hours that followed were like something out of a movie. I still felt like I was waiting for the other shoe to drop, but I couldn't stop myself from falling for her if I tried.

Rhey stirred as I carried her down the path to my cabin, sleepily blinking up at me.

"Did I fall asleep?" Her voice was raspy and low, drowsy with sleep.

"Mhmm." I nodded, keeping my eyes on the path.

Earlier today, I'd teased her about bending her over the porch railing and ripping her dress off, but now I wasn't so sure I was in the mood for something frantic.

Rhey had cast a spell over me earlier as we swayed in each other's arms whenever the music slowed. Her body curled into mine naturally, feeling like we were one. It was like this world didn't seem so out of touch. She made me crave the feeling of her soft skin beneath my fingertips, of breathing her in and watching her eyes as I slipped inside her.

"It still seems hazy out here," she whispered, combing her fingers through the hair on the back of my head. I loved how she seemed to want to touch me as much as I wanted to do the same to her.

She'd been the first person I'd let close since my skin grafts healed, and they didn't seem to bother her. Jay had been horrified by the ugly pink skin every time he'd peeled back a dressing, both in the hospital and once I was staying at his place. He never said anything, but I saw the looks in the bathroom mirror, and someone who'd once been my jovial, affectionate brother hadn't hugged me in months. Not that my sour mood had lifted until a few days ago, so I guess I couldn't blame him entirely for being standoffish.

195

My own mother looked at me with pity and hugged me like I was made of glass, but this gorgeous creature in my arms hadn't even flinched and touched me like she wanted to. Like she wanted me.

"Sometimes it takes a while for the smoke to dissipate. It was good to control the fire when the winds died down, but it might be a few more days until the smoke clears out so we can see the stars again."

She arched an eyebrow as I stepped onto the porch, the light next to the door illuminating her grin. "Someone promised to make me see stars earlier. I believe we have a date with a porch railing."

"Maybe another night," I said, lowering her to her feet by the front door.

"Why not now?" she asked, nodding toward the rail I'd wanted to bend her over earlier.

"Because the air quality still isn't great out here, and there are plenty of other places inside that cabin to break in first. But don't worry, sweetheart, I always keep my promises."

"Hmm," she hummed, stepping close and slipping her palm behind my neck. She tugged, and I leaned forward, bracing my hand on the door above her head as she rose to whisper in my ear. "Does my good boy want to lay me out on that kitchen island and have a late-night snack?"

"I am feeling a bit *hungry*," I growled in her ear, loving the way she kept asking me for what she wanted. It was undeniably sexy when a woman took control of her own pleasure.

I reached beside her hip, turning the door handle and pushing the door in slightly before I grasped the backs of her thighs and lifted her.

She giggled as I carried her across the room, setting her on the edge of the island. I moved to grab the nearly empty fruit basket from behind her, but she put her hand on my chest.

"I've always wanted to do this," she giggled, reaching behind her to push the basket off with a sweep of her arm, the two apples that'd been inside rolling across the floor. Next was the stack of mail I'd brought back with me from the post office, cascading to the floor on the far side of the island.

"And I've always wanted to do this," I responded, placing my palms on her knees and slowly sliding them up her thighs underneath the material of her dress. Dragging a knuckle down her bare slit when I reached the apex of her thighs, I relished in the breathy moan she let out. Moving my hands to her hips, I yanked her to the edge of the counter.

"Pretty sure you've already done that...multiple times," she teased, leaning back to brace her palms against the countertop.

"But I haven't done this," I responded, backing my hands out of her dress and gripping the fabric on either side of the slit in the material. With one swift yank, the stitches gave way, making a satisfying sound as it ripped to her navel.

"Well, you did promise."

"And I'll buy you a dozen more if you let me rip them off you like this," I growled, yanking again and revealing the swells of her bare breasts. Halle-*fucking*-lujah for sundresses and no bras.

"Just going to leave it like this?" she asked, looking pointedly at the last few inches of material barely holding the sides of her dress together.

"What do you want from me, Rhey?" I asked, tracing the back of my finger along the underside of one breast, enjoying the breathy whimper she couldn't keep inside.

"Rip it," she demanded, tipping her head backward and moaning when the material gave way. I lowered the straps down her arms, leaving the destroyed dress in a puddle beneath her naked body.

"Fuck," I groaned, taking in how hot she looked perched on the edge of my kitchen island, the moonlight caressing her spectacular curvy body from the window behind me.

"Not yet," she teased, reaching up to unbutton my top two buttons. She bit the corner of her lip as she toyed with the third button, looking up at me.

"Do it," I growled, knowing what she wanted.

Her smile grew, and she grasped the sides of my shirt in the opening, the sound of buttons flying making us both laugh as I looked down at the three buttons she'd managed to pop off my shirt. I reached down to untuck it from my jeans, my hands pushing hers out of the way to rip it the rest of the way open.

"Oh no, your shirt is ruined. Guess you'll have to take it off," she laughed, and I shook my head at her, unbuttoning the cuffs and shrugging off the damaged material. "Now the belt."

She grasped the end of my belt after I unbuckled it, slowly drawing it toward her. I watched as she folded it in half, playfully cracking the leather in front of herself. "Have you ever been spanked, Tripp?"

"There's a first time for everything," I mused, unbuttoning my jeans.

Rhey hooked a finger in the waistband of my boxer briefs, teasingly dragging her fingertip across the head of my hard cock. "Maybe I'll bend you over this island next."

"Maybe." I grasped her hand, lifting it to kiss her palm. "But it won't be tonight."

Dropping to my knees, I yanked her forward, taking a slow lick up the center of her slit, groaning as I realized exactly how wet she was.

Her fingers dug into my hair, gripping hard and holding me in place as I licked and sucked her sensitive flesh, groaning into her pussy. The sounds of her moans and whimpers just spurred me on, my beard scraping against her skin in a way that was sure to leave marks.

"Oh fuck," she moaned, cupping the back of my head as she panted, watching me with rapt attention. "Fingers, fuck me with your fingers."

Leaning back to draw in a breath, I brought two fingers to her pussy, curling them inside until she drew in a sharp breath, letting out a loud moan as she clenched around them.

"Like that, baby?" I asked, knowing I hit the spot when her eyes rolled back in her head, her arms shaking as she struggled to hold herself up. "Are you going to come for me, beautiful girl?"

"Oh God, yes," she keened, her entire body arching as she fell over the edge, milking my fingers. Once the pulses subsided, I removed them slowly and placed them into my mouth while I watched her catch her breath.

I was hard as fuck, but I'd wait to see if she wanted me to fuck her on the counter or take her back to my bed. With how amped up I was, I was down for both.

"Why are your pants still on?" she laughed, reaching down to yank me toward her by a belt loop.

"Someone hasn't told me to take them off." I arched an eyebrow, and she shook her head at me, but her smile showed she liked it when I waited for her to tell me what to do.

"Well, I'm telling you now, lose the jeans *and* the underwear."

She sat up, helping me slide the worn denim and cotton down, my hard cock bobbing in the space between us. Her warm palm encircled my shaft, and I groaned, watching her draw me between her spread legs.

"Now I need you to fuck me until you come inside me."

Slowly shifting my hips forward, I slid through her wetness; the head dipping inside of her. "And if I don't want to fuck you?"

"Pretty sure you already are," she whispered, inching forward to take me in further.

"This isn't fucking, baby. This is me loving on you." I hadn't meant to say that word like this, but I didn't regret it. There was nothing more that I wanted right now than to love her with my body. Show her how addicted I'd become to her. To the smiles and the way she looked at me. Even when I wanted to throttle her for putting herself in danger.

I wanted it all with her.

"Then love me." Her voice was breathy as she wrapped her legs around my waist, drawing me into her fully. I braced my hands on

199

either side of her hips, capturing her lips with mine as I drew back, plunging forward again and again.

Rhey was right there with me, rocking into my movements, gripping my hair, tracing my cheeks with her fingers, digging her nails into my chest, our mouths only parting to gasp in shaky breaths before we dove back in.

"I'm gonna come again," she whimpered, wrapping her hands around my waist and rocking into my thrusts, clinging to me like she needed me as much as I needed her.

"Let go, sweetheart," I whispered into her ear, grasping her hips and holding her still while I picked up the pace, pistoning my hips into the cradle of her thighs.

Her neck arched back, her body shaking as she fell over the edge, squeezing me with her release.

"Come in me," she cried, watching me holding back, my hips faltering with the intense pleasure as the aftershocks of her orgasm rippled around my cock. "Please."

"Hold on," I panted, pulling her close and burying my face in her neck as my thrusts picked up. She wrapped her arms around my waist, her fingers clenching my lower back, beneath the damaged skin. She dug her nails in as she panted against my chest, little moans escaping her lips with each thrust. Spurred on, I groaned into her neck, loving that she wasn't afraid to be rough with me. "Fuck, sweetheart, I love your marks on me."

Losing myself in the feeling of her body, I groaned against the soft, sweaty skin of her neck, plunging in all the way before I lost myself, emptying myself inside her warm, supple body.

"If that was loving me," she breathed, pushing the sweaty hair off my forehead. "Then next time, maybe you need to hate me a little."

I laughed, enjoying the way she giggled along with me. "Not sure that's possible, but I can give it my best shot."

"But right now you need to take me to bed," she yawned, bracing her palms on the counter behind her.

Tracing the back of one knuckle across her breast, I leaned in to kiss her softly before I pulled away.

Leaning down to pull off my boots, I left them with the pile of clothes on the kitchen floor with my socks, jeans and underwear.

Scooping up Rhey's warm, pliant, naked body, I kept her close as I navigated the path through the dimly lit cabin to my bed. Depositing her on the soft cotton, I smiled, climbing in behind her before I pulled the sheets over our sated bodies.

This was what I'd been missing. A connection with a woman that seemed more than just superficial. The ability to curl myself around someone I'd just shared something intense with and interlace our fingers on her stomach without it feeling forced. Without having to ask, I knew she'd be here when I woke up, ready to face whatever tomorrow threw at us.

I knew we still had so many unspoken things between us, but the more time we spent together, the more I craved it. Then there was the not so inconsequential task of figuring out the details around where she'd be living long term, but I wasn't going anywhere, and I hoped she wouldn't either.

"See you in the morning, sweetheart," I whispered, kissing her shoulder and enjoying the way she wiggled her hips to get closer to me.

This living arrangement might be temporary in her eyes, but I was going to put up a fight to convince her she belonged here with me.

It might have been crazy fast and a bit reckless, but what hadn't been with us at this point?

Maybe we all needed a bit of recklessness in our lives. Rhey was my little bit of chaos. And I'd never regret her.

Chapter
Twenty-Three

Annie

B EING AT THE RANCH with Tripp made it hard to believe that I'd ever spent my life anywhere else—with anyone else. It was peaceful in a way that I didn't know I needed.

When we woke up to a beautiful blue sky, it finally felt like the chaos of the past few days was finally behind us. The smoke wasn't entirely gone, but the haze had lifted enough so that it was easier to stay outside for longer periods of time.

I still had a few more days until I needed to return to reality—aka my job at the bar—and I was determined to focus on the uninterrupted time with him. Even if I was currently cleaning stalls in the barn and up to my elbows in horseshit.

"You sure you don't want a job?" Marty teased, watching me attempt to smoothly maneuver a wheelbarrow down the aisle between the rows of stalls, while simultaneously trying to hold my breath. He and the rest of the ranch hands may have been nose blind to horse manure, but I was not. That shit—literally—was pungent and huge. "You're only at the bar during the evenings. I could use a few extra hands around here once the season picks back up. And from what I remember, you used to be pretty good in a saddle."

"It's been years since I rode, and I think I prefer the animals I serve to be of the party variety—not the shits bigger than my fist variety."

He laughed, and I smiled at the sound because I was sure everyone in town had aged significantly in the last four days and needed to be reminded that while some of us may have lost everything, we still had each other. And ridiculous poop jokes.

"Let's hope you don't know the bathroom habits of the people you serve at the bar," he teased, shouldering me out of the way to take the wheelbarrow. It was the latest load I'd helped Tripp cart out of the horse stalls and felt like the millionth trip I'd made down this aisle with a pile of crap.

"You wouldn't believe half the things I've seen. Drunk people definitely have the ability to revert to their nasty baser selves."

The horses were still being temporarily housed at the fairgrounds. So, the ranch staff not supervising them there were trying to get the barn back into shape for when they were ready to come home. While the lodge was currently deserted, Marty had told us that the next week was a full house after the fourth.

We'd all been a little worried that the fire would scare away the tourists for the rest of the summer, but once they'd let people with upcoming reservations know things were under control, very few of them had canceled their trips. And any remaining openings had already been filled. Tripp and Marty were supposed to go on a ride of the western edge of the ranch later in the week to assess the trails for damage, but a majority of the ranch was intact, including the cabins to the north we'd taken overnight refuge in.

Tripp was anxious to get Phi back to the ranch. He'd spent ten minutes on the phone with the equine vet this morning asking all kinds of questions. The smoke inhalation during the fire didn't seem to have done any permanent damage to her lungs. She'd just have to spend the next month taking it easy in the barn to recover as a precaution.

I still had a bit of a cough when I spent too much time outside, and Reese had tried to get me to come get checked out at the hospital, but I felt fine otherwise. At least my lungs did. Other parts of me were a bit tender from repetitive use, but I didn't regret how they'd gotten that way for a damn minute.

"Well, if you change your mind, the barn door will always be open to you. Although I'm sure I can wear you down if you're living on the property."

"I, uh…" my voice trailed off, unsure if he was upset because my room at the lodge had been unoccupied the last few nights in favor of the cabin in the woods behind it.

"I hear my new manager got a mattress delivered last week, hope he bought a good one," Marty teased, bouncing his eyebrows. "You know, since none of the ones in the lodge have been used recently. When I came looking for you during breakfast, Charley told me the room she put you up in was suspiciously empty this morning."

"Oh my God, Dad, leave her alone!" I hadn't even realized Charley was at the ranch today, but I appreciated her coming to my rescue, because while I'd known Marty since I was a kid, I wasn't exactly keen on sharing mattress assessments with him. "She can stay wherever she wants, and it's none of your damn business."

"Just sayin'," he chuckled with a shrug. "But that's okay because we have new guests comin' in on the fifth and as of right now, we're booked solid, so I was gonna have to kick you out, anyway. How gracious of Tripp to take a lady in distress into his home."

"Who's in distress?" the man in question asked, wiping the back of a leather glove covered hand across his sweat and dirt-streaked forehead.

While my first instincts were to say *my ovaries*, I had a feeling that was not the answer to his question. Even if it was true.

No matter what this man was wearing, it was seriously unfair the effect he had on me. I only hoped I held even half the appeal to him. And the tight denim jeans hugging his strong thighs added to a straw speckled plaid shirt that stuck to his muscles in all the right places was a seriously dangerous combination when you added a cowboy hat, some leather boots and a smirk.

"Nice of you to offer up your bed to our little Annie here," Marty teased, winking at his ranch manager and laughing when Tripp's cheeks tinted just the tiniest bit of pink. "Real selfless to sacrifice your comfort like that. Since I'm guessing you're staying on that lumpy old couch in the living room."

Charley snorted, and I unsuccessfully held in a giggle when Tripp tried to stutter through a response.

"Well, you see, sir... it *is* a king-sized mattress. So, there's plenty of room for both of us to sleep without any problems."

"Pretty sure the two of you could make a twin sized bed work without a problem, too," Marty guffawed, and Tripp's composure slipped once he realized his boss was just teasing him. "Just don't keep my horses or my guests up at night, and you're fine."

Once her dad walked away to harass some other employees, Charley pulled me aside, shooing Tripp away with her glove-covered hands. "Girl talk. No sweaty, stinky boys allowed."

When she'd dragged me far enough out of earshot, she turned on me with an expectant look. "Have you been ignoring all our texts?"

"What?" I absently patted my back pocket until I remembered I still didn't have a phone. Which honestly wasn't as bad as I thought it'd be. What had seemed like a necessity in my life before was easier to live without when you were enjoying the person you were spending most of your time with. "Oh... no. My phone was lost when Tripp rescued me, and I haven't been able to replace it yet. That's why I called Hudson from Tripp's phone to check in."

"Gotcha. Well, maybe I need to get his number to get ahold of you. Hudson was trying to see if you wanted to come in tomorrow night for a little while. Should be slow with the holiday, but since fireworks are still prohibited with the burn ban right now, it might pick up in the evening once people get bored."

Hesitating, I didn't want to agree to anything. Selfishly, I wanted to spend a little more one-on-one time with Tripp, but I didn't want to assume he felt the same way. I knew his family lived nearby, and post wildfire, their emotions were still running high. Maybe they wanted time with Tripp, and maybe that time wouldn't include me.

"I'll think about it. I can call Hudson to let him know later once I figure out what my plans are."

She looked over my shoulder, her grin widening. Turning to follow her gaze, I smiled as I took in the man leaning against the wall, his gloved hands propped on the handle of a stall shovel.

"I have a feeling your plans are gonna involve a whole lot of that man," she teased. "Don't forget to write my dad a thank you note for his matchmaking skills. Who knew bringing on someone to lighten his workload would lead to *love at first horseback rescue*?"

"Not me," I laughed, shaking my head. Part of me had just resigned to being alone. Now I had all kinds of crazy thoughts running through my mind, each getting just a little too far ahead of itself.

"I'm gonna assume since you don't have a phone, you haven't heard from Reid's cousin?"

Charley knew *of* Jayden from when he came into the bar, but since he was closer to Reid, and not as much with Hudson, I wasn't sure how well she knew him personally. Jay was quite a bit older than her, so it wasn't like she ran in the same circles as him before she started dating my boss.

"Last I knew, he was still up in Breckenridge," I commented offhandedly, feeling a little guilty that I hadn't made more of an effort to check in with him. But that's not how things were between us. Especially not lately. "He's been trying to get some chef to come down here to help him open the restaurant. But Jay's been tight-lipped about things."

"Gotcha," she replied, nodding toward Tripp. "Well, just be careful. Once he gets back to town, things might get a little more complicated for you. I'm sure Hazel can have Reid talk to him if you need him to."

Shaking my head, I glanced at Tripp out of the corner of my eye, glad he was giving us space to talk. "Tripp knows I was involved with someone. But I'm ending it when Jay gets back to town. I mean, it's kind of been over for months, anyway."

"Just be careful. I know things were casual with you and Jay, but men can get territorial when they think their toys are about to be taken away." I gave her a look, and she held her hands up. "I wasn't saying you were a toy, per se. But the comparison works. I just don't want to see your friendship blow up because he's jealous."

"Things weren't like that between us. It was never an exclusive arrangement." To be honest, I wasn't sure if Jayden could be jealous. Even after seven years together, he still never truly showed me the real him. The only people who seemed to get the real side of him were his best friend Colette and the ex from college he never talked about.

"Well, I'm glad Tripp found you, because this is the happiest I think I've ever seen you." She thankfully let the conversation go, brushing off her jeans before she left her parting shot. "But I'll still fuck him up if he hurts you."

Chapter
Twenty-Four

Annie

TRIPP AND I HEADED into town late in the afternoon, and with the 4th fast approaching, it didn't look like as much of a ghost town as it had previously. It still wasn't as busy as I'd seen it in years past, but maybe Sage Springs had a chance of bouncing back with the fire completely suppressed. Watching the people milling about as we drove past, I admired the resilience of this community. How, despite our tragedies, people were still coming out to support local businesses and celebrate the holiday.

And now maybe assholes with fireworks would respect red flag warnings and burn bans now that they'd seen the aftermath of their stupid decisions.

"Do you want to check in with Reese?" Tripp asked, his thumb tracing distracting patterns on the inside of my knee. His hands seemed to gravitate toward me whenever he was near. And I craved the overt affection after years of being involved but not in an actual relationship.

"She's usually on shift by now, and I know she volunteered to work the holiday tomorrow, so I'll check in with her after. I'm sure she's got her hands full with Baker."

He stopped at a light, squeezing my knee and flashing me with a grin. "Or she's got her hands full *of* Baker."

"Or maybe both, he's at the hospital a lot since he works the rig with Rhodes. Technically, Elias is an EMT, right?"

"Yeah, he's wildly overqualified. I think he was a trauma doc at a hospital before he moved back here with Emi, but he needed something he could have predictable hours with. The hospital didn't have any openings, so he got some additional certifications and took over the vacant EMT position at the station."

Nodding, I realized it seemed to be a theme with the fire department. "Seems like he might not be the only one overqualified for his job."

Tripp nodded, squeezing the hand on the steering wheel before he spoke again. "The Chief offered me a field training officer position."

While I'd only seen him in action briefly, I could see that being a good fit for him. "So, does that mean you're going to be leaving the ranch?"

Managing a ranch may not have been what he'd been doing with his career before he moved back to Sage Springs, but it suited him. He seemed at ease working with Marty.

"The Chief said it can be a permanent part-time position that could transition into a full-time assignment when there are new officers to train. He's fine if I need to drop back to volunteer status, too. I still need to talk to Marty, but I think it might be a good fit. I'd get to train new officers, which I enjoyed doing while I was stationed at the national park but not have to be on full-time duty."

"Sounds like the best of both worlds." The selfish part of me felt a little relieved knowing that he wouldn't be going back to the fire department full time. I knew he loved his job, and it'd been his life for a really long time, but knowing he'd be in a position that didn't put him in danger quite as often was a relief.

"And now that I've settled in, I don't want to leave the ranch. I still have a lot to learn to take over for Marty when he wants to retire, and I'm ready for the responsibility. I've been in crisis mode for so long that a change of pace sounds nice."

He'd worked hard for a long time and deserved to choose his own path from now on. I just hoped I could walk by his side on that path.

"What about you?" he asked, glancing over at me. "Is the bar your long-term goal?"

It was hard to answer that question, helping Hudson find his footing at the bar had been all I knew for the last seven years. We both had a background in restaurant management, but I'd gravitated toward bar service where Hudson had taken over all the administrative duties. He still occasionally worked the bar, but he'd settled into the background, relying on me to pick up the slack.

"I think I need to sit down and talk to Hudson about my role once I go back. I'll admit I've been a bit of a workaholic since my responsibilities outside the bar didn't take up much of my time." Reese was really the only person I prioritized until now, and her hours were crazier than mine. "My sister isn't much better, and since she's the only family I have left, I threw myself into my job."

"Would you want to stay there full time?" My mind briefly flitted to Jayden's offer to help him design the drink menu for the restaurant, but even I knew that'd never happen now, even if I had been interested. If Charley thought jealousy was going to be an issue once I told him our situationship was done, then I doubted he'd want me involved in the expansion of his business.

"Yeah, I think there's a possibility of bringing on some new bartenders and teaching them what I know. Maybe scale my late-night hours into a more reasonable schedule now that I may actually have a social life outside of that place."

He chuckled, smiling at me while he shifted the truck into park outside the general store downtown. I couldn't keep surviving on borrowed clothes, and the dress he'd bought me to go dancing was now in a heap in the bottom of his trash can, so I needed to find something to wear.

"Speaking of social life," he murmured, turning to face me and pulling my hand across the center console. "Would you go somewhere with me tomorrow?"

"Why do you sound so nervous?" I asked, squeezing his fingers until he made eye contact with me. "We've spent the last several days together. Afraid I'm gonna get sick of you?"

"You don't have to spend all your time with me if you don't want to." He suddenly looked nervous, and I wasn't sure where else he thought I'd go.

"I never said that. And where else am I going to go? Homeless, remember?" I teased trying to lighten the mood, but his jaw still looked tense.

"I wouldn't stop you if you wanted to go hang out with your friends. I've kind of been monopolizing your time. And I've been pushy about asking you to stay with me."

"And I have enjoyed every fucking minute of it, Tripp. While I could move into the apartment above the bar like Hudson offered, I kinda like staying with you on the ranch. It's quiet. And I feel like I'm on vacation sharing that big king sized bed with you instead of freaking out that everything I own, including my truck, is gone."

A hint of a smile replaced his serious demeanor, and I was glad we could talk like this. We could both let our insecurities show and not be judged by the other for them.

"Your insurance will—"

"My insurance will take care of it," I interrupted, unbothered by the logistics at this point. "And I know you'll hold my hand when I have to go see what happened to my home. I may literally only own the clothes on my back right now, but I'm not going anywhere if I have a say in it. I'm happy to stay right where I am—with you."

"Technically, you're not wearing your own clothes right now," he teased, tugging at the wrist on the shirt I'd stolen from his closet this morning.

"Okay, Mr. Literal. You know what I mean."

"So, is that a yes?" he asked, circling back to where this conversation started.

Arching an eyebrow, I tilted my head to make eye contact. "You haven't told me what we're doing."

He took a deep breath, and I held mine, wondering why he was getting so weird about asking me to go somewhere with him. "My aunt and uncle are having a get together for the fourth. Their place isn't too far from the ranch, so we could even ride over if the weather holds out. Marty is bringing some horses back over this afternoon."

I paused, smiling at him. Silly man, who was clearly overthinking things right now. "You want me to meet your family?"

"I guess, yeah. Now that I'm closer geographically, my parents have been putting more pressure on me to come to things like this. But I also don't like the idea of leaving you at the ranch alone."

I thought back to Hudson's offer for me to pick up a shift at the bar tomorrow night. It would be the easier, emotionally safer option. Before meeting Tripp I wouldn't have hesitated saying yes to an extra shift, but now...

"Are you sure that wouldn't be weird to show up with a random person?"

"My brothers and cousins always bring friends. There's usually a ton of people there," he explained, rubbing his thumb across the back of my hand while he stared down at our interlocked fingers.

"And that's what I am to you? A friend?" I asked quietly. While I knew we were a little past the *just friends* stage, I wanted to make sure I knew exactly who he wanted me to be tomorrow. I knew things between us had been moving fast, but it'd be a disappointment if we weren't on the same page if I was asked tomorrow.

"Putting me on the spot, huh?" he chuckled, letting go of my hand to use a finger to tilt my chin up. His eyes bore into mine and I tried not to flinch, letting him see I was genuinely asking what I was to him.

"You're the one who brought this up."

"And if I wanted you to be more than a friend?"

My smile was involuntary, and thankfully he returned it. Butterflies danced in my stomach when I thought about the last few days and how natural everything felt with him. "Are we defining this now?"

"This situation hasn't exactly been conventional, but I want to continue seeing you. See where this goes. I enjoy spending time with you. And I think we seem to have a good time together."

Nodding, I tried to maintain my composure. The last thing he needed to see was me crying in relief that he reciprocated the feelings that scared me. "We have more than a good time together."

"Good enough that you'd come with me to this thing as my date?"

"Hmm," I mused, deciding to tease him a little. "I might need some convincing. You've made a pretty good case, but I might need a bit more lip service."

"Happy to put my lips to work. Just tell me where you'd like them," he murmured, leaning in and sinking his fingers into my loose hair. "Might put in some tongue service, too."

"You seem to have a good handle on how to argue your case," I whispered back, leaning in until our lips touched. "I might be almost convinced."

The tip of his nose brushed against mine, his thumb smoothing back the hair on my temple while I fisted the front of his shirt. Our breath mingled in the space between us, the tension building before he pressed his lips fully to mine.

The butterflies I'd felt in his presence since our first stilted conversation took flight, and my body came alive as he kissed me thoroughly, his tongue pushing forward to mingle with mine until we were both pulling away with our chests heaving.

He rested his forehead against mine when he pulled away, fingers gently combing through my hair. "Now let's go find you something to wear. I'll try not to rip it off this time."

"I won't argue if you can't help yourself. Just maybe save it for when you get me home. Don't want your family to think I corrupted you."

"Then we've got a deal," he agreed, tilting his head and pushing forward to capture my lips again.

Chapter
Twenty-Five

Tristan

EARLY FEBRUARY

*M*Y EYES SCANNED THE *screen, assessing the footage that was being relayed to base from the helicopter flyover. The wind speeds were continuing to fluctuate, but there was a clear increase in sustained gusts that were going to blow the embers directly at the hikers who'd abandoned their camp. There was clear visibility from the aerial shots that continued coming through.*

"This isn't good," Pace grunted from my right, shaking his head. "Why in the fuck would those people go down a trail clearly marked closed?"

"Because they don't have any common sense." That was what half our job was, fixing peoples' lapses in judgment that most often resulted in catastrophe. Yes, wildfires were naturally occurring and could put even the most suspecting person in danger unintentionally, but a majority of our careers were spent rescuing people from their own shitty ass decisions.

"The Deputy Chief just sent us updated stats on the weather conditions. I don't like the shift in these wind gusts. Are we going to be able to keep this away from them?" he huffed. "And why in the hell did the burn boss okay the burn plan with these wind conditions?"

"Again," I responded, shaking my head. "People don't have common sense. But we don't have time to analyze the dumbasses, we have a job to do if we don't want fatalities on this one."

"You're right," he sighed, pressing the button to the side of the control panel that would alert the pilots on the flight deck that they needed to prepare for takeoff immediately.

After the horn blared through the building, the inside of the base station locker room was a frantic flurry of activity as our group of ten smoke jumpers on duty suited up and checked the gear before hustling to our awaiting aircraft. After sixteen years on the job, everything was second nature, but I checked every pocket and every strap of my harness, just in case. Even veterans made mistakes, and every piece of gear we carried was essential, meaning mistakes could cost a life.

"We ready to do this?" Pace asked from my side as we exited the side of the hangar, the light breeze at base command a tease against my face compared to what I knew we'd be jumping into.

"Don't think we have a fucking choice," I grunted, my focus on running through the list of things I checked before each mission. Every single one of us had a ritual we followed, and not fucking talking was mine. I needed to be in the right headspace to jump, and right now I was irrationally pissed that someone in our organization caused this fire unnecessarily.

Anyone running a controlled burn knew to watch wind speeds and weather advisories before they lit the first line, which meant the burn boss had epically fucked this one up. Not to mention whoever closed the trails that were closest to the burn area didn't do a good enough fucking job apparently, since we had a half a dozen hikers now trapped by a fire they couldn't control without our help.

"We fucking got this," he said, holding his glove covered fist out for a bump. I tapped it and hauled myself up the stairs into the aircraft, sliding across the seat to my designated spot. The adrenaline rush on the way to a jump was unlike anything I'd ever experienced, every cell in my body buzzing as the last member of my crew boarded.

We were all quiet as the plane took flight, the radio chatter of the spotters indistinguishable over the roar of the engines from where I was sitting.

Once we reached the drop site, our team was like a well-oiled machine, each jumper waiting for their cue until they leaped from the door one by one until I was the last man left. Double checking the strap on my helmet, I waddled my way to the open door, the sound of the wind rushing through the airplane almost deafening. Grabbing the stationary pole by the door, I waited for the spotter to give me the go ahead.

When his fist connected with my shoulder, I was gone, free falling with the wind at my face, scanning the horizon line for the little blue dots of my colleague's parachutes.

We were to set the fire line between the burn and the stranded hikers, keeping it away from them until the wind conditions improved for an aerial rescue. Having done hundreds of jumps, my brain was on autopilot, running through the checklist of things I needed to do as soon as I hit the ground.

Deploying my parachute, my heart rate slowed as my body bounced, and I grabbed the handles, steering into the wind to get near the drop zone. Studying the ground, I could see where the front line of the fire was, a pillar of smoke in the air marking it in the distance.

Scanning the spotty tree line, my eyes widened when I noticed a flash of color that shouldn't have been there. As the ground came closer and closer, I tried to focus, but my eyes were drawn back to the bright purple dot in the forest, way too close to the smoke.

A gust of wind caught my parachute, and I steered against it, ready to battle the winds to reach my final destination and steer away from the fire, but as I crossed over where the purple dot had been, I saw flashes of arms waving through the branches.

"Fuck." There was someone out there.

We were too far out for anyone to know that one hiker wasn't with the group they'd steered away from the fire, and since I was the last man on the ground, and my crew was far enough away they didn't know we still had a civilian in danger.

I wasn't a search and rescue firefighter. It wasn't my job to rescue people from burning buildings or wildfires, but fuck if I was gonna let someone remain in danger on my watch.

My adrenaline was pumping as I steered toward the trees, knowing I was about to get the fuck beat out of me. When I plunged through the canopy, I was thankful for my gear, the heavily padded suit and helmet protecting me from the tree branches as I fell.

It still knocked the wind out of me when my chute hooked overhead and my body bounced in the air, suspended about six feet off the ground.

Reaching for my front pack, I grabbed my knife, cutting the lines of my parachute and bending my knees for the impact with the forest floor.

The sound of a feminine shout carrying through the haze had me jumping up, jogging toward the sound of her voice. Blood rushed in my ears as I hustled as fast as my heavy packs would allow through the smoke, no time to throw off my extra gear.

"Where are you?" I yelled, hoping I was heading in the right direction, but I could barely see, the smoke burning my eyes as I scanned through the trees, the distinct red glow of the fire much closer than I wanted to see it.

"Here!" the voice echoed back, and I turned, picking my way through the underbrush toward a steep hill. I slogged my way down it, trying not to let my heavy gear throw off my center of balance.

"Just keep yelling!" I shouted, knowing I needed to find this person and get them the fuck out of here before that fire got any closer.

Her voice carried over the rush of the wind and the roaring crackle of the fire. I followed it as I scanned for the purple dot I'd seen overhead.

Breaking through a cluster of trees about halfway down the hill, I saw her on the ground, clutching her leg while she sat yards away from a battered purple tent that had been stretched out over the ground but was clearly not set up on the steep hillside. I had to admire the quick thinking on her part. It was a bright marker that could clearly grab attention from the air, but holy fuck.

"What the fuck are you doing out here by yourself?" I yelled, assessing the situation. While we were all required to complete mandatory emergency medical training each year during the off season, I didn't have the equipment to properly set a bone or splint a leg.

"I fell down this embankment and I think I broke my leg. They were going to send someone back for me, but it's been hours, and I tried to walk, but I kept falling, and—"

I held up my hand, cutting her off. "So, it's broken?"

She nodded; tear tracks visible on her dirt-smeared cheeks. "Alright, here's what we're going to do. I've got a fire shelter in my gear and I'm gonna help you climb into it. That fire line is way too close to us, and I can't carry you out of here safely."

"You're going to leave me?" she whimpered, her breathing picking up.

"Not unless I need to," I replied, shaking my head, but as the wind blew, and embers danced in front of my face, catching on the canopy overhead and sparking the branches, I knew I might have to if she had my only fire shelter.

Activating the beacon on my gear that would broadcast my location, I made sure the little blinking light engaged, the chirp it emitted almost drowned out by the sound of the fire as it flashed up the hill toward us. I dropped my packs to the ground beside me, but kept my outer suit on, reaching down to yank out what I needed.

"But we need to move, now," I urged, my voice loud over the roar of the approaching fire. Pulling out the pouch my shelter was housed in and ripping off the Velcro, I shook out the material. "I'm gonna have you roll over and pull this over your legs. Keep your feet hooked in the bottom pouch and use your forearms to hold down the top, cover your face with your hands and keep your mouth low to the ground."

"Oh my God, oh my God," she whimpered, rocking in place, but we didn't have time to waste as the heat from the fire blew in our direction with the next gust of wind.

"This is probably gonna hurt," I yelled, turning her and pulling the end of the shelter over her feet and legs. "Hold on!"

She grabbed the top of the shelter and pulled it over her head, her body disappearing beneath the reflective foil.

Glancing behind me, my eyes widened as I watched the wind carry the fire higher, heading directly for us. I grabbed the pouch with my fire-resistant blanket and my neck shield and turned back to where I came from.

Without time to waste, I moved up the hill, my legs burning with the extra weight of my suit.

The deafening sound of the fire followed me, but I knew there was no looking back. When I reached the peak of the hill, I sprinted across the open space, my eyes zeroed in on the break in the trees ahead. If I could get to an open field, I might stay far enough away from the fast approaching blaze.

But I didn't make it, the sound of a deafening crack sounding over-head, the ground shaking beneath me. Suddenly, I was falling, the breath knocked out of my lungs as I hit the ground, stars dancing in my field of vision.

Blinking against the haze, I tried to roll, but I was pinned down, something heavy against my back.

"Fuck," I grunted, trying to move, but it was impossible with the weight of whatever part of the tree had fallen on me.

As the seconds ticked by, the roar of the fire grew louder, sparks dancing on the breeze in my limited field of vision. Not knowing how close it was to me, I flexed my hands, testing my range of motion to see if I'd broken anything in my arms when I fell. With shaky fingers, I pulled off my helmet, and my eyes widened when I saw the dark red marks on the inside padding.

My adrenaline was pumping too hard for the pain to register, but my glove came back with streaks of blood when I ran it across my forehead. But I couldn't focus on where I was injured, because the heat coming from behind me was a more pressing issue than some cuts or broken bones.

Reaching down to grab where I'd dropped my back up fire blanket and neck protector, I cautiously yanked the protector over my head, securing it as well as I could before I awkwardly pulled the blanket over my shoulders without letting the wind drag it out of my hands.

I pulled it in tight, tucking my face to the ground and trying to take shallow breaths as the noise got louder, the heat of the fire licking up my covered legs.

Flashes of my life started running through my mind as the roaring blaze crossed over me. My family. The somber look on my mother's face when I told her I was leaving Sage Springs all those years ago to jump out of planes for a living. My brothers and memories of growing up trying so hard to be the role model I always felt compelled to be for them.

Spotty flashes of all the women I'd been with over the years were a blur, and I realized I hadn't been in love with any of them. And I yearned to find someone who would finally see who I was and what I was passionate about. That despite my rough edges and scars, I just wanted someone to love and return it without conditions or hesitation.

As the pain registered across my back, the intense heat licking up my spine and making me scream into the fabric beneath my mouth, I clenched my eyes tight and let the darkness take me, hoping that this wasn't the *last moment I'd spend alive, because I had so much more I wanted to experience.*

Chapter
Twenty-Six

Annie

M Y EYES FLUTTERED OPEN, and I blinked in the dim morning light, trying to process my surroundings to figure out why I'd awoken before the sun was fully up. Tripp's body trembled beside me as a pained, muffled groan welled from his chest. His fingers flexed against my side and my eyes widened, worry filling my chest.

Turning to face him, I traced my finger down the scar that ran along his hairline. His face was burrowed into the pillow beneath his head, but it didn't stop me from studying both the beauty and pain so clearly there.

"Tripp," I whispered, combing my fingers through his hair. "What's wrong, baby?"

His breathing was choppy as he lay with his eyes clenched tightly, another groan echoing into the dim morning as his back arched.

"No..." he whimpered, and I burrowed closer, trying to turn his head to the side. He was clearly dreaming and judging by the pinched expression and the sounds coming from his lips, it was not a pleasant one.

"You're okay," I whispered, finally getting him to relinquish his grip on the pillow so I could turn his face.

"No, no, no..." he groaned, curling in on himself.

Climbing to my knees, I leaned over him, framing his face. "Tripp, wake up. You're okay, you're safe. Just breathe."

Tripp's eyes opened, but they held the vacant stare he'd had right before I kissed him in the barn again. They weren't the warm deep blue I was used to, and it startled me how cold his expression was before he blinked hard, turning his face away from me.

"Tripp, please," I begged, watching his body tremble. Relying on the techniques I knew could pull him from the flashbacks, I slipped my leg over his waist, gently rolled him to his back and covered his body with mine like a weighted blanket. I stroked his hair and whispered in his ear, tears leaking out the corners of my eyes as he shook beneath me.

Eventually, his body relaxed, a large, calloused hand settling on my lower back with his lips grazing my forehead.

"Thank you." His voice was raspy, but I could tell from the tone that he appreciated I didn't let the moments he slipped into those memories scare me away. If anything, they made me want to cling to him tighter. And acknowledge that at one moment in time, he might have been taken away before I ever met him.

This kind, genuine, sarcastic, gentle man would have ceased to exist, and I would have been waiting for someone to finally *see* me that was already gone. And the feelings that had been building inside me for days, and continued to flourish, would have been taken away before I got to experience them. All because of a selfless act that saved someone else's life.

As we clung to each other, I wasn't even sure I deserved him, but I was going to try to be what he needed, even when it was heartbreaking.

"Are you okay?" I whispered into the skin of his shoulder, refusing to relinquish my hold on him.

His fingertips traced down my spine, lingering in the dip of my lower back before he fanned them and grasped my butt, pulling me even tighter against him.

"I am now. Thank you for staying."

Nodding against his chest, I tried not to get emotional, but I'd never experienced this soul-deep connection to someone where I just wanted to be with them all the time. I knew people would try to write it off as infatuation, that I hadn't known him long enough to develop real, true feelings. But I would tell those same people to take a fucking hike, because sometimes....*sometimes* you just knew when you found the other half of yourself, and there wasn't any explaining it.

"I don't want to be anywhere else." At his satisfied hum in response, my body melted into his chest, ear pressed tightly to the warm skin, just listening to his heart's steady thrum.

"Can we just not leave the bed today?" he whispered, continuing to trace patterns on my back with his fingertips.

"We can do whatever you want to do today," I replied, content to remain how we were, cuddled in our warm cocoon inside his quiet cabin. "But if you still want to go to the barbecue, you know I'll be there holding your hand the entire time."

He was quiet for a few moments, and I almost wondered if he was falling asleep again before his deep voice broke through my thoughts.

"I didn't know it'd happen so soon, and I didn't know it'd be you, but I prayed for you before I blacked out." His whispered confession brought goosebumps to my skin, and I shivered as he pulled me in tighter.

"Hmm?"

He pressed a fingertip to my chin, urging me to tilt my head up to look into his eyes.

"In those last few moments before the fire reached me, I prayed I would find someone like you. Someone who would care about me, even the ugly parts."

Unable to hold back the tears, I nodded, drawing in a shaky breath. While I hadn't been close to fulfilling the family curse until a few days ago, I'd been secretly yearning for the same thing, but also hiding from it.

I didn't want to hide anymore.

"Tripp, I..." My lip quivered and I couldn't respond, too overwhelmed by the unfamiliar emotions flowing through me for him.

The morning I went to that festival and encountered this grumpy, brooding firefighter who had zero interest in small talk, I hadn't realized I was meeting the man I was going to fall hard for a few days later.

"Maybe coming back home wasn't running away. Maybe it *was* coming home. To you."

He arched his neck, warm lips caressing mine while his muscular arms tightened around my body. He held me close—like I might be as much of a lifeline for him as he'd been for me.

"I need you," he whispered against my lips, reaching down to grasp my waist as his hips pressed up into me. "Please. I just—"

Placing a fingertip on his lips, I shifted my hips until he was poised at my entrance. "You don't need to beg. You know I'm yours."

That might be as close as we'd get to a confession of love this morning, but as I took him inside my body and rocked against him, chasing something I'd never been able to find before, I knew that we both felt it.

Sweet and passionate seemed to melt away as he held me tighter and shifted to sit upright against the headboard. His large hands grasped my hips, and I gasped as he thrust up from the mattress hard. It coaxed me into a fast pace that had me breaking the once quiet atmosphere with my loud cries.

I couldn't control how he made me feel—wild like the fire we'd both escaped, but beautiful and in control in a way that no one ever had.

"That's it," he groaned, throwing his head back against the headboard as I rotated my hips and met every thrust, my fingernails raking down the taut muscles of his chest. "You fucking own me, Rhey. Mark me."

Digging in deeper, I watched the marks blossom on his pale skin, trailing down to where we were connected. He watched me with hooded eyes, his grip possessive as he steered me closer and closer to the edge.

"I wanna feel you, sweetheart," he panted, his chest heaving. "Just keep lovin' on me until you come."

I wanted to laugh at the way his voice dropped into a southern accent when he said *lovin' on me,* but I was already there, falling apart as he held me, calling out his name like a prayer and he was the only one who could save me.

"Fuck," he groaned, his grip almost painful as he held me still moments later, pulsing deep inside as he filled me with his release.

I collapsed against his chest, trying to catch my breath while he held me to him, combing his fingers through my chaotic hair. My fingertips traced the marks I'd left on his skin, smiling at the drowsy hum coming from his chest as I did.

"Now that you've gotten me sufficiently dirty, you ready to get cleaned up?" he teased, and I laughed, leaning back to look him in the eye.

"Pretty sure you're the one who made the mess." Lifting off him, we both watched the evidence of that mess leak onto his lap with matching smiles.

And when I glanced up and met his eyes, I smiled even wider at the naughty tilt of his eyebrow when he dipped a finger through it and extended it in my direction. "And I intend to make a few more messes before we go to sleep tonight if you keep looking at me like that, Ms. Thomas."

"Challenge accepted," I goaded, pulling his finger to my mouth and sucking suggestively before I climbed off him, rolling to the side of the bed. My giggles carried behind me at his deep, masculine groan that followed on my way toward the bathroom. "You coming to get clean with me, dirty boy?"

"THERE'S STILL TIME FOR me to turn around," Tripp murmured, his fingers flexing on my bare knee. While I'd always have a fondness for the blue dress he'd destroyed the night we went dancing, I was taking full advantage of the seasonably warm weather and had worn another new sundress. And yet again, the man had stolen my panties. But I wasn't about to kink shame, because truth be told...I loved it.

I'd gotten so accustomed to my ritual of wearing band tees and ripped jeans at the bar, I wasn't used to embracing my femininity like when I was with him. But when we'd gone to the general store the other day, Tripp's enthusiasm every time I added a new dress to the shopping pile had me buying several dresses I never would have looked twice at before.

"I told you earlier we could stay home if you weren't feeling up to it." And I meant it, if he didn't want to go socializing, I wouldn't make him.

"No," he sighed, blowing out a breath. "I know we need to go. My mom has been harassing me to come visit since the fire, but I didn't want to leave you alone. Just try not to mention exactly how close to the fire line we were, I've put her through enough close calls this year."

"You realize I'm an adult, right?" I teased, laying my hand over his and interlacing our fingers. "While my self-appointed babysitter is kind of a hunk, I don't actually need one."

He flashed me the side eye, and I laughed, loving how he could call me out with a single raised eyebrow.

"I survived fine all by myself until you came along."

"Not sure how," he laughed, blowing me a kiss. "You're a mess, sweetheart."

"For your information, I can hold my own with a bar full of drunks, I think I can handle some overeager family members."

"Don't say I didn't warn you."

Tripp had turned northeast after leaving the ranch, but I was still trying to figure out if I recognized where he was taking me. After a few miles, he turned off on a gravel road, following a long and winding path through the trees that opened to a large two-story house styled like a log cabin.

There was a cluster of cars parked in an open field off to the side of the house, but it was the familiar black motorcycle sitting near the house that had me side eyeing Tripp.

"This is your aunt and uncle's house?"

"Yeah. They moved out here about five or six years ago. Our family has owned this land for a long time, but they never wanted to sell it to developers. I've only been here a few times, but they kind of took over as the host of family gatherings during the summer since they have a pool and a huge fire pit."

He slipped out of the driver's seat, meeting me at my open door and offering me a hand down from the truck. I'd worn a pair of slip-on sneakers, so at least I didn't have to deal with heels outside, but it was nice that he was still trying to be a gentleman. Although I had a feeling that it was just who he was without trying.

Hand in hand, he led me around the side of the house; the music getting louder as we turned the corner, and the backyard came into view. There was a good-sized clearing behind the house that slowly blended into the surrounding forest.

"Annie?" Hazel's surprised voice carried from the edge of the pool, and my eyes widened when I saw Reid standing right behind her, his head tilted to the side as he stared at us. Hazel glanced over her shoulder at her much taller boyfriend and some kind of unspoken communication passed between them. He nodded and stepped away to head toward a makeshift bar set up on the back patio.

Hazel wrapped a towel around her waist, slid her feet into a pair of sandals on the pool deck and headed in my direction.

"I'm gonna need to steal your guest," she told Tripp as she hooked her arm in mine and steered me back toward where we'd just come from. "Reid is over by the bar if you want to get a drink, *Tripp*."

"Where are you taking me?" I asked as she walked around the side of the house and led me to the covered front porch.

"Annie, what are you doing here?" She didn't look mad, just curious. But there was a certain edge to her question that suddenly had me on alert.

"Tripp invited me. This is his aunt and uncle's place." Suddenly, puzzle pieces that hadn't seemed to fit before now started clicking into place.

"And this is Reid's *parents'* house," she said pointedly, knowing that it'd confirm my suspicions.

Oh, fuck. How did I not see it until now?

Maybe because I was blinded by a distractingly charming, brooding firefighter and hadn't stopped to think about how small Sage Springs really could be sometimes.

"Fuck."

Her eyes widened, and she slowly nodded her head. "Yeah, fuck. Kind of like I'm assuming you've been doing with *Tripp*, judging by the relaxed smiles on both of your faces and the interlocked hands I just witnessed."

"Why didn't you tell me he was Reid's cousin at the festival?" She'd been in the medical tent with us after I collapsed, you'd think this would have been something she would have told me.

Oh, by the way, the hot firefighter you've been flirting with all morning, who also carried you unconscious through a festival full of over half the town's residents, is the older brother of the guy you've been casually screwing for the last seven years.

"I didn't know. His family calls him Tristan. How was I supposed to know that Tripp and Tristan were the same person? I don't exactly keep tabs on the new recruits at the fire station. He hasn't been home much the last several years, and he barely left Jay's apartment while he was recovering from his accident," she replied, and I tried to scan my memories of the last several days for other clues.

You'd think I would have connected the dots that the reason he felt so familiar was because, until a few months ago, I'd been sleeping with his brother. Or that he was a firefighter who was injured and returned home to a community that, while it had almost ten thousand residents, wasn't that big since a good chunk of those were people who owned a rental home here.

"Oh, my God. What am I supposed to tell him?" Now that my brain had put together the pieces, there wasn't any shoving this kind of discovery back into a neat little box.

"Does he know you were seeing *you know who*?"

"Haz," I whined, suddenly wanting to flee. "Do you think I would freak out this much if he knew I was sleeping with *him*?"

"Okay, probably not. But he knows you weren't celibate, right?"

I nodded, but I could feel the anxiety building in my system.

Meeting Tripp—*Tristan*—had felt like it was meant to happen. Like we had both just been in a holding pattern in our lives until we found each other. When Hazel and I had talked in February while things had become complicated between her and Reid. I'd told her all about how Jayden was just a placeholder, and I knew I was the same for him. We weren't emotionally invested in each other like people in a genuine relationship were. Friends but not soul mates.

We'd both been on the same page, but now the page had turned.

"Just...wait here. I'm gonna go get Reid. Maybe he can give you some advice about how to handle this, because we both know this is too much for my chaotic brain to handle. I could barely handle sneaking around with my brother's best friend and the fictional persona he created to convince me to fall in love with him."

She disappeared into the house, and I stepped down onto the driveway, pacing back and forth while I waited. I had no idea what Reid would say to excuse himself from his cousin, but I hoped the several dozen family members in the backyard would distract him long enough so I could figure out the predicament I'd gotten myself into.

Tripp was right. I *was* a mess. And this mess was about to lose him.

Closing my eyes, I tipped my face up, letting the sun warm my cheeks as I tried to figure out how to keep him once he discovered exactly who I was.

He hadn't put the pieces together either. Which meant he was just as oblivious as I was, or Jayden hadn't told him about me. That wouldn't have upset me if this were anyone else, but now I felt like it was a vital piece of information that could have prevented this.

But the longer I paced, the more I realized I didn't want to prevent this.

I *didn't* regret our time together.

I *wouldn't* change the fact that I was falling for him.

And I *couldn't* imagine my future without him.

The screen door opened behind me, and I blew out a breath as a pair of hands grasped my waist, a face tucking into my neck. But instead of the scruff that'd left marks on me this morning, the skin was smooth, my heart stopping when I realized the person behind me wasn't the man I needed right now.

"I missed you, Annie," he hummed into my skin, and my eyes shot open, panic flowing through my veins when my eyes connected with those of the man coming around the side of the house. Tripp was a few feet away, a beer bottle halfway to his mouth, and a look of confusion painted across his handsome features.

Oh, shit.

Chapter
Twenty~Seven

Tristan

*W*HAT THE ACTUAL FUCK, was the only thought in my brain as I stared at Rhey in the middle of the gravel drive, my brother's hands possessively holding her waist while he whispered in her ear.

She looked downright panicked, and I suddenly felt like a gigantic fool.

How could I not have seen this coming? Of course, the woman who'd seemed like my perfect match had been fucking my brother for who knew how long. Because that was just how my fucking life worked.

I find someone who finally made me feel like I might have some purpose in my life, and she just gets ripped away. By my spoiled, emotionally stunted brother, who took nothing in his life seriously.

Taking a deep breath, I tilted the bottle in my hand toward the ground and poured out the beer I hadn't even had a chance to enjoy. Calmly walking toward the front porch, I placed the bottle on the railing and turned for my truck. I could catch up with my family later. Right now, I needed to leave before I exploded. The anger was right there, barely restrained beneath the surface, and I knew I'd say something I'd regret if I stayed here and had to watch him touch her.

Without looking in their direction, I made a beeline for the driver's side door, my hand pausing on the handle when she called out to me.

"Tripp?" Her broken voice had my fist clenching at my side. "You're just leaving?"

"Why are you calling him Tripp?" Jayden laughed, and I glanced up, watching her attempt to extract his hands from her waist. "And why do you give a shit if he leaves?"

"Because I—"

He didn't relinquish his grip on her, and I saw red, cutting her off. "Get your fucking hands off her. She doesn't want you to touch her."

Jay's eyes widened as he looked between the two of us, his eyes lingering. I knew he could sense the tension; my squared shoulders and clenched jaw, letting him know I meant every word. Then his eyes went to Rhey—*Annie*—with her arms wrapped around her chest like she was holding herself together. Her heartbroken look gutted me, as the realization came that my reaction was hurting her more than his.

"Why wouldn't she want me to...?" he trailed off with a frown, looking down at her. Her watery eyes met mine, and I shook my head, removing my hand from the door handle.

He reached for her shoulder, but I growled when she flinched.

"I told you not to fucking touch her."

He spun, marching toward me with a look I was very familiar with drawn across his smug face. "And why wouldn't she want me to touch her, *Tristan*? Last I checked, she was *my* friend, and a whole lot fucking more. Since when do you speak for her?"

"Jay, stop. We need to talk," she pleaded quietly. I hadn't even noticed her follow us to the far side of the truck.

Glancing toward the house, I saw Reid and Hazel just inside the front door, attempting to give us privacy. But I knew if Jay's voice got any louder, the rest of the family on the other side of the house likely wouldn't extend the same courtesy.

"No, Annie, I want him to fucking answer me. Why are you so concerned with me touching her? Cause I've done a lot more than just touch her waist or her shoulder, and she never had a problem with it before."

"Jay," she hissed, stepping in my direction, her eyes pleading. "Don't."

"It's none of your business why, but you need to take a fucking hint. When a woman removes her hands from you and says stop—you fucking listen."

His eyes narrowed as he stepped forward, his chest brushing against mine.

My knuckles cracked loudly when my fists tightened, trying to hold back, but I was still on edge from the flashback this morning and would happily punch my brother in the fucking face if he so much as breathed in her direction too heavily.

While neither of their names had actually been mentioned, I could connect the dots that she was the girl he'd been hooking up with. She may have been his months ago, but she wasn't anymore.

"Did you fuck my girlfriend while I was out of town?" he growled, grabbing a fistful of my shirt collar.

Glancing past his face, I locked eyes with Rhey, and almost fucking laid him out when I saw the tears streaked down her cheeks.

"Who I fuck is none of your business. And the same goes for her. You may have *been* involved with her, but you don't own her, and you better treat her with some god damned respect."

His face turned red, and I knew he was about to blow, but I wasn't about to let him disrespect her because he had his fucking feelings hurt. Or more likely his ego, because I still wasn't convinced he actually had feelings for her. He may have been throwing a tantrum right now, but he seemed more concerned with me touching something he perceived as his than how his behavior was affecting her.

Not that I was much better, because I was prepared to leave her here with him a few minutes ago. Maybe I *wasn't* any better than him.

"Maybe she likes it when I disrespect her," he hissed, and I growled in response, shoving hard against his chest until he stumbled back. Rhey quickly stepped to the side as his body moved backward, so he didn't knock her over.

"Maybe you need to fucking watch it before I kick your ass."

"Like you could, old man," he taunted, lunging in my direction, but Reid was suddenly there, catching him around the waist and hauling him backward.

"What the fuck is wrong with you, Jay?" he growled, dragging him toward the porch. "Can we not pick fights in the front fucking yard on a holiday? Do you know how much shit you'd be in right now if our mothers heard you talking about Annie like that?"

"But he..."

"But he, nothing, you fucking asshole." Reid dragged him up the steps, pinning me down with a look that would have been frightening had I not been as angry as I was right now. "Get your asses inside this house before someone hears you."

"I'm not going anywhere with him," Jay hissed, fighting against our cousin's hold. They may have been of similar build, but Reid was scary when he was mad.

"You don't have a fucking choice," Reid growled, pushing him inside when he got to the front door. "The two of you are going upstairs to talk before you turn this into a three-ring circus, and you're both going to calm the fuck down and work this out before I let you leave the guest bedroom."

Hazel stomped toward me, pushing past and knocking her shoulder against mine, as she headed toward Annie. She was crying beside the truck, and I instantly felt like shit as I watched her friend wrap her arms around her.

They disappeared out of sight just before I turned and followed Reid as he pushed my brother up the staircase, thankful the people in the backyard hadn't noticed Jay's dramatic hissy fit.

"Do I need to find one of those huge T-shirts our moms used to shove us into together as children until we could get along? Cause I'll stuff your asses into one if I have to." Reid marched my brother down the hallway with a tight hold on the back of his shirt and pulled open a door at the front of the house, hopefully out of earshot of the people in the backyard.

E.L. KOSLO

"Why am I the one being manhandled?" Jay whined, bracing one hand against the door frame and trying to shrug off Reid's tight grip. "I'm the innocent one here."

Growling, I fought the urge to use my foot to get him inside and pointed. I was about to lose my shit.

"Because you were raised better than this," Reid hissed, shoving my brother inside. "What you just did to Annie was disrespectful as fuck."

"But she—"

"She didn't know who I fucking was, dipshit." And since I honestly hadn't given a shit who warmed my brother's bed, I hadn't put the details together. Until now. "And I thought she was just a bartender you hired to run your booth at the festival. You never talked about her, how was I supposed to know what kind of arrangement you two used to have?"

"Used to?" He rounded on me as soon as I followed him through the doorway, shoving his palm into my shoulder.

"Yeah, used to, asshole. When was the last time you two were together?"

He paused, a line forming between his brows. "It's...been a few months. But that's your fault too, because you have been sucking all the oxygen out of my place for the last few months."

"Thanks, asshole," I muttered, pacing in front of the window. "Nice to know how much of an inconvenience I was to you while I was recovering from nearly dying."

Glancing out the pane of glass, I could barely make out where Rhey was still wrapped around Hazel with her head down behind a few of the cars. Fuck, I wasn't even sure what to feel right now.

"That's not..." he sighed, scrubbing his hands over his face roughly. "You know I was okay with you staying there, but I couldn't exactly invite her over to fuck with you there. I'm not a total asshole."

"You sure about that?" His mouth opened and then closed again as he swallowed down whatever answer he was about to shoot back at me. "Cause you're acting like one right now."

240

"Well," Reid interrupted from the doorway. "Now that you two are talking instead of yelling, I'm gonna leave you to it before people come looking for us. Try not to kill each other."

"No promises," I shot back, and our cousin shook his head, quietly pulling the door closed. This wasn't the first time he'd had to referee a blow up with one of my brothers. The Harding men were short-tempered and competitive, which didn't always make for the most level-headed conversations when one of us was riled up.

"I just don't understand how you two could do this to me?" he hissed, and I rolled my eyes. Always the fucking victim, and he knew it pushed all my buttons.

"Are you in love with her? Or just fucking her?" I growled, pinning my brother with a look that even had him shrinking back.

As the baby of the family, Jay had spent half his life getting what he wanted because he thought he deserved it. Well, fuck that shit. I wasn't giving this up without a fight. I wasn't giving *her* up without a fight.

She wasn't some toy he'd claimed first and refused to share. She'd never been his. Not really. Not in any way that mattered.

Not in the way I felt every time I saw her.

I'd been where he was. Feeling possession of a woman that I couldn't—or wouldn't—commit to. I'd had my fair share of friends with benefits over the years. You weren't unmarried and closing in on forty without having been in relationships, friendly, physical or otherwise.

But I'd also seen a few of those same women fall in love with someone who wasn't me. And I didn't act like a jealous little prick and selfishly hold on to someone when I couldn't give them what they needed.

And there was one thing I knew for sure. Annie deserved to be loved. And I was gonna be the undeserving fucker who gave it to her. Gave her the part of me I'd never truly given to someone else.

Sure, I thought I'd been in love once or twice. But not like this. Not to where I wanted to tear my fucking baby brother to shreds at the thought of him going anywhere near her.

"Oh, so you steal my girlfriend while I'm out of town and suddenly *I'm* the bad guy?" he scoffed.

"I didn't steal anything, you selfish little prick. She told me about this guy she'd been hooking up with who would never be more than a friend. Wasn't aware that made her your girlfriend."

He paused, tilting his head as he looked up. "She told you about me?"

"Well, yeah. Rhey—Annie—is really fucking loyal. She wanted me to know that there had been someone else before we took things too far. I thought she was your fucking employee, not your hookup. Although I guess with your track record, I'm not sure why I'm surprised."

"And what did she tell you about the guy she'd been with?" His tone wasn't accusatory, and it gave me hope that maybe he'd listen to reason.

"That she'd been in a situationship—whatever they're calling it these days—with a guy she'd known since high school, but she didn't have feelings for him beyond friendship."

He nodded, looking down. "And you didn't think to exchange names?"

"Why the fuck would I want to know the name of the guy whose hookup I was falling for?"

He nodded absently, staring at the ground for a beat before he returned his gaze to me. "You're falling for her?"

I shook my head and saw his fists instantly ball at his sides. "Not falling, dude, *fallen*. I'm already there. And if that means you hate me, then so be it, because I know you don't love her. You haven't loved anyone since—"

"Please don't say her name," he choked out, turning away from me and thrusting his fist toward the wall. I laughed humorlessly as he shook out his hand, cursing under his breath.

"And that's how I know you don't love Annie, because otherwise you wouldn't give a shit if I mentioned—"

He turned toward me, glaring as I held my hands up and clamped my mouth shut. But when the tension drained from his shoulders, I knew I'd made my point.

"Maybe you're right. But she's still my friend. She deserves someone who loves her. If you hurt her, I'll fucking kill you."

"Aw...it's cute you think you could do any damage with those fake pretty boy muscles you like to post all over the internet," I chuckled, knowing it'd rile him up.

"Didn't stop your girlfriend from holding onto those muscles while she rode my..."

He trailed off laughing when I growled and lunged at him, wrapping my forearm across his throat with my lips at his ear. "Say another word, fucker. I dare you."

"Word," he choked out, laughing as he ducked out of my hold. He turned to face me and nodded at the window. I followed his gaze and saw the flash of the taillights of a Jeep headed down the gravel drive away from the house. I wasn't sure whose car that was, but I knew Rhey was inside it right now. "Well, don't just stand there, dumbass. Go after her. If you love her, go fucking tell her."

Without hesitating, I pulled the truck keys from my pocket and headed for the door, my brother's amused voice following me into the hallway.

"And I'm the one who's a dipshit..."

Chapter
Twenty-Eight

Annie

"**Y**OU SURE YOU DON'T want me to take you back to the ranch?" Hazel asked, turning her Jeep onto the main road and heading toward town. "It's on the way, if you need to get something. You know Hudson would understand if you don't feel up to running the bar tonight. Tripp will probably come to look for—"

"No." My voice was curt as I cut her off. Shaking my head, I watched the trees pass while I stared blankly out the window. "I've already started over from nothing once this week, what difference is twice going to make?"

"You're not starting over, Annie. I'm sure once they talk, and things calm down a bit, he'll want to see you." She may have been certain, but I wasn't so convinced. "You don't look at a woman like that and just walk away from her."

Biting the inside of my lip, I fought back my remaining tears, determined to not show up at the bar a sobbing mess. People were already going to feel sorry for me when they found out about my cabin, I didn't need to add in the fact that I got dumped by both Harding brothers on the same day. Not that whatever Jay and I had been doing for years was more than a friendship with perks. The rift I'd created was going to cause ripples across town that I'd never live down.

It was the situation with Tripp that was going to crush me if I let it. And I wouldn't let it. I'd survived heartbreak before, and I'd survive it again. Even if that brooding bastard had taken a huge chunk of me into that house earlier, and I was terrified I'd never get back.

His scars were on the surface—visible to everyone, but mine were a dark secret I pushed deep inside and never let anyone else see.

"You know you're welcome to stay in the apartment for as long as you need, but don't use it as an excuse to run from something good. You'll regret it if you do. Running away from your problems never works, trust me, I've done it enough to have expert level avoidance certification."

"There's nothing left to run from, Haz," I murmured, suddenly wishing I was going into the bar with my usual armor of jeans and a T-shirt. The dress that had felt liberating to wear a few hours ago left me feeling exposed.

"And here I thought they handed out PhDs in wisdom when they gave you permission to serve alcohol, but apparently all they handed you was the inability to see what's right in front of your face."

Biting my tongue, I returned to looking out the window on the quick trip to the bar, closing my eyes and trying to center myself when I saw the parking lot full of cars. It was time for me to turn on the charm and forget there was a gaping hole in my chest.

Once she parked, I opened the door to leave, but she placed her hand on my shoulder. "If you need me, call from the bar phone and I'll come back to get you."

Unable to look at her for fear I'd burst into tears again, I nodded, closing the door without a word.

The back hallway was quiet when I let myself in the door to the kitchen, the familiar smell of fried food making my stomach turn instead of comforting me like it usually did. While I didn't always love being here, this place was like home to me. It was the one thing that had been constant in my adult life, and while I couldn't control the people who patronized it, I could control my workspace.

Hudson was in the office at his desk when I passed by the door. I'd hoped to go unnoticed, but he called my name when I tried to slip past him.

"Annie? I thought you had something else going on this afternoon?" he asked, glancing up at me from the stack of papers on his desk with a frown. It may have been a holiday, but there was always paperwork to do when you were the boss. "I may have to be here, but you don't."

"Plans changed, so I thought I'd take you up on your offer for some hours."

He tilted his head to the side, eyes scanning my face in a way that made me feel exposed. Hudson Rivera may have been oblivious to social cues sometimes, but he wasn't an idiot.

"You sure you're feeling up to it? I just offered because I didn't know what your plans were. Thought having a distraction might keep your mind off things."

I knew he was talking about the fire, and that my sister and I had probably lost everything, but I needed the bar to keep my mind away from how my social life had spectacularly exploded. With Jay being swamped with the restaurant expansion at the distillery and Tripp admitting he rarely came in here, I was hoping I could just ignore them until they forgot I existed.

If only it was that easy to erase the time I'd spent with both. Jay had been a distraction from my loneliness for years, and Tripp had felt like the beginning of something real. A person I could let down my walls with and connect to on a deeper level.

He may have been understanding when he found out I hadn't exactly been celibate before we met, but I had a feeling his attitude might have been a little different if he knew the man I'd been involved with was his brother.

There was an underlying tension between the two of them I hadn't expected. Tripp seemed more concerned with how his brother had treated me earlier—although I'd deserved it. I *should* have ended things with Jay before I let my feelings for Tripp develop as much as they had, and maybe if we'd done a little more talking and a little less flirting, we'd have discovered this connection before things blew up like they had.

He'd been prepared to just get in his truck and drive away. To leave without a word and not give me a chance to speak with him. If Jay hadn't acted like a jackass, he would have. But I wouldn't give him the chance to break my heart.

Hazel had been reluctant to leave, trying to get me to wait until they came back outside, but I could read the room. Neither of them wanted me there.

"Annie? You okay?" Hudson asked, closing his laptop and pushing back from his chair.

With my chin quivering, I nodded, knowing my friend would see right through me if I opened my mouth right now.

He stepped in front of me, tipping my chin up with a finger, and I couldn't stop the tear that escaped. Hudson had known me since I was a melancholy, gangly preteen, and while he could be a bit of a grump, he'd been a loyal friend for half my life. While a hint of his last name might be on the *River Run Tavern* sign out front, we'd turned this place into what it was today together.

"There's no shame in taking a break," he whispered, wrapping his arm around my shoulder and tucking my head into his chest. "You've had enough thrown at you in the last week, don't pile on more because you feel guilty for taking some time off."

"I'm okay," I replied, but my voice cracked, so he pulled me in tighter, kissing the top of my head. Being with Charley over the last several months had softened him, and I appreciated the hug more than he knew.

I drew in a shaky breath and tried to push the look on Tripp's face earlier when he'd rounded the corner of the house from my mind, because he wasn't my concern right now. Not anymore.

"We both know you're lying, but I'll let it go for now. Food service has been slow, but the bar could probably use a restock. Apparently, since fireworks have been banned, that means you have to sneak off and use copious amounts of alcohol to escape your family members and not explosives," he joked, but he wasn't exactly wrong. I just didn't have any family members left to escape, and I rarely drank, so I used avoidance as my method of distraction from my problems.

"Well, since I know your best friend and your sister are at his parents' house, I guess I don't need to knock before I go into the storage room," I muttered, and my forehead bounced against his chest when he let out a chuckle. There had been an incident in there right before Hazel moved out with the two of them doing something at least partially unclothed. I didn't ask many questions, but Reid had insisted he was just trying to correct bad memories.

"Thank fuck they moved into his apartment together," he grumbled, and I couldn't hold back the giggle. "People need to quit doing kinky shit in my bar."

He hadn't been as resistant to his formerly slutty best friend shacking up with his baby sister as we'd all expected. Sometimes when people just made sense together, it was easier to put away the hurt feelings.

If only that applied to my situation. I knew technically I'd done nothing wrong since I wasn't in an exclusive situationship when I met Tripp, but the timing of finding out who Jay was to him was kind of a clusterfuck. Although I couldn't change how hard I'd fallen for Tripp, or Tristan, or whoever he was to everyone else.

To me, he'd had the potential to be everything.

Only relying on the universe dealing me with a fair hand hadn't exactly worked out in the past. Going through adolescence with a traumatized younger sister and a grandmother struggling to balance two kids who'd lost their parents while dealing with the grief of losing her son had been hard. Maybe that was why I'd leaned on Jay so much.

He'd been there through the hard parts, and when he wasn't acting like a jealous asshole, he was a good friend. A friend that I could probably now add to the tally of people I'd lost. But I was the one dead to him, not the other way around.

"I've got some things to finish up in here while Charley's spending the afternoon with her dad at the ranch, so if you'll get the bar back in order while I do that, the new bartender can stay on service for the night shift until they need you. It's been steady today, but not swamped."

"Sounds good," I said, reluctantly stepping out of his hold. "Let's hope you didn't fuck up my organizational system too much while I was gone."

"Don't worry, your job is secure," he chuckled, stepping back into the office. "I wouldn't know what to do with this place without you. It's bad enough Hazel abandoned us to go draw naughty pictures, if you left, I'd be screwed."

At least one man in my life couldn't live without me—even if it wasn't the one I wanted.

Leaving Hudson in the office to finish his paperwork, I made my way to the front, absently scanning the tables for familiar faces, pausing when I recognized the man sitting in the corner booth. Baker nodded when he saw me standing there, but quickly returned his attention to the papers on the table. I wondered what the story was behind him being here alone and not at his apartment or his parents' house for the holiday, but I was sure my sister had a part in him coming here.

While some of our regulars had taken up residence on the stools at the bar, there weren't many other faces I could pick out of the crowd, which was a relief.

"There's our favorite firecracker," one of them joked, tipping his glass in my direction, but they were busy watching a baseball game on the television screen mounted on the wall above the bar.

"Nah, Haz is the firecracker nowadays since she took up with that bad boy next door. This one is more like a sparkler—flashy and mesmerizing, but she won't do too much damage. Now that Charley... she's like a mortar. Don't treat her with caution and she'll blow you to smithereens," another chimed in.

"Now gentlemen, I know you were taught better than to compare women to inanimate objects," I teased, but they didn't seem fazed, returning to arguing over which team was hitting better in the game they were watching.

"Hey, Ann," the newest bartender on our roster, Noah, greeted as I stepped behind the bar. "I didn't know you were on tonight."

"Technically, unless you need me, I'm not here. But I'll work on getting stuff restocked back here while you do your thing. I'm not here to cramp your style. But if you need me or want to take a break, I can step in."

He nodded, moving to the opposite end of the bar, where he turned on the charm and greeted a group of young women with a dimpled smile.

"You have a hot date tonight?" A deep voice asked, and I blinked as I looked up, straight into Baker's amused hazel-hued eyes.

"Um, no. Not exactly. No dates for me. Not anymore."

He swiveled his bar stool side to side as he rested his elbows on the bar top, fingers steepled under his chin.

"Well, you can't just drop that kind of comment and expect me not to be curious. What did cowboy do?"

He hadn't done anything other than rescue the wrong woman.

"What makes you think it's his fault?"

"Isn't it always the guy's fault?" he laughed, but there was an edge to it. I'd never outright asked what went on all those years ago between him and my sister, but since she held a grudge like no one else, I had a feeling he'd done something she deemed unforgiveable.

His older sister Addi and I had been in the same friend group in high school, but we'd lost touch once she left for college a year before me, and I'd never reached out to see if she knew anything.

"Not always," I sighed, picking up a cloth and wiping at a nonexistent spot on the counter. "Some women are capable of screwing things up all on their own by making reckless decisions."

"You've always seemed pretty cautious, kind of like the other Thomas sister I know. I have a hard time believing you're all that reckless."

That might have been true a week ago, but all the decisions I'd made since the festival had been wildly out of character. Still, I was

251

having a hard time regretting most of them. It felt good to do what I wanted for once.

"You'd be surprised..." I trailed off.

"Dude was down bad at the festival for you. He couldn't keep his eyes off you. I even warned him how much trouble you and your sister were, but he couldn't help himself. We all saw how he looked at you the other night too and you can't fake that kind of chemistry. He's an idiot if he walks away now."

My cheeks flushed at Baker's comments and as I recalled Tripp's intensely focused gaze as he'd moved through the festival crowd on his way to help me. Right before the first time I embarrassed myself by passing out.

"I think my sister is right, you are delusional," I replied, but he just laughed in response.

"Your sister *is* always right, but I'm not that delusional. Just you wait and see."

Leaning back, I scanned the spare bottles underneath the counter, making an inventory in my head of what needed replenishment. "Since you're here, why don't you put those muscles to good use and help me carry crates out from the storage room."

"And why should I do that?" he asked, quirking one eyebrow.

"Because I know all my sister's secrets and if you want to get in her good graces, I might be able to help."

"Don't know all her secrets," he muttered, spinning backward and hopping off the stool. He held out his arm, gesturing toward the hallway that led to the storage rooms. "Grace before beauty."

"Did you just call yourself beautiful?" I laughed, shaking my head. He was just as ridiculous as I remembered, but maybe having him as a distraction for a little while would keep my mind off things I didn't want to think about.

"I know my assets," he responded with a grin, following me down the hallway.

Baker was a dutiful assistant, holding crates while I pulled bottles down and recorded what stock was left on the clipboard Hudson used for inventory.

He didn't harass me about Tripp anymore, deciding to tell funny stories from the fire station to fill the silence, careful to avoid mentioning the handsome cowboy firefighter who was the elephant in the room.

"Annie, are you back here?" Hudson's voice carried down the hallway and I put the bottle I'd just pulled down in the crate on Baker's lap.

Poking my head out the doorway, I frowned as I saw Charley dressed in barn clothes dotted with straw following Hudson down the hallway. "Hey, what's up? Does Noah need me out front?"

"Someone needs you out front," Charley said, a mischievous grin tugging at her lips.

"We're in the middle of something right now," I replied, gesturing to the imposing firefighter—holding a crate full of liquor—who'd followed me into the hallway.

"Hi, Baker," Charley greeted, and he winked at her in return. Hudson narrowed his eyes at the younger man, but let it go.

"Annie, you need to go out front. Because they can't stay out there all night, and they're asking for you."

"Who is asking for me?"

"Just, don't worry about it." Walking past Hudson, Charley grabbed my arm and towed me down the hallway. Curious stares followed us toward the front doors of the bar, and I frowned as I saw several people abruptly sitting who had been looking at something outside through the windows along the front of the building.

Pausing at the front door, I pulled Charley to a stop. "Seriously, who's out there? I have no desire to be fodder for the gossip train this week."

"Too late for that now," she replied, pushing open the door and grabbing a hold of my wrist to tug me into the parking lot.

While I'd been expecting one of two men to be out there, waiting to yell at me for being an idiot, that wasn't exactly all that was waiting for me in the parking lot.

Chapter
Twenty-Nine

Tristan

H URRYING DOWN THE WOODEN steps, I rounded the corner for the front door, my chest slamming into my cousin's shoulder.

"Dude, where's the fire?" he chuckled, grasping me by the shoulders.

Footsteps thundered down the stairs behind me, and I braced for the impact, but Jay skirted around us, flinging the front door open.

"Fuck, did she leave?" he asked, looking back at our cousin expectantly.

Reid glanced between the two of us, a hesitant smile pulling at his lips. "You two gonna play nice now?"

"Where did Annie go?" he asked again, practically bouncing in place. If I wasn't still irritated by the way he'd talked to and about her earlier, I might have found it comical. The dude was almost as hyper as his golden retriever, Jameson, sometimes.

"Didn't answer my question, Jay," Reid drawled, and I shook my head, pulling out my phone before I remembered she still didn't have a replacement phone. A frown formed as I tried to think about where she would go.

"Yeah, yeah. He screwed my—" his voice cut off abruptly at the dark look I aimed in his direction. She might not be mine, but she sure as hell wasn't his.

"If he stops talking about women like property, we're good."

"I'm sorry. We're good," he replied, gesturing toward me impatiently. "You gonna just stand there, asshat, or are you going to go after her?"

Reid crossed his arms and narrowed his eyes at me. "I take it you're planning to go find your girl?"

"I..."

Would she even want me to? I suddenly wasn't convinced. Maybe I'd just been romanticizing our time together. Now that we'd come out of our forced proximity and the adrenaline had worn off, maybe being involved with me would be too much. I couldn't control who I was related to, but I could see how this situation would feel impossible for her. She just didn't stick around long enough for me to tell her I didn't care that she'd been involved with him.

"Hazel isn't exactly happy with either of your behavior," he said, eyes still narrowed.

"Where did your girlfriend take her?" Jay asked, crossing his arms and staring right back at Reid.

"Not sure I should tell either of you, because that girl has been through enough and doesn't need more of your competitive bullshit."

"Did Hazel take your balls with her?" Jay asked, stepping forward.

I tried not to laugh at the way our cousin raised an eyebrow. Jay had apparently decided to poke yet another bear today.

"What is your fucking problem?" Reid asked, stepping forward and placing the back of his hand on Jay's forehead. "Nope, no fever. So why exactly are you coming for everyone's throat today? And you better not make some joke about needing to get laid, cause I won't hold Tristan back this time if you do."

"I'm just..." he sighed, deflating a little. "I need something to distract me right now, and since I thought I'd be able to come home and blow off some—"

"Nope," I cut him off, shaking my head. "Not going down that path again."

"Fine. You want to know what's wrong? I just had to literally get down on my knees and beg the woman I thought I was going to marry someday to come work with me, and she laughed in my face. *Again*. She laughed in my face again for the second time in as many months."

My eyes widened, and I met Reid's gaze. There was only one woman he'd ever been in a serious relationship with. While I knew she was a chef, I also never thought Jay would ever talk to her—or about her—again after his meltdown when he heard she'd gotten married abroad six years ago.

"So, she said no?" I asked, unsure how the topic swung so wildly away from what'd happened with Rhey earlier, but also kind of invested in the answer to this question. If he wasn't fixated on his former friend with benefits, then maybe he'd be okay with her being something more than that to me.

He shook his head, pacing by the front door. "No. She said yes, after she stopped laughing at me. But then she started again right after she let her feral kid shoot me in the face with a water gun."

"And she's moving here to help you open the restaurant?" Reid asked cautiously.

"That's the plan. There was a unit available in my building, so I put down the security deposit yesterday when I got back to town." Jay sounded like he was annoyed, but he almost seemed strangely excited by the fact his ex was going to be living close by.

"Mack is going to live in the same building as you—with a kid? Are you going to be able to handle that?" I asked, knowing part of the reason he acted like he did was because of her. And that while he'd been devastated by her abrupt departure to a study abroad program shortly after he'd confessed he wanted to drop out of culinary school, it was her getting married to one of her instructors and having a baby right away that'd really done him in.

"Yeah, she's in a two bedroom with Hardy. He starts kindergarten in the fall. So, she's moving in soon."

"I thought you weren't breaking ground until next spring?" Reid asked. He'd been helping Jayden out at the distillery when he needed it. Now that I was healed, he promised to get me up to speed on how much his operation had expanded, but it sounded like he was going to have his hands full.

"I'm not. But she wants to be involved when my architect buddy comes in to draft the construction plans. Apparently, she doesn't trust me to know how to put together a commercial kitchen properly."

Reid laughed at Jay's irritation, but I could see where Mack was coming from. When Jay was younger, he had the tendency to follow the thrill, and when culinary school had turned into more work than he thought it'd be, he dropped out. While I could admit he'd matured since then and seemed to be dedicated to perfecting his craft at the distillery, he still didn't have enough experience in a commercial kitchen to know what a professional chef needed.

"Enough talking about how I'm going to regret my decision to bring her on, why are we just standing around?" Jay asked, gesturing toward the front door again.

"I don't even know where she went." Looking at Reid, he shrugged his shoulders, but I had a feeling one call to Hazel, and he'd know exactly where his girlfriend had taken Rhey.

"Do you even know what you're going to say to her?" he asked.

"I'm gonna ask her to not hold the family I was born into against me and remind her I knew she was with someone before me." Jay shook his head, but I had a feeling he knew he'd fucked the way he'd initially handled this up spectacularly. For someone who claimed to be her friend, he hadn't treated her with much respect. "And that I don't give a fuck if my brother saw her first."

"Saw her naked," Jay muttered under his breath, but he had the decency to look embarrassed when I stared him down.

I should have listened to Rhey earlier instead of walking away. But the sight of my brother with his hands all over her had been enough to send me into fight-or-flight mode—only she beat me to the flight part.

Jay cleared his throat. "I know we talked it out upstairs, but please be careful with her. She's lost a lot in her life, and there are scars buried deep that she hides from everyone. I think that's part of why she stayed with me so long, she knew I was safe because I didn't expect love to be a part of our relationship."

Pausing, I gripped the back of my neck, and the lingering nerve pain surfaced as my skin stretched. It was background noise to my thoughts. I hadn't been lying to him, I'd already fallen hard for this woman, and if she wasn't capable of the same...

"If she doesn't want—"

"Fuck," my brother cursed, shaking his head. "Just keep fucking today up, don't I? Tris, I wasn't implying that she couldn't love you, I just want to make sure she isn't just someone to pass time for you. She looked devastated when she thought you were going to leave, so if you don't feel the same..."

"I do." I didn't even have to think about it. She wasn't someone I could walk away from now, and maybe never.

We'd clearly bonded during some stressful situations, and there were still so many things I wanted to learn about her... But I felt like I could finally breathe around her, though. And that wasn't something I could just move on from without even trying. "She's..." *the love of my life.*

"Then let's go," he said with a smile, but the sliding glass door to the back patio opened, and our moms walked through before I could follow him out the front.

"And where do you think you're going without giving me a hug, Tristan?" my mom, Clara, teased, holding her arms open.

When I looked toward my brother on the front porch and back to her waiting, she lifted an eyebrow, and I knew I wasn't getting out of this house without a distraction.

Shaking my head, I resisted the urge to punch my smirking cousin in the arm on the way past and wrapped my arms around the woman who'd raised me. She laid her head on my chest, squeezing tight, but keeping her arms around my waist and away from my scars.

"Someone told me you brought a date," she said once she released me.

"About that…" I trailed off, but she crossed her arms, giving me a look I was very familiar with.

"Well, where is she?"

Glancing over my shoulder, I could barely see my brother ducked down near the rear passenger side of my truck, clearly trying to avoid being seen by our mother. Chicken shit.

"Is she out front? We're really not that scary, Tris," she laughed, moving to skirt around me on a mission to ambush my supposed date. "Why is your brother trying to hide behind your truck?"

"I'm staying out of this," Reid laughed, hooking his arm with his mom's and leading her out the back door. "Let's go find you a fresh drink, mama."

When I returned my gaze to the front door, my mom was marching across the front yard, my brother trying to escape behind another car.

"Jayden Lucas, what did you do now?" she yelled, hands braced on her waist as she paused a short distance away from him. Jay was notorious for trying to hide from people when he'd done something, so she knew the signs when he was up to no good, even as a grown adult.

"Why do you people always assume I did something?" he hollered back, and I laughed loudly, heading for the driver's side of the truck. While I would love to watch her give him shit, I had a woman to convince that my feelings for her hadn't changed.

"Because you're an idiot," our mom yelled back, her gaze focused on him.

Letting him provide a diversion, I pulled open the driver's side door and started the truck, keeping my gaze focused on my mirrors while I turned around. My mom had stepped off the front porch, eyes lasered in on my ridiculous brother, and I considered his distraction a small token toward repairing the damage his behavior had done earlier.

Now, I had a girl to get.

O NLY AFTER I PULLED the truck up to the cabin did I realize a significant flaw in the plan to find Rhey. I didn't know where the fuck she was—and she still didn't have a cell phone.

I already knew she wasn't inside before opening the door, but her presence lingered in the air. My eyes found her ruined dress hung over the lip of the kitchen trash can, the hairbrush she'd used this morning still lying on my nightstand, and her dirty work boots sitting on the tray by the front door which meant she hadn't stopped here first to claim her things. But I couldn't just sit here and wait for her to return.

Sitting down on my bed, I pulled up a text message with Reid, hoping he'd tell me where Hazel took her.

Tristan: She's not at the ranch.

Reid: I know.

Tristan: Can you ask Hazel where she took her?

Reid: You gonna use the information wisely?

Tristan: Jay is a dick and you're holding it against me?

Reid: You were about to get in that truck and leave her there.

Tristan: I didn't want to take my anger at my brother out on her.

Reid: You don't run away when you love someone.

Tristan: Since when are you a love guru?

261

Reid: *Since a woman chased me down for leaving before we had the hard conversations.*

Tristan: *I know I helped screw this up, but I've never felt this way about a woman before. Please tell me where to find her.*

Reid: *Answer the door, the cavalry is on the way.*

Frowning at my phone, I tried to figure out what the hell that meant, until someone started pounding on the front door.

"Tripp, get your ass out here!"

Charley West was standing on my front porch, her hot pink tipped blonde pigtails riddled with pieces of straw.

"Finally," she sighed, grabbing my arm and towing me onto the porch. "Let's get moving. Hazel called and told me what happened. Time for damage control."

"What?" I laughed, following along as she towed me toward the barn.

Seraphina was saddled up and waiting on the walkway outside the barn, the horse nickering softly when she saw me.

"Why is Phi saddled? She's supposed to be resting," I asked, running my hand down her mane.

"Because she needs to help with your grand gesture," Charley replied, rolling her eyes.

"Grand gesture?"

She sighed, nudging me out of the way with her hip. "Annie is fully prepared to hide until she thinks this has blown over. She asked Hazel if she could stay at the apartment and implied that she'd already started over once this week and would do it again if she had to."

"Fuck." Maybe my hope that she'd come back to the ranch wouldn't pan out.

"Yeah, *Tripp*, fuck. You kinda fucked this up if she doesn't know how you feel about her. And don't even get me started on your idiot brother."

Turning toward her, I frowned. If she'd known who I was… "Why didn't you tell her who I was if you knew?"

"Because not everything is about you, Tristan," she shot back with a dramatic eye roll. "I didn't know who you were until this morning. When my dad only referred to you as Tripp, I didn't stop to connect the dots that you were Reid's cousin. And I was kind of busy helping my dad get his ranch—*my childhood home*—ready for a fire to potentially burn everything to the ground."

"Noted," I replied, backing down. "I only thought she was someone who worked with him at the distillery. He never told me about her specifically. I knew he had a long-time friend who he hooked up with, but I'd have remembered if he'd ever mentioned her name."

"And now we've got work to do since y'all seemed to only be communicating with your private parts over the last few days instead of sharing your family trees. So, here's what you're going to do…"

Chapter
Thirty

Tristan

I SEVERELY UNDERESTIMATED THE number of people that would be out wandering around downtown Sage Springs during a national holiday when Charley convinced me we needed to stop in town for flowers. And how many of them would take pictures of a man riding a horse down main street in the middle of the afternoon with his shirt unbuttoned and a bouquet tucked in his saddlebag.

Charley was in a West Peak Ranch pickup truck behind me, and every time I turned toward her, she'd just waved while simultaneously laughing her ass off.

Despite the early July heat, Seraphina seemed in good spirits, happy to be out of her stall. Charley and Marty had assured me that the equine vet was okay with light exercise, so if I didn't push her too hard, a walk through town wouldn't overtax her lungs.

As I moved her reins to the side, steering her toward the River Run Tavern where Annie worked, my eyes widened when I saw a handful of my fellow firefighters gathered in the drive of the fire station washing one of the three engines we kept there.

"Ow, ow!" a deep, masculine voice yelled right before a chorus of loud whistles tore through the air from the officers washing the truck. "Check out that hunky cowboy!"

Chief Wilson, who was typically a stoic man, held a wet cloth in his fist while he yelled loudly enough a few pedestrians stopped to watch. "Call the fire department, boys! We've got a blaze rolling through. Oh wait, we are the fire department. Better get the hose!"

Steering Phi across the road to the far side, I hoped my typically mellow horse wouldn't be spooked by the spray of water when my chuckling boss aimed the nozzle of a garden hose toward us.

She nickered, turning her head to look at me, and if a horse could roll her eyes, I knew she would have. "I know, pretty girl. You're being very tolerant of this nonsense."

"Get a move on," Charley yelled from the truck behind me, and the handful of firefighters waved, laughing as I turned Phi toward the bar.

The pedestrian traffic thinned out even more the further we got to the edge of town. But when I looked at the parking lot of the bar, it was more than half full.

I led Phi to the side of the building as Charley parked the truck, hopping out to run around the back of the building. She came back with an empty bucket, filling it with the spigot beside the side door.

"Remind me again why I agreed to this?" I asked as she put the bucket on the ground in front of the horse, running her hand down her mane while Phi took a drink.

"Because you *luuurve* her and you're trying to make an impression."

"And I couldn't have done that just walking through the bar and asking to talk to her?" Now that I was here, sitting atop a horse in the gravel parking lot of a bar on the fourth of July in the mountains of Colorado on an unseasonably warm day, I was second guessing that this was a good idea to win back a woman's affection.

"You've never done this grand gesture thing before, have you?" she teased, but she wasn't wrong.

"Never needed to before."

She rolled her eyes, pulling the bucket against the side of the building once Phi had drunk her fill. "Go wait by the front doors and I'll go get her."

"Are you sure it's okay that we're doing this?" I asked, nodding toward a couple of patrons who'd stopped in the parking lot to stare at us.

"I let the owner play with my boobs on a regular basis. He won't give a fuck as long as the cops don't get called."

"Not sure I needed to know that," I muttered, realizing how right my boss had been about his strong-willed daughter. When she told you to do something, you didn't push back.

"And if you play your cards right, then maybe Annie will let you see hers later tonight." She mimed cupping a set of boobs, and I shook my head, not exactly sure how this was my life right now. Charley pointed toward the front of the building again before she typed in a code on the side door and slipped inside.

Steering Phi out front, I waited just outside the doors, trying not to pay attention to the heads I watched pop up in the front windows the longer we stood there. Depending on who was in the bar right now, my entire family might know what I was doing within minutes.

The only thing I had going for me right now was that, after being gone from Sage Springs for as long as I'd been, some of my observers might not know who I was. Maybe if I kept my hat tilted forward, I could conceal my identity.

But who was I kidding? Probably not in a town this size.

The sound of Phi's tail swishing behind my back almost lulled me into a trance with the sun beating down from overhead, but my pulse started racing the second the door pushed outward.

Rhey's red-rimmed eyes widened as she paused in the doorway with her arms crossed. Seeing the evidence of her tears gutted me, but she stood with her head held high, still so strong even when I knew my actions had upset her. Charley not so gently nudged her further outside when she didn't show any signs of moving, and I was thankful for the intervention.

"What are you...?" she trailed off, her eyes bouncing between Phi and me.

"Howdy, ma'am." My voice was deeper than usual with nerves, but I cleared my throat while she just stared at me. "Someone told me that there might be a damsel in distress in need of a ride this afternoon."

Charley slapped her hand across her mouth, but the giggles escaped anyway, and Baker appeared in the doorway behind her, shaking his head.

"Dude, no. That was cheesy as fuck," he laughed, pulling out his phone and holding it up.

Turning the hand still holding the reins, I discreetly flipped him the middle finger, and he laughed harder, but I wasn't looking at him. I was watching *her*.

Rhey's fingers hovered in front of her quivering lips, and I tried to fight the urge to dismount and pull her into my arms when her voice shook. "Why are you here?"

"Because I'm not ready for this to be over yet." I extended a hand toward her, ignoring the crowd that was forming behind Charley and Baker in the doorway.

"But what about—"

Shaking my head, I cut her off. "I don't care. You're worth it, Rhey. And I'm not leaving until you give me a chance to make it right."

"You didn't do anything wrong, I—"

"And neither did you, no matter what my asshole brother says." My heart pounded as I watched the emotions flicker across her features, the most prominent one being fear. "Sweetheart, I don't want to move on from you. I want to move on *with* you."

She hesitated, and I extended my hand further in her direction. "Come take a ride with me?"

"I'm working," she protested weakly.

But Charley was right behind her, extending a boot into Rhey's butt to urge her forward. "No, you're not. Don't make me tell Hudson to fire you."

Rhey turned her head, eyes widening when she saw all the people standing in the entrance of the bar and dotted throughout the parking lot, watching me humiliate myself to get her attention.

"Don't look at them, Rhey. Look at me." She hesitantly returned her gaze to me and our eyes locked, her posture relaxing as our unspoken connection took over.

That's right, sweetheart. I'm not letting you run from me.

"Ready to go for that ride now?" I asked, and her eyebrow raised suggestively, a chuckle escaping me. Shaking my head, I couldn't resist teasing her since she wasn't running away again. "Not that kinda ride. *Yet.*"

The crowd behind her laughed, but I didn't pay attention to them as she stepped forward—eyes locked with mine—fingers grazing mine as she stopped beside Phi, using her other hand to pet her neck. The horse nudged Rhey in the shoulder with the side of her face, nickering as if to say *get on already.*

I kicked one of my boots out of the stirrup and held Rhey's hand as she used it to step up; her face inches from mine. Leaning in, I whispered in her ear. "I know you're scared right now, and to be honest, so am I. But I'm done running from the things that scare me, and I hope you are, too."

She smiled, tipping her head until her forehead rested against mine, causing my hat to shift back. "Thank you for coming to find me."

Her breath caught as I tilted my face, lips lingering beside her mouth. "Anywhere, anytime. You need me, and I'll always be there to rescue you. Even if it's from yourself."

Her hand grasped the back of my neck, and she pulled me closer, lips grazing my ear. "I'm not sure how to get on this horse without flashing half this parking lot."

I laughed loudly, wrapping one arm around her waist as I pulled the reins to the side, turning Phi to face away from the bar. "I got you."

Thankfully, all the months I trained to keep in peak physical condition in my previous life meant I could both brace my hands on her waist and lift her while she slipped her leg over the saddle in front of me. We both smoothed out her dress, and I watched over her shoulder as she tucked the material between her legs and underneath those luscious thighs.

"You ready to go home?" I whispered in her ear and sighed when she leaned back into my chest.

"You're welcome!" Charley's loud voice cut through the air, and I shook my head as Rhey giggled in front of me.

Turning Phi back to face the bar, I tipped my hat, raising my voice for the benefit of the crowd. "Thanks for the public humiliation, we're gonna head home now."

Deciding I'd had enough ridicule from my co-workers, I took the much shorter route back to the ranch without going through downtown—and past the station. Rhey's hand rested on top of the one I had braced against her stomach for the quiet ride along the outskirts of town.

As the horse passed the lodge, her pace increased when she realized how close to home she was. "Easy, girl," I teased, pulling back on the reins to slow her pace. It was bad enough that I was asking her to ride double again when she was supposed to be recovering. But she *was* kind of my wing woman, so I could understand why Charley insisted it had to be Seraphina.

Rhey's fingers tightened over mine when I slowed the horse outside the barn, looking around for signs of anyone inside. The expansive building was silent as I walked her inside, pulling back on the reins to halt her outside of a stall.

"You okay?" I murmured, smiling at Rhey's shaky nod, before I pulled my hat off, reaching over to hook it on the post next to Phi's stall door.

My hair was a sweaty mess, but I didn't care, and I hoped she wouldn't either, as I tucked my face into her neck, inhaling her sweet scent. When I woke up this morning, I didn't expect our whole day to be thrown for a loop in the form of a mistaken identity gone wrong. But my day ended with her back in my arms, and that's exactly where I wanted her to stay.

Chapter
Thirty-One

R HEY STILL SEEMED A little skittish as I sat behind her on Seraphina in the barn. I couldn't exactly blame her. It'd been a bit of
a shock to learn that my brother was the friend from high school
she'd been hooking up with for years. And to have the discovery
happen completely unexpectedly led to the three of us epically
fucking things up. Jay was probably the one who escalated things
the most unnecessarily, but I knew my tendency to put my head
down and walk away from conflict hadn't helped.

"I'm sorry I tried to leave," I whispered into her skin, tracing
my lips along the side of her neck. She leaned her head back
against my shoulder, guiding my hand higher until I felt her heart
thudding beneath my palm.

"I'm sorry I left," she replied, melting against my chest as we sat
quietly atop the horse in the dimly lit barn. "I was scared that you'd
be angry with me."

"I wasn't angry with you. I was angry at how he was talking to
you...about you." It still made my blood run a little hot when I
recalled the crushed look on her face when Jay started lashing out
as he realized something had happened between Rhey and me
when he was out of town. "You never lied to me, sweetheart. So,
I have no reason to be mad. I knew the score going in, and I still
pursued you. And I wouldn't change what happened between us
either. If he has a problem with that, then so be it."

"But I don't want to come between you and your family. I
couldn't live with myself if you lost your brother over me. I'm—"

"Worth it," I interrupted, wrapping my arms around her tighter. "You are worth more to me than you give yourself credit for. With you, I finally feel like I might move on with my life and be happier than I was before. I thought it ended underneath that tree, and now I have you. It was worth every bit of that pain and grief to find something I want more than to be a jumper."

"I'm scared," she whispered, her inhale shaky, and I could tell she was right on the cusp of being overwhelmed enough to cry.

"So am I." I whispered the words against her neck, my lips lingering on her pulse point. "But I think I could love you, and while that scares the fuck out of me, I don't want to let it go."

She sniffled, a drop of wetness rolling down the back of my hand as I realized she'd given in to the tears she'd been trying to hold back. "I don't think I'd survive losing you too."

My heart broke as her voice trailed off into a soft cry, and I shifted, turning her face in my direction. I used my fingertips to catch her tears before I leaned in, softly pressing my lips to hers. When I pulled back, I dipped my head to keep eye contact. "I'm not planning to go anywhere, anytime soon. Not unless you tell me to go."

She nodded, sniffling again and trying to stem the tears rolling down her cheeks. She'd lost so many people in her life, and I knew she was scared, but I wouldn't let a little fear deter me from pursuing what I wanted. I never had, and I wasn't starting now. I wasn't stopping until I got what I needed, and that was building a new life with her by my side.

"What do we do now?" she asked, wiping her cheeks with her fingertips.

"Well, right now I should probably get this saddle off Phi, but you're waiting for me because I'm not letting you out of my sight right now." She rolled her eyes, but I leaned in, placing a kiss against her wet cheek. "I don't trust you not to wander into danger if I don't keep track of you."

"A girl gets stranded on a deserted road in peril once and she never hears the end of it."

273

"A gorgeous woman intentionally puts herself in danger multiple times in a few days' span and I have to come to her rescue more than once," I teased, squeezing her waist.

"My favorite hero," she whispered, laying the side of her face against mine.

"Your favorite sweaty hero that wants to get out of this sweltering barn and take a shower before I do unspeakable things to you now that you're back where you belong."

Phi was a good girl and held still while I slipped off the back of the saddle, extending my hands up to help Rhey dismount. She fell into my arms, and I tightened them around her waist, my nose grazing her chin. She laughed when I didn't put her down, leaning back to look into my eyes.

"I think I could love you too," she confessed, and I sighed, letting her slip lower in my grip until our lips were level.

"Good," I whispered into them, our breath mingling as hers pulled into a smile against mine. "I was worried it'd take you a while to catch up."

Not giving her time for a retort, I surged forward, kissing her hard as I backed her against the barn wall, pouring every ounce of relief into reconnecting with her.

WHILE I WANTED NOTHING more than to fuck away the stress of the day, I knew it was more important that Rhey and I talk about everything that had happened before we let ourselves get distracted.

Even if she was looking gorgeous—stretched out on my bed in just a towel—watching me dry my chest after our shower. While our hands *had* wandered as we kissed underneath the spray of the shower until the water ran cold, I'd tried to keep my baser instincts at bay. She deserved a genuine conversation about where our relationship went from here. I knew where I wanted it to go, but I also didn't want any other surprises.

"Is it time for you to do those unspeakable things to me now?" she asked, crooking a finger and beckoning me toward her like the siren she was.

Climbing onto the mattress, I tried not to laugh at how her eyes lit up as I stalked toward her. The way she looked at me had me falling harder and harder the more time we spent together. I'd never felt as wanted as I did with her. The fleeting thought that she might have looked at Jay the same way at one time had me groaning and falling to her side on the mattress.

"That didn't sound like a sexy groan," she mused, turning to her side and tracing her fingers down the damp skin on my back. "Everything okay?"

Turning my face, I looked over at her, hating I'd put that little crease between her eyebrows again. Sometimes being honorable was a gigantic cockblock.

"Maybe we should talk."

Her eyes flashed with something that looked like fear as she shifted away from me and sat upright against the headboard, clutching her towel to her chest.

"Not that kind of talk," I murmured, reaching for her hand and tugging until she settled on her side, mirroring how I was lying on top of the covers. Lifting her hand toward me, I kissed her palm and settled it on my chest as I scooted in close to drape my hand over her hip. "I just don't want the tough conversations to get clouded by my desire to fuck you into this mattress until you can't remember your own name."

Her eyes widened, and she tilted her head to the side. "I don't know, forgetting my own name sounds pretty good right now."

Leaning forward, I kissed her nose, shaking my head at yet another one of her dirty comebacks. While I wanted nothing more than to lose myself in our connection, I didn't want the emotional one to suffer because we were too afraid—or too distracted—to talk.

"I want you to know that I'm not just interested in a fling with you. I know we talked about how this felt different, but I also know how guarded you can be sometimes. I'm laying my cards on the table. I want a relationship with you." She opened her mouth to respond, but I put my fingers over her mouth so I could finish. "While he wasn't exactly thrilled about finding out about us at first, I told Jay the same thing. You aren't a distraction in a new town; you're the reason I want to stay."

"He's not mad?" she asked, her gaze trained on where her fingers played with my chest hair. Crooking a finger, I tilted her chin so she'd look at me.

"Jay is gonna have plenty of distractions on his plate here soon. He's the one who encouraged me to go after you when I told him how I feel about you." And provided the interference so I could escape our mother and having to explain why my date had run away from the family barbecue.

"I don't want to cause problems with your family. I know how important they are to you," she murmured, averting her eyes.

"Rhey, sweetheart…" She tried to pull away, but I banded my arms around her back, pulling her further into my chest. "You're important to me, too. And while it might be a little awkward for a while, I still want you to meet my family."

"Do they—"

Cutting her off with my mouth, I captured her lips, kissing her until we were both breathless. "Reid is the only one besides my dumbass brother who knows what happened."

Rhey's body relaxed in my hold as I kissed her again, her anxiety melting with each pass of my lips. When we finally came up for air, she still looked worried, but there was some relief lingering in her gaze.

"It's gonna be so awkward when I meet them," she whined, burying her face in my chest. I combed my fingers through her hair, enjoying the way she burrowed closer with each caress.

"No, it's not. Because they never need to know. You gave me the impression that you and Jay kept things discreet as far as my family was involved, so unless you feel the need to tell them, I won't say a word. And I'll make sure my ding dong brother doesn't either."

"Are you sure it's not too much?" she asked, shifting back so she could look into my eyes.

"While you are a lot," I teased, tickling her side when she tried to escape. "You're definitely not too much. Not for me. Leaving you isn't in my plan; I can tell you that much."

"Sometimes plans change," she whispered, her eyelashes fluttering as a tear streaked down her cheek.

She sniffled, reaching up to wipe away another tear, and my heart broke as she finally let me see through the mask she tried to hide behind.

"Do you want to talk about it?" I whispered. She'd heard enough of my trauma and helped me cope with it, and I wanted her to trust me enough to do the same for her.

"You don't want to hear ab—"

I blanketed my body over hers as I rolled her onto her back, staring into her eyes. "Don't blow off your own feelings. Because I absolutely want you to talk to me. I want to hear your stories, even if they're hard. I want to *know* you, Rhey. The real you. Not the one you try to hide behind."

"I don't even know where to start," she whispered as she wrapped her arms around my neck, her fingers lingering as they traced the outline of my scars. While I'd thought they were disgusting a few months ago, and no woman would want a broken man, she never hesitated to touch me.

"What happened to your parents?" She'd told me about living with her grandmother, but other than Jay's veiled comments about her losing people, she'd never talked about them.

She shifted beneath me, turning her body to face away from mine, but she was quick to tug me closer, so I curled around her back, my lips against her shoulder as she began to talk.

"I was twelve when they died. And to be honest, when I had to leave behind my life and move here to live with my grandmother, I hated them. I hated they left us..." her voice trailed off in a broken whisper as she sniffled. "And I hated I had to be strong for Reese, because she fell apart once they were gone."

While she sounded sad, her voice was clearer as she talked about growing up in a big city, and how it'd seemed like she had the perfect parents and the perfect life...until she didn't. She broke down again as she talked about the accident, and how their grandmother had shown up in the middle of the night with the police. About Reese's panic attacks and how she pushed down her own grief to be strong for her sister as they tried to fit into a small town where they didn't know anyone.

She told me stories about a younger Baker and briefly skimmed over how she dated my brother before they left for college. I chimed in with sarcastic comments about how much of a dumbass he'd been at eighteen and she just laughed as she told me things I knew he'd hate me knowing. It should have been weird that he'd been with her for so long, but I could see how easy it would be to get caught up in something familiar when you were trying to protect your heart.

"It sounds like he was a good friend to you," I whispered, my fingers toying with the towel covering her stomach. "So, I guess I don't have to kill him for disrespecting you earlier. Even though I really want to."

She rolled in my arms, her hand covering my cheek as she scooted up, so our faces were level. "I never once felt about him like I feel about you."

"I can just cut off his airway a little, make him sweat," I teased with a little growl, but she shook her head.

Her fingers tangled with mine as she slowly drew my hand to wrap around her throat. "If you're cutting off anyone's airway, it better be mine."

Shaking my head, I tried to resist the urge to squeeze, but her eyes lit up as I applied just a bit of pressure. "Feeling reckless again?"

"Well, someone did promise to make me forget my name," she whispered, pulling the towel out from between us and throwing a leg over my hip.

She giggled as I pinned her to the bed, kissing her firmly before I slipped inside her warm body, doing my best to give her what she wanted.

While I knew things were still a bit complicated, as long as she was in my arms, the only detail that mattered was us being together.

Epilogue:
Part One

Annie

T HE FRONT EDGE OF the truck dipped, bouncing back up again on its slow ascent up the pockmarked, deserted road. My eyes widened as I scanned the scenery outside the window at what looked like charred toothpicks protruding out of a sea of ash. The sides of the road that had once been full of lush conifer trees were now a desolate contrast to what they'd been previously. This place had once signified safety to me, especially after what happened to my parents, but now it only represented devastation.

Tripp's fingers tightened on my knee as he followed at a safe distance behind the Sage Springs fire department pickup truck in front of us, being navigated by Baker. While we'd offered to let Reese ride up with us, she'd opted to stay in the truck with him after meeting us at the ranch. There was still a weird vibe between them, and I knew my sister was hiding something, but I'd been too busy with work and spending time with Tripp to pry answers out of her.

"You sure you're ready for this?" he asked, the scrape of the calluses on his thumb against my bare skin oddly comforting. "It's okay if you're not. If you feel overwhelmed, we can go right back to the ranch and try again another day."

"I'll be okay." My voice was hoarse, but I'd already cried once this morning, so I wasn't eager to start again. "I need to do this. *We* need to do this, and I'm not letting Reese go through it alone."

Looking over, we made eye contact, but he quickly refocused his attention on the road, navigating around the dips as the truck in front of us slowed. "Needing to do something doesn't make it easy.

281

Let us know if you need a break. Not everything has to be done today. This will take a while to sort out."

But I already knew that, having dealt with the insurance company for the last few weeks. A claims specialist would come out now that the fire department was letting residents get to their lots, but it'd be months until we could start rebuilding. And then, depending on when we started, progress would be determined by the winter weather.

"It could be a year from now before a new cabin is built."

He shifted the truck into park, turning toward me and pulling my hand into his lap. "You know what my opinion is about that."

Sighing, I let my head drop forward dramatically. "And I've told you repeatedly that moving in together after we've only known each other for a month seems a bit reckless."

Not that I'd made any moves to find somewhere else to stay. I'd taken over Tripp's closet and we hadn't slept apart since the day he rescued me from the fire. I'd once thought living with someone romantically seemed like a lot of work, but it wasn't. Our lives, despite schedules that sometimes clashed, had meshed seamlessly.

"Since when has something being reckless stopped you?" he teased. But, in all honesty, I had been dreading the thought of looking for an apartment in town.

Since we still had a few months to go in the fall tourism season, most of the cabin rentals were booked. Things would probably slow down a bit in late fall, but they'd pick right back up for ski season. And since so many residents who'd lived on the ridge had been affected, rentals were already scarce.

"I'm not making any decisions today."

He nodded, lifting my hand to his mouth and kissing my palm. "And I'm hoping you won't for a while."

The idea of staying in his small cabin at the ranch had merit. I didn't need a lot of space since I didn't have much. We'd been told our cabin was unsalvageable from the fire and we'd also been warned that there might not be much to save from the rubble, so it wasn't like we couldn't make it work living in a one bedroom. Tripp has already put plans in motion to refurbish the dated kitchen and expand the cabin to add another bedroom if needed.

Other than a few trips into town for new clothes and toiletries, I'd been able to make do with very little. While I was devastated to lose family heirlooms, I'd learned long ago that sometimes physical reminders of a person you lost only made the ache of their absence worse. I'd cherish the memories of time spent with my parents and my grandmother much longer than the belongings they'd left behind.

The sound of car doors slamming drew my attention to the truck in front of us, and I glanced up, watching my sister fall into Baker's arms from the passenger side. She burrowed into his chest, and he wrapped his arms around her, cupping the back of her head as he stared in our direction.

Watching him tilt his head backward, I picked up on the hint and took a deep breath before I reached for the door handle. I could feel the tears building behind my eyelids, but I knew I needed to be strong right now for my sister.

"I'll get the supplies," Tripp called out as I stepped onto what had once been our driveway.

Seeing pictures of it had been a shock but actually seeing the damage with my own two eyes were two wildly different things. There wasn't anything that could have prepared me for seeing what had been my home for almost twenty years as a charred pile of rubble and ash.

The stone fireplace in the center was mostly intact, a solemn pillar in the black heap that spread out around it.

While I'd been determined to do this without falling apart, I couldn't stop the tears that streaked down my cheeks as I slowly walked toward what had once been my home.

I could feel Tripp's presence behind me. Ready to spring into action if he thought I needed him. His steadiness was a support I was depending on. But he couldn't fix this.

He couldn't change what happened that day, and in some ways, it had changed my life and Reese's in ways that we might have needed.

I'd been rescued by a man who had become my partner, someone to grow a life with. And my sister had rekindled a friendship with someone who had once been lost to her. She wouldn't be leaning on Baker like she had if she had plans to cut him out again.

The late July heat had finally let up in the last week, but the sun felt oppressive on the exposed skin of my arms. It was weird that a place that had been surrounded by vibrant tall trees was now exposed and bleak.

Footsteps crunched behind me, pausing as I felt a small, warm body settle against my side, a loud sniffle drawing my attention to my sister as she hooked her arm around mine. The tears came in earnest as we just stood there, mourning another loss together.

Flashes of us as girls standing arm in arm in a shadowy cemetery raced through my head. I still refused to visit that place almost twenty years later, because my parents weren't really there. More memories resurfaced of us sitting beside our grandmother's bed, holding hands as she slipped away. Reese and I had scattered her ashes in the very forest that lay destroyed in front of us.

"What are we going to do?" she whimpered, letting the tears roll down her cheeks. She looked exhausted, and I wondered if this was the thing that would finally break her. Reese had nightmares and panic attacks for years after our parents died, and if anything would break that tough armor of hers, it'd be almost dying in a house fire.

Turning, I cupped her face, rubbing my thumbs along her wet cheeks. "We're going to be fine. I promise. We've made it through worse than this and come out the other side that much stronger. This will be no different."

Her eyes closed, a shuddery breath escaping as she nodded, her hand settling on her stomach. We'd been in this position countless times over the years, me calming the panic in a room that no longer existed a few feet away.

Baker lingered a few feet away, eyes never leaving my sister, and I knew if anyone could take my place and calm my sister when she felt lost, it'd be him. Despite all his inappropriate jokes and goofball demeanor, he was a good man. If Reese let him in, I knew he'd love her with all he had.

"I'm not sure if I can do this..." she whimpered, a fresh round of tears rolling over my thumbs.

"You can," I whispered, pulling her toward me and tucking her face against my neck. Hot tears ran down my arm, but I didn't care, because my baby sister needed to let this out. She'd buried so many feelings over the years, and I knew she needed to let the emotions out before she completely shut down. "*We* can. We have to keep going, but you don't need to do it alone. We're all here for you, Reesey."

Her arms tightened, and I closed my eyes, resting my cheek on her forehead as she let it out. All the grief we'd both been holding back for years.

A pair of hands settled on my shoulders, a warm chest at my back, Tripp providing silent support until we were ready to do what we came here to do.

He was the friend and lover I never expected, and while it'd been hard to open up to him at first, he was the first person I wanted to talk to in the morning, and we often fell asleep wrapped up in each other after whispering for hours in bed. We'd even talked extensively about all the ways our lives could have overlapped growing up in the same community, and how it was kind of crazy that we'd never met, even by accident.

But I was almost glad we hadn't before now. Back then, I'd been wrapped up in just going through the motions. I wasn't ready for him, and from the sound of it, he wasn't ready for me either. While the circumstances almost seemed a little too far-fetched, it'd taken a few literal acts of God for us to be in the same place at the same time. The *right* time.

"Are you ready?" I whispered into the top of my sister's head.

After a shaky sigh and a nod of her head, she pulled away, swiping the backs of her hands across her cheeks, her typical mask falling back into place.

Reese turned toward the remnants of our home, her hand finding mine as we walked forward. Baker flanked her other side, his hand reaching for hers. Tripp followed behind me with his hand in the center of my back.

July had come roaring in with a vengeance, burning everything we'd known to the ground, but we were coming out the other side with the support of two men who neither of us had expected to be the ones to pull us out of the ashes.

Epilogue:
Part Two

Annie

THE INSIDE OF THE truck smelled like sweat and smoke, my cheeks and neck hot despite the air conditioning blowing out of the vents. I was sure I probably had a bit of sunburn from being outside for the last several hours, but that was the last thing on my mind as we followed the fire department truck back down the ridge.

Baker turned right toward town, Reese waving from the passenger side window as we waited to cross traffic and head in the other direction back to the ranch.

"You sure you don't want to go into town for dinner?" Tripp asked, his fingers squeezing my knee. Covering his hand with mine, I stroked my thumb across his knuckles, letting out a tired sigh.

"No. I'm ready to go home." The quirk at the corner of his mouth was the only sign that he liked me referring to the ranch as home, but that's what it was coming to feel like.

I may have protested when he mentioned living together, but it felt right to go to bed with him every night and wake up with him every morning—even if I kept saying it was temporary. It seemed foolish to let some arbitrary timeline dictate what was right and what wasn't. If how my life had unfolded had taught me anything, it was not to take time with the people you loved for granted.

Neither of us had mentioned our confessions a few weeks ago, but every day I spent with him, I could feel the weight of what we'd told each other. We *could* love each other, because we already did.

Every lingering touch, every long look, every small thing we did for each other showed more love than saying the actual words.

"What are you in the mood for tonight?" I asked, trying to recall the contents of his small fridge.

"Are we talking about food, or..." he trailed off with a naughty lilt to his voice, and I smiled, suddenly a little ravenous for something myself. If you'd have told me this morning that I'd be desperate for him to touch me after spending hours sifting through the burned remnants of my life, I'd have thought it was crazy talk. But the realization of how differently the entire situation could have turned out had me suddenly craving connection.

"The sun should be down by the time we shower," I said, suggestively stroking the length of his thumb.

"And it is supposed to be nice out tonight..."

"Perfect for stargazing." He met my grin, turning the truck down the gravel access road that would take us to the barn without passing the main lodge. Most of the guests for this week had already checked out this morning, so I wasn't worried about Tripp getting caught up, but I wanted him all to myself right now.

He slowed the truck next to the path leading to his cabin, shifting it into park before he pointed toward my door. "Go shower—*alone*—and put on one of those sundresses you bought last week. I'll go park the truck and check on Phi, because I know if I follow you in there right now, we'll never make it outside."

Laughing, I climbed out of the pickup, watching the taillights disappear down the gravel road before I followed the walking path and let myself into the cabin.

Deciding not to turn on the lights, I headed to the small washing machine tucked in the hall closet, stripping down and throwing my filthy clothes into it before I escaped into the bathroom. Closing my eyes, I let the quiet calm me while I waited for the spray to warm.

I could hear Tripp banging around in the kitchen while I showered, letting the water wash away the grief that had plagued me this morning.

E.L. KOSLO

While we hadn't been able to find much, Reese and I had both left with a few mementos of our childhood that had survived the fire. Baker had uncovered a fire safe in the rubble of the closet of our grandmother's old bedroom, but since we didn't know where the keys were, he was taking it back to the fire station to crack. When we'd settled her estate upon her death, all the important paperwork had been at the bank in town and her lawyer's office, so I wasn't even sure what was in there.

Tripp wasn't in the bedroom when I finished drying off, but I found a dark green floral sundress laying on the haphazardly made bed. Pulling it over my head, I quickly ran a brush through my wet hair and dried it as well as I could with my towel.

Padding into the living room barefoot, I smiled at the lit candles on the kitchen island next to a glass of wine and a piece of paper. At first glance, my previously ultra-serious firefighter might not have seemed like he'd be into romance, but he had game.

His deep voice projected from across the living room, and I turned, spying him sitting in the battered leather armchair with his shirt unbuttoned. "If you stand there much longer, I'm not going to be able to resist ripping another dress off you."

He looked deliciously rugged, and I licked my lips as I took a step onto the living room rug.

"Nope." He held his palm in my direction as he stood up. "Don't you dare come over here. I've got plans."

"Plans can change," I murmured, watching him walk toward me with hungry eyes. There was something about a sweaty, dirt covered man that made my pulse race.

"Not tonight, sweetheart," he whispered, stopping a few feet in front of me. The muscles of his chest rippled as he took a deep breath, and I clenched my fists, fighting the urge to run my nails down his abs. While he'd been in good shape when we met, now that he was working full time, his physique made my mouth water. "Take that wine and wait for me on the porch. There's a covered plate out there with some things for you to nibble on while I get changed."

Reaching forward, I hooked a finger in his belt, drawing him forward until his warm breath fanned across my forehead. "And if I want to nibble on something else?"

"Rhey," his voice rumbled, and I shivered at the warning, loving it when he showed how much I affected him. "You get that wine, go sit on that porch, and think about all the things you want me to do to you while I take a shower, and if you're a really *good girl*, then maybe I'll do some of them when I'm done."

"Promise?" I asked in a breathy whisper.

He grinned, laying a soft kiss on my forehead, still refusing to touch me. "Go. Now."

Turning, I watched him over my shoulder as I walked away, drawing the hem of my dress upward so he could see I wasn't wearing anything underneath. His groan echoed down the hallway as he spun and disappeared, the sound of his dirty clothes hitting the floor making me smile.

The note on the island next to the wine only had four words scribbled on it—*wait for me outside*—and a hastily drawn arrow pointing toward the porch.

I left the outside lights off, not wanting to attract bugs, and lit the small citronella candle in the middle of the table. While we'd had a brief reprieve after the fire, the mosquitos were back out in full force, especially with our proximity to the river.

The trees rustled with a light breeze, but it was still warm outside as the sun sank beneath the horizon in the west, illuminating the surrounding forest in a pinkish orange glow. We couldn't see the mountains through the trees from here, but I liked how even though we were close to the ranch, it felt private.

Marty had teased me about working for him whenever I saw him, but I just didn't see myself adding something else to my plate. I already spent half my weeknights at the bar, and that was enough for now. Noah had been picking up more shifts, so the responsibility to run the bar didn't fall squarely on my shoulders anymore, and the break from all the late nights was nice. Especially when I got to curl up on the worn couch with Tripp after he came home to talk about our days. It'd been years since I just sat back and relaxed for even a short period.

The sounds of the crickets had almost lulled me to sleep when the cabin door opened. I turned my head, watching a fresh smelling Tripp step outside with his shirt unbuttoned and bare feet. He looked relaxed, and I smiled as I watched him inhale a deep breath with his eyes closed.

"Nice night out," he murmured, glancing at me with a soft smile on his lips. He seemed happier than when I'd met him, and despite the drama along the way, I could say I was, too.

"Perfect for stargazing."

An eyebrow arched as he stepped toward me, holding out his hand. "Among other things."

Grasping his hand, I let him pull me up, settling my palms on his warm, damp chest. "And what might those be?"

He leaned in, resting his lips on my forehead as his hands crept underneath the hem of my dress, his large palms cupping the swells of my ass. "Didn't I promise I'd bend you over that railing?"

"That you did," I murmured, unable to keep the eagerness out of my voice.

His chest shook against my palms as he chuckled, pulling my hips forward. "Someone sounds excited about that. But I could have sworn you were asleep when I walked out here. Are you sure you were spending your time thinking about things for me to do to you?"

"Mm hmm," I replied, pushing to my toes and nipping his earlobe with my teeth. He turned his face, groaning into my neck as he banded his arms around me. "I want you to hold my arms behind my back while you fuck me from behind up against that railing."

"Mmm," he hummed, latching onto my neck with his lips and sucking until my hips rocked forward, his hard cock pressing against my stomach through his jeans. "And then what?"

"After I come, I want you to pin me to the front door and kiss me until you can't hold back anymore and come inside me."

"And what if someone hears us?" Neither of us were particularly quiet, but I would try if I needed to be.

"Then you can put your palm over my mouth, but don't you dare stop."

Tripp released my hips, letting me slide back down his chest until my feet touched the worn wood. He stared at me with barely masked attraction, his eyes trailing down the dress I was wearing.

"Don't you dare rip this one," I warned, but he just laughed, grasping my hand and spinning me to face away from him.

He walked me toward the railing, gently turning my elbow so the back of my hand rested against my lower back. Repeating the motion on the other side, he overlapped my hands, squeezing before he stepped back. My pulse raced at the sound of his clothes rustling, his heavy belt buckle making a thud as it hit the wood beneath his feet.

His skin was warm as he stepped forward, pressing his chest into my arms while his hands drew up the sides of my dress. He tucked the material beneath my arms, one of his rough hands trailing over my stomach and dipping between my legs as I arched my neck back, resting my head against his chest.

Soft skin grazed my palm, and I felt his cock twitch against my hands as he played with my clit, teasing lower and then spreading the moisture until I was whimpering.

"You ready for my cock, sweetheart?" he asked, his lips trailing down my neck. He then guided me forward and bent me over the railing, my body shaking with anticipation. One of his large hands clamped down on my wrists, urging me to bend further.

"Please," I gasped when the head of his cock dragged through the lips of my pussy, dipping inside teasingly as the hairs on his thighs tickled the backs of my legs.

"Sounds like you want something." His voice was a dark tease as he shifted, pressing inside me fully in one smooth thrust. "Don't worry, I know exactly what you need."

My chest heaved and my shoulders burned as he used the leverage on my arms to pull me into each thrust, grunting each time he plunged inside. His sounds alone were enough to send me climbing, my building climax causing my toes to curl and my legs to shake. I was completely at his mercy.

Even when he was fucking the shit out of me, the railing of the porch digging into my hips hard enough to leave marks, he was careful, giving me as much as he knew I could handle. Normally, I needed more stimulation to get there, but he knew, his warm chest flattening against my back, his free hand sliding down my hip to press against my clit as he circled his hips, driving me insane as my eyes clenched.

"Oh fuck," I panted, trying to breathe as I felt the familiar flutters start, my legs almost giving out as the orgasm crashed through me.

"Fuck, you just got so wet," he groaned into my neck, thrusting lightly until he felt the pulses slow. Laying a soft kiss on my cheek, he pulled back, releasing my hands and rubbing my shoulders before he slipped from inside me.

I whimpered at the loss, but he was quick to turn me, hoisting me up his body and wrapping my shaky legs wrapped around his waist. His lips claimed mine in a scorching kiss as he walked toward the front door. He pressed my back into the wood, reluctantly letting me breathe as he reached between us, lining his cock back up and thrusting inside hard enough I involuntarily moaned loudly into the warm night air.

"Quiet, baby," he whispered, his fingers grazing my lips as he held my weight with one arm. "I don't want to have to cover your mouth and smother those pretty sounds you make."

Tucking his face into my neck, he returned both hands to my ass, groaning as he flexed forward. My hands slipped into his hair, cradling the back of his head as he fucked me, groaning into my skin as he got closer and closer. The sheer strength of his body was mesmerizing as he held me up and drove his powerful hips into the cradle of my thighs. Tracing one hand over his shoulder, my fingers outlined his scars, feeling the muscles flex as he poured every ounce of passion he had for me into my body.

Unable to wait any longer, my lips found his ear, my voice hoarse as I told him the thing I'd been holding back for weeks. "I love you."

Tripp's hips paused as he leaned back, my pulse hammering in my ears. His eyes met mine, a soft smile pulling at the corners of his full mouth. "You do?"

Nodding, I felt a tear slip down my cheek, but his thumb was there to catch it, his lips meeting mine a moment later as he thrust into me hard enough to make me gasp.

"I love you so fucking much," he panted against my mouth after he released my lips. "*So* fucking much."

Nodding, I kissed him again, my palms holding his cheeks as he started fucking me again, chasing his release with my body. His feral groan when he came had my arms wrapping around him and pulling him tightly against me while we both caught our breath.

"Does this mean you're staying?" he whispered into my chest, and I laughed, relieved to have my feelings out in the open.

"Probably."

"Such a brat," he laughed, pinching me. "You know you belong here."

But he wasn't wrong. I did belong here. With him. At the ranch. Wherever life took us from here, as long as it was together.

"You might need to convince me," I whispered into his cheek.

He leaned back, holding my waist as I untangled myself, standing on shaky legs pressed up against the door with him looming over me.

"And how might I do that?" His grin was teasing, and I knew he was humoring me. "Does it involve a lot of what we just did? Because if it does, then I'm all in for all the convincing you need."

"You only love me because of these sundresses," I teased, using my hands to straighten the hem of my now wrinkled dress. "Once I have to cover up for winter, you won't like me as much."

"I *love* you no matter what you wear. Even when you're filthy and you smell like horseshit," he whispered, using his fingertips to tuck my hair behind my ears. "I want you to stay. Not just because you don't have any other options. I want to wake up with you every morning and go to bed with you every night. I want to go on rides with you and growl at guys who hit on you at the bar."

"Sounds somewhat appealing," I murmured, tracing my fingers through his chest hair while his arms flexed next to my face as he gripped the top of the door frame. "I always have had a thing for possessive cowboys."

He groaned, hating the nickname from the fire station he still hadn't been able to escape, but he had kind of embraced the part. "You're not allowed to call me that."

"But you *are* a cowboy," I teased, scratching my fingers through his stubble. "You ride horses and do manly things on a ranch every day."

"You ride too." He'd even picked out one of the trail horses to be my unofficial mount—with Marty's permission, of course. "Does that make you a cowgirl?"

"Maybe," I replied with a shrug. "I kinda prefer riding the cowboy myself."

He shook his head with an eye roll, pecking me on the nose before leaning down to pull up his pants. "This cowboy needs to be fed and watered before anything is getting ridden."

"Save a horse, give a cowgirl a ride," I giggled, wrapping my arms around his neck.

"Not sure that's how the saying goes." But he reached down to hoist me against his chest anyway before he opened the door at my back. "But I'll let you ride whatever you want once you get some meat in me."

"Pretty sure the meat goes inside me."

His laughter warmed my chest as he carried me inside *our* home, kicking the door shut behind us. "You're terrible, Rhey."

Leaning my head back, I ran my fingertips across the fading scar on his forehead. "But you love me."

"I do." He nodded, right before he kissed me again. "Sometimes you're ridiculous, but I love you anyway."

Carrying me further inside, he set me down on the kitchen island while he set to work. I couldn't keep the smile from my face as I watched him pull together dinner, briefly escaping to retrieve my wine glass from the porch for a refill.

A month ago, I'd never seen him coming, but now, I couldn't imagine my future without this man.

THE END

Also By E.L. KOSLO

THE DIRTY WORDS SERIES

Foreplay on Words (Amazon)

Book One of The Dirty Words Series
Evan and Chase
Preview of Foreplay on Words: https://BookHip.com/WCJHJGA

Mark my Words (Amazon)

Book Two of The Dirty Words Series
Sam and Kristine
Preview of Mark my Words: https://BookHip.com/QHWGXTZ

Bound by Words (Amazon)

Book Three of The Dirty Words Series
Nathan and Kelly
Preview of Bound by Words: https://BookHip.com/NRRHRBN

More Than Words (Amazon)

Book Four of The Dirty Words Series
Adrian and Isobel
Preview of More Than Words: https://BookHip.com/TARMSTL
.
.

MASKED MEN OF SAGE SPRINGS

Accidental Abduction (Amazon)

Book One in the Masked Men of Sage Springs Series
Hudson and Charley
Preview of Accidental Abduction: https://bookhip.com/CDPWX
AB
Coming to audio soon!

Illicit Illustration (Amazon)

Book Two in the Masked Men of Sage Springs Series
Reid and Hazel
Preview of Illicit Illustration: https://bookhip.com/CDPWXAB

Smokin' Situation (Amazon)

Book Three in the Masked Men of Sage Springs Series
Annie and Tristan
Preview of Smokin' Situation: https://bookhip.com/FCDAKTZ
.
.

STANDALONES

The Midnight Voyeur (Amazon)

Now available in Duet audio featuring Branden Davis-Butler, Cole Eubanks and Troy Duran: https://books2read.com/themidnightvoyeur
(Wide at all audio retailers)
Spicy, taboo, reverse age-gap, stand-alone – Ginny
Preview The Midnight Voyeur: https://BookHip.com/SZXGKKQ

The Mystery Correspondent (Amazon)

Steamy Christmas novella, stand-alone – Ryder and Stella
Preview of The Mystery Correspondent: https://BookHip.com/XPBVAMB

Meet Him at the Altar

New Adult coming of age, written like a romcom/mystery
Kendall & The Groom
Preview of Meet Him at the Altar available on ELKoslo.com

Acknowledgments

FIRST AND FOREMOST, THANK you so much to all the readers for your continued love, support, encouragement, and enthusiasm for each one of my books. I truly couldn't do this without you.

Eternal gratitude for my alpha reader team. You special group of ladies keep me sane, motivated and on the tracks when my brain tries to go rogue. Katie, you will never truly understand how much your friendship means to me and how none of my books would be as special as they are without your beautiful soul. You help me craft plots and characters that are truly meaningful and I love you to pieces. Kelly, thank you for always enthusiastically jumping into the chaos that are my rough drafts and finding the things I miss. And for always making me giggle when you claim dibs on another book boyfriend by licking them to establish your ownership. Nikki, I love all your comments and how you always fit me into your busy schedule the second I tell you I have new chapters ready. Jody, thank you for embracing my chaos and supporting me when I doubt myself. Your encouragement and motivation mean the world to me.

Special shout out to my lovely PR ladies, Jane and Nicole for working hard to get this book into the hands of readers who love spicy romantic comedies about slightly submissive, brooding, cowboy-firefighters.

And I definitely cannot do this without all the ARC readers on my team who enthusiastically share my books and leave thoughtful, insightful reviews. I'm always terrified to send new book babies out into the world, and you help me keep the imposter syndrome at bay.

Special thanks to Brittni, who has now edited my 10th project, which is kind of insane. You help me shape the chaos into something beautiful for people to connect with. And you are never afraid to tell me when I need to get back to work. Thank you for jumping in and getting this book ready even when my brain did not want to cooperate. My books and my writing would not be where they are today without you.

Thank you, mom, for continuing to read my books even when I'm not sure I can look you in the eye after knowing you've read some of these spicy scenes. Your love of reading and romance novels sparked this journey, and I'm forever thankful for you.

And last, but certainly not least, thank you to my husband who I know will probably never read this, but who has supported my writing journey without hesitation even if he would much rather read books about war and chaos than a romance novel.

.

Make sure to follow me on Instagram - @ELKoslo_writes, Tiktok - @elkoslowrites and sign up for my newsletter at ELKoslo.com

.

I hope you enjoyed Annie & Tristan's story, if you would leave a review with your thoughts, it'd mean the world to me—Until next time,

.

E. L. Koslo

Social Media

Website: ELKoslo.com

Instagram: @elkoslo_writes
Threads: @elkoslo_writes
TikTok: @elkoslowrites & @elkosloauthor

Facebook: E.L. Koslo
Page: EL Koslo Romance Writer
Private Reader Group: E.L. Koslo's Dirty Words Brigade

Pinterest: @elkoslo

X: @ELKoslo
BlueSky: https://bsky.app/profile/elkoslowrites.bsky.social

Amazon: amazon.com/author/e.l.koslo

Linktree: linktr.ee.Elkoslo

Newsletter: https://elkoslo.beehiiv.com/

About
E.L. KOSLO

FIND THE FUNNY IN YOUR LIFE.

E.L. writes spicy romantic comedies with a variety of cinnamon roll heroes and strong heroines. She grew up in the midwest US, married her college sweetheart, now lives in one of those flyover states with her four spirited children and emotional support/writing companion Bernedoodle, Quinn. Banter and second-hand embarrassment are her jam, so be prepared to laugh with or at her characters.

Her novels combine her love of steamy romance, awkward but loveable leading males, and headstrong heroines with a dash of humor and a little bit of kink.

www.ingramcontent.com/pod-product-compliance
Lightning Source LLC
Chambersburg PA
CBHW020410260626
47156CB00007B/2313